"Max—I'm not your wife."

Abby struggled to find the words, awed by his presence. He was a tall, powerful man dressed in a simple, dark T-shirt and faded jeans. "I—I'm Abby, Abby Clarke. Kellie's twin sister."

"Twin..."

"I know Kellie told you I was her little sister, and I am. But only by a few minutes."

Max heard what Kellie said—surely this *was* Kellie— and wondered if he was hallucinating. Too many sleepless nights. Then again, according to his housekeeper, she'd come down with the flu. Maybe she was feverish.

Without conscious thought, he put out his hand to feel her forehead, but she pulled away from him. He clenched his hands at his sides. "Whether you like it or not, Kellie, I—"

"I'm *not* Kellie," she insisted in a surprisingly forceful voice. "I'm Abby, and I'm trying to reach Kellie." Gesturing toward the phone, she added, "She's supposed to be in France."

Max eyed the woman who was his wife but seemed a total stranger to him. "You're not making sense, Kellie."

"I told you—that's because I'm Abby, and the reason I'm sick is...I'm pregnant."

Dear Reader,

I've been through the "nine months later" experience four times, and each time I gave birth to my darling babies, I considered it a miracle. As I prepared to write this story, I found myself reliving those months of waiting and wondering. I began to envision a character who would go through those same highs and lows of pregnancy, and suddenly my heroine, Abby, took on life.

I loved writing about Abby, who is an identical twin to her sister, Kellie. Because of the uniqueness of being a twin— being one of two people formed from the same cell—Abby is no ordinary heroine.

If any of you readers out there are identical twins, you know what I'm talking about. There's a bond between twins that shapes their destinies in intriguing and sometimes mysterious ways. In *The Wrong Twin*, I've explored that world, imagined one such destiny. These sisters are so connected on every level, their communication so refined—despite more than a year's separation—that their experiences often defy logic.

If you're surprised or shocked or even incredulous about some of what happens in this book, let me assure you that I've written nothing I can't document from existing studies on identical twins or from interviews with twins and their families.

I hope you'll find Abby's story a fascinating journey into a world most of us don't know much about. And I hope you'll enjoy sharing the complex, emotional experience of her pregnancy—as well as her growing love for an extraordinary man.

Sincerely,

Rebecca Winters

Rebecca Winters

The Wrong Twin

Harlequin Books

TORONTO • NEW YORK • LONDON
AMSTERDAM • PARIS • SYDNEY • HAMBURG
STOCKHOLM • ATHENS • TOKYO • MILAN
MADRID • WARSAW • BUDAPEST • AUCKLAND

ISBN 0-373-70636-7

THE WRONG TWIN

Copyright © 1995 by Rebecca Winters.

Printed in U.S.A.

ABOUT THE AUTHOR

Rebecca Winters is a writer, teacher and mother of four. She's a graduate of the University of Utah and has also studied at schools in Switzerland and France, including the Sorbonne. Rebecca is currently teaching French and Spanish to junior high school students—but despite her busy schedule, she always finds time to write! She's won a number of awards—including the *Romantic Times* award and the Readers' Choice award—for her Harlequin Romances and has become well-known for her dramatic, highly emotional and often unusual stories. This is her first Superromance—watch for her second, *A Man for All Time*, this summer.

In loving memory of

Isolde Carlsen

Whose valiant spirit
was an inspiration
to us all.

We'll miss you, Isolde.

CHAPTER ONE

NOW THAT ABBY CLARKE knew, she had to tell Philippe right away. He'd be flying into New York next week, but she couldn't wait that long to share her news—she was eight weeks pregnant. He'd be a father in February.

As ill as she felt with what she now knew was morning sickness, the joy of carrying a child inside her—Philippe's child—seemed a miracle.

This pregnancy was the most wonderful thing that had ever happened to her. Soon she'd have a baby of her own, a child to hold and love and teach. Someone who would share the wonder of life with her. Seven months sounded too long to wait!

It didn't matter that the doctor was concerned about her high blood pressure and had ordered her to bed for part of each day. Once Philippe learned the truth, he'd want to help. He would understand why she had to quit her job and would insist on their getting married at once so he could take care of her.

With determination, she punched in the unlisted phone number she'd wrested from Philippe's private secretary, Georges Tronier, and waited for the call to go through.

"Allo?" an unfamiliar female voice finally answered.

"May I please speak to Philippe Moreau?" Abby asked in fluent French.

"He is not here. Do you wish to speak to Madame Moreau?"

Growing more and more anxious, Abby let out a dispirited sigh. "No. I wouldn't want to disturb his mother."

"No, no. You misunderstand. His mother has been dead these last five years, God rest her soul. I was referring to his wife, Delphine."

Wife?

"She is out in the garden with their newest little granddaughter. If you wish, I'll call madame to the phone."

Abby broke out in a cold sweat, exacerbating the terrible nausea that had been plaguing her all day.

To think she, Abby, was the "other woman"! To think she was the "mistress," living in the United States, while his wife and family thrived in the south of France! No fuss, no muss, as long as Abby didn't press to join him there.

"Allo? Are you still there? Do you—"

Cutting off the Moreaus' maid, Abby replaced the receiver and clung to the edge of the bed while the world swam around her.

Dear God. The oldest trick in the world and she'd fallen for it.

Philippe, with his soulful Gallic eyes and romantic disposition, always insisting he come to Abby, not the other way around. How many times had he assured her that one day he would take her to his château, that one day he would introduce her to his mother?

Abby pressed her hand against her heart, trying to ease the pain.

She had to talk to Kellie! ''Please, please answer,'' Abby prayed as she punched in her twin sister's number, ignoring Kellie's rule that they only call each other once a month.

It rang four times before she heard, ''No one's here right now. Please leave a message and someone will get back to you.''

''Damn.''

Abby slammed down the receiver, the adrenaline surging through her. If she hadn't become pregnant, who knew how long she might have continued in the relationship before begging Philippe for a commitment? How long would she have given her trust to this man?

Abby couldn't believe that the same kind of betrayal that happened to hundreds, *thousands*, of women around the world every day had happened to her.

Side by side with her anger and grief grew an overwhelming sense of shame. She'd been caught like countless others, and now, like them, she was pregnant, alone. Forced to find some sort of job she could do at home. With few savings to see her through her pregnancy, let alone the rest of her life.

But one thing was absolutely certain. *She wanted this baby.* Though it wouldn't have a father, her child would never suffer. There would be an endless outpouring of love from Abby and her family. When her sister and stepmother, Giselle, heard the news, they'd be overjoyed. And they'd join forces to help her raise her little boy or girl, a child Philippe would never know about.

Abby had to credit Georges who, when he heard her voice, must have taken pity on her and known exactly what he was doing when he'd relinquished that private phone number.

Maybe she wasn't the first person to be embroiled in an extramarital affair with his boss. Perhaps there was another unsuspecting female in Philippe's life right now. Abby would never know.

She didn't *want* to know. She didn't want anything more to do with him.

The ringing in her ears intensified and the taste of bile propelled her to the bathroom. Again. She'd already been sick once today.

She needed Kellie. Why wasn't she home? When there was nothing more in her stomach to lose, Abby wandered through her claustrophobic apartment, trying to figure out where she would put a crib and all the paraphernalia a baby required. Not to mention how she'd pay for all these things.

Her sudden hysterical laughter turned into tears, and she buried her face in her hands, sobbing.

She wasn't sure how long she'd been standing there when it dawned on her that someone was knocking on her door. She knew it couldn't be Philippe, because he always called before coming by the apartment.

She never opened her door unless the person on the other side identified him or herself. It was an unwritten law of the building that she and her neighbors always phoned before dropping in.

When the knocking persisted, Abby tiptoed to the entrance and listened, not wanting to give away her presence.

"Romulus?" a familiar voice called out. "You're still as paranoid as ever. Open up. I know you're in there."

"Remus?" Abby cried out the second half of the secret code she and Kellie had used since the seventh grade, when they'd learned about the famous twins of Rome. "Thank God you've come!"

With trembling fingers she unfastened the locks and threw open the door. "I've been trying to reach you. All I got was your answering machine saying you were out. I can't believe you're here!"

She dragged her sister into the room, and between tears and joyous laughter, they hugged each other fiercely.

Abby shook her head and clung to Kellie's hands, still dazed to see her mirror image standing in front of her.

"How did you get past the doorm—" Abby stopped in midsentence. "Of course!" She scoffed at her own stupidity. "He thought you were me."

"I've caught you at a bad time, haven't I." Kellie didn't miss much.

Abby nodded, wiping her eyes. "How could Max bear to let you go? Or did he come to New York with you? Will I finally get to meet him?"

"He doesn't know I'm here. He's been gone almost five weeks on a witness-protection case that could take up to three months."

"What kind of marriage is that?"

"The kind Max and I want." Kellie smiled and released Abby so she could shut the door. "We do our own thing when we're apart and it suits us perfectly well."

"How do you stand it, Kellie? I couldn't live with a man whose life was in constant danger."

"Max has always been capable of taking care of himself. He's the most confident man I've ever known. And he's got such a sense of adventure. That's why ranching isn't enough for him and he became a deputy marshal, too."

Abby shook her head in disbelief. Then she smiled. She'd prayed to talk to her sister, and like a miracle, Kellie had materialized. "It's been a whole year since we've seen each other! I know what Giselle said about how we should try to lead separate lives, but only phoning each other once a month is ridiculous, Kellie. It's no good."

"I agree. It's horrible being apart from you, Abby." She tossed her purse on the couch.

Abby followed the movement with her eyes, marveling at her sister's unconscious grace and beauty. For just a moment, though, it looked as though Kellie had swayed on her feet a little. But it was probably Abby's imagination. She still felt a little unsteady after her bout of vomiting.

"Why didn't you say something before, Kellie? I've been dying to visit you."

"You *know* why. Giselle said Mother used to encourage us to be together too much, to be too much alike. She thought we ought to try to become more independent. In one respect she was right. If you and I hadn't decided to take separate vacations last summer, I would never have met Max, nor you, Philippe."

And I might not have felt so alone and abandoned that I fell for the first attractive man to come along, Abby thought with sudden insight.

They stared at each other. Kellie broke the silence first. "I'm sorry if I've carried Giselle's suggestion too far. I'm here to make up for it."

"I love you." Abby reached out and hugged her sister again.

Kellie squeezed her back. "You're a knockout, Abby. All that red hair and green eyes. Those long gorgeous legs. Just like mine." Kellie grinned wickedly without an ounce of modesty. "But *franchement, ma chère,* you look, 'ow do I say it?" She mimicked a French accent. "So, so *horrible.*" She raised her shoulders in an exaggerated shrug and sank onto the couch.

Abby chuckled in spite of the gravity of her situation, enjoying her sister's acting ability almost as much as she respected her honesty. There was no one else in the world like her. Like *them.* Another "self" walking around, two minds like one. Two human beings formed from the same cell.

"I was just going to tell you the same thing, *ma chère,*" Abby mimicked back. "You seem to be having a pretty bad day yourself," she went on in a more serious tone. "How come you look so drained, so...fragile?"

"Have you tried taking a commercial flight lately—flying across the U.S. in a sardine can with a kamikaze pilot?" Kellie said dryly, shaking her head back so her cloud of red hair swirled gently before settling on her shoulders. At the movement, her hand gripped the armrest hard enough to make her knuckles turn white.

Abby's smile faded. "Come on. It's truth time. What's wrong? You're feeling dizzy, aren't you?"

"My periods are bad again, the way they were when we first started having them. I'm pretty impossible to live with when it's PMS time. The medication's helping, but one of the side effects is that it makes me a little light-headed. What's your excuse?"

"I'm afraid the exact opposite. I—I'm pregnant."

"Oh, Abby!"

Her sister stared at Abby's flat stomach. Since she'd left the obstetrician's office two hours ago, Abby had run her hand over it a dozen times or more, still unable to believe a life had started growing inside her.

"Our handsome Frenchman from the Midi?"

"Our very *married* handsome Frenchman."

Kellie's features froze. "Damn the man for all eternity. Have you told him yet?" she asked fiercely.

"I was going to, but he wasn't home. Did I care to speak to madame? His mother? I asked. No, no, the maid tells me. She's passed on. I mean his *wife,* who's outside with their newest grandchild." Abby's voice quavered, and she couldn't hold back the wrenching sobs.

"Oh, come here." Kellie held out her arms and Abby ran into them. They sat close together, hugging for a long time until Abby's tears had dried.

"Would you believe that just last week Philippe said he was going to see his widowed mother in Cap D'Agde, and . . . and maybe on the next visit he'd take me with him so she and I could get to know each other?"

"Abby, honey, I'm so sorry."

"I should have seen it coming. He's older. Very sophisticated. Like Louis Jourdan. Remember him in *Gigi?* Our favorite movie? Philippe's a lot like that. I was flattered when he said he wanted to see me. He told me he'd married young, that it had ended years ago. I naturally assumed—"

"Don't blame yourself," Kellie broke in. "You're a beautiful, desirable, loving woman. He doesn't deserve you."

Abby sniffed. "I agree."

"Are you going to tell him about the baby?"

"No. I've decided not to. Do you think I'm awful?"

"No. You've made the right decision, little sister," she teased gently, reminding Abby of the day their mother had told them that Kellie had been born first, making her the older by about fifteen minutes. She'd considered herself Abby's protector ever since. "Philippe doesn't deserve to know about a child he never had any intention of fathering or acknowledging."

"What makes me so angry is that we talked about the future, about children. He hadn't proposed yet, but I was so certain he was leading up to it." Abby's voice grew shaky again.

"Where is the *crétin* now?"

Abby loved it when her sister cursed in French. Even now, it made her grin. "Probably in another woman's bed," she muttered with uncharacteristic cynicism.

"Probably."

"Not his wife's," they said in unison, exactly as they'd done countless times throughout their lives, their thoughts perfectly in tune it was almost frightening. Suddenly they were both laughing, and it acted as a much-needed catharsis.

But when their mirth subsided, Kellie was all business. "Have you seen a doctor?"

Abby nodded. "On my lunch hour, in fact. That's why I was trying to reach you."

Her sister's eyes narrowed. "Tell me everything. Come on. Out with it."

"Oh, Kellie...things couldn't get much worse." Relieved that she could unburden her fears to the one person who loved her unconditionally, Abby told her what the doctor had said, leaving nothing out.

"I don't know what I'm going to do. He explained that if I don't want to lose this baby, I have to stay in bed part of every day until the danger passes. Which means I've got to give up my translating job and find some kind of work I can do at home. I don't know where to start."

"That part's easy. You're going to leave this apartment and fly out to the ranch in the morning."

"No, Kellie. I couldn't do that."

"Don't be selfish. We're in this together now. I have a vested interest in my own little niece or nephew. Who knows? Maybe you're carrying twins. Mother didn't know until we were born." Abby almost fainted at the thought. "Besides, you don't have a choice, not when there's a risk to your health, as well as the baby's."

Abby could be stubborn, too. "This isn't your problem, Kellie."

"Are you going to sit there and tell me you wouldn't do the same thing for me if our positions were reversed? Max makes a wonderful living. Since our marriage, I haven't had to worry about money.''

"That's just the point. You have a husband to consider. I don't.''

"Neither do I,'' Kellie fired back. "Not at the moment, anyway. Abby, I'm not talking about a nine-month stay.''

"Then what do you mean?''

"I mean,'' she began with a lift of one brow, "you need to get your wits together so you can make a decision about the rest of your life. You can't do it here in this postage-stamp apartment when you're worried sick about money and no job!

"What I'm suggesting is that you stay at the ranch for a few weeks. Let our housekeeper, Ida, pamper you, and in no time at all, you'll come up with a solution we can both live with. How's that?''

Abby frowned. "It sounds wonderful, except that you're talking as if you're not going to be there.''

"I won't be.''

"Kellie—''

"I'm on my way to Europe for a couple of weeks. I'm worried about Giselle, so I've decided to try and make contact with her while Max is away.''

"I've been anxious about her, too. I wish I could go with you,'' Abby muttered. She still missed those long talks with their stepmother, a wonderful French-woman whom their father had married several years after their mother had died of cancer. Unfortunately everything changed again when their father had suffered a fatal heart attack and Giselle married Paul Beliveau. "She hasn't written me in weeks."

"Nor me." Kellie sighed. "She probably doesn't dare with that monster of a husband."

"It must have come as a horrendous shock to him to discover Giselle was raising two headstrong seventeen-year-old stepdaughters. He really hated us."

"I think he hated anyone he couldn't control, especially since we reminded him that Giselle had loved and married Daddy first. It still amazes me that we were able to stay with her until we were twenty-two. Thank heavens she found us those translating jobs here."

"Can you imagine what her life has been like since then?"

"I can't stop thinking about it."

"From all indications," said Abby, "she's a battered wife."

"That's why I'm not going to wait any longer. I'd hoped you and I could fly there together, but since that's out, I'll go alone."

"You'll have to be careful, Kellie." Abby stood up and gazed down at her sister.

"Don't worry. I've worked out a plan. If I can just get her away from the house for five minutes, I'll talk her into going to a shelter or getting some counseling."

Abby felt tears smarting her eyes. "Poor Giselle, and I can't even help her at a time like this. This—"

she gestured at her stomach "—has changed my life forever."

Kellie rose to her feet, too, and placed both hands on Abby's shoulders. "Are you saying you don't want this baby?"

"You know better than that." Abby lifted her head. "I just can't bear being a burden to you and Max."

"Then don't be. Two weeks should give you enough time to think about the kind of work you could do at home. There are dozens of companies needing translators for textbooks and the like."

"That may be true, but free-lancing is hard work and you have to be aggressive to find jobs."

"Which is exactly why you need to be at the ranch free from other cares. You can lie in bed all day and make phone calls. With your credentials, you'll come up with something concrete in no time."

"Oh, Kellie." Abby ran a hand through her hair. "You make it sound so easy, but I just couldn't do it. I'd be too embarrassed to show up at the ranch expecting to be waited on. What will they think of the long-lost sister who didn't even come to your wedding? I'm sure my nonappearance didn't make a good impression on anybody, particularly Max."

"Well, we did get married very quickly. But it's my fault you weren't at the wedding, Abby. You were in France on a contract for that computer company, and I told you to stay there. It was because of what Giselle told me—that if my marriage was going to get off to the best start, I should keep away from you for a while." She paused for a moment, frowning. "And, Abby, don't be shocked, but I have a confession. Max knows I have a sister—but he doesn't know we're twins. Originally I didn't tell him on Giselle's advice, and then . . . it never seemed the right time. So I decided to wait until you could meet each other. . . ." Her voice trailed off.

"He doesn't know we're twins?" Abby repeated hoarsely. "Oh, Kellie, how could you?"

"I'm sorry, Abby. But you have to admit that until we lived our own separate lives, our closeness always sabotaged our relationships with men."

"That's true, but you're *married* now," Abby murmured, still feeling disturbed—and betrayed—by Kellie's revelation. She did understand it, though. For their own good, Giselle had seen to it that they read the latest available literature on identical-twin studies. She felt they'd lead healthier emotional lives if they understood the drawbacks, as well as benefits, of being connected on so many levels.

"You're right. I've been stupid. Forgive me?"

"What do you think?"

"I've missed you, Romulus."

"I've missed you, too, Remus. The problem is, if I show up at the ranch, everyone will be scandalized to think you had a twin all this time and kept it a secret."

"No, they won't. *Not if you pretend to be me.*"

Kellie had a mischievous look in her eye. Abby had seen it a thousand times before, and it'd always landed them in trouble.

"Aren't we a little old for that sort of thing?"

"Yes. But that's what makes it fun, and I haven't had that much fun since we job-shared a whole year at the *crémerie* in Neuilly and no one ever found out."

"And Monsieur LeClerc and his son tried to start affairs with both of us."

Their chuckles grew into full-bodied laughter. Without a word, they both sat down on the couch, crossing their right legs over their left—which made them laugh even harder.

It always fascinated Abby that their bodily gestures were identical, that, without discussion, they often made the same movements at the same time, that they slept on their stomachs on the same side of the bed. From an early age they discovered that they both preferred to lie on their right sides, left leg bent and right leg extended.

For that matter, they wore the same French perfume, read the same historical biographies and mysteries, preferred Brahms to all the classical composers and craved authentic canneloni. The list went on and on.

"Let's do it, Abby. What harm could there be?"

"Possibly none, but I want to know the real reason you're suggesting a switch. I'm your other self, remember? Let's get down to the truth."

"You're no fun." But Kellie smiled as she said it. "All right. The truth is, Max would be upset if he knew I was going to see Giselle without him. After everything I've told him about Paul, he's afraid my interference could make matters worse. Though he's never said it out loud, I think Max is afraid Paul might do *me* harm."

"Maybe he's right."

"No." Kellie shook her head. "Paul never laid a finger on you or me. Max is just being overprotective. That's his line of work, after all. And it's why I'm determined to see Giselle again while Max is still away from the ranch. This is his longest case to date, so it's the perfect time for me to fly to Paris, check things out and get back before he even knows I'm gone. I don't want him worried."

"I don't blame you. But from what you've told me, your housekeeper and her husband are devoted to Max. Won't they tell him about your trip?"

"That's why Ida and Jesse don't have a clue where I am right now."

"You're kidding."

"No. I didn't want to say anything until I'd seen you first. But I'd hoped you could take time off and we'd go visit Giselle together. Then I would've phoned Ida and told her you and I missed each other so much I decided to fly to New York and stay with you for a week or two. She'd never read anything alarming into that, and Max would be pleased—he's wondered why we haven't gotten together before now."

Abby rubbed her temples where she could feel the beginnings of a headache. "There's nothing I'd rather do than go with you. I'm sorry my condition has ruined your plans."

"Nothing's ruined. Not if you'll pretend to be me for a week or two. Jesse and Ida will never catch on, because they think you're my *younger* sister, which of course you are. In fact, you'll scarcely have to see them, except when Ida brings you your meals."

Staring hard at her sister, Abby said, "You're really serious about this, aren't you?"

Kellie nodded. "I am. Giselle is too important to me, to both of us. I've got to find out if she's all right. But it's imperative that Max not know what's happening. I don't want him distracted while he's out on this case. It's dangerous enough being someone's bodyguard. If Max were to lose his concentration even for a moment, he could be killed, along with the people he's protecting."

Abby heard the love and the fear for her husband in Kellie's voice. Between Giselle's troubling silence and Max's vulnerability, Abby could feel herself succumbing to her sister's wishes.

"What possible excuse would I give Jesse and Ida for staying in bed?"

"Tell them you've got the flu and the doctor in Rexburg has given you strict instructions to rest."

"What if they realize I'm not you?"

"If they do catch on, tell them we were just joking. Explain that it's something we always used to do. Tell them I'm taking a much-needed vacation in New York. Say that you couldn't come for a visit until now, and we thought this was a good way to meet them, and to find out what my life is like now. Then apologize for deceiving them. They're terrific people, and they'll get over it."

Abby didn't like the sound of that. "What if Max comes home before you're back?"

"He won't. I told you—he's in the middle of a three-month stint."

"But suppose he does. Won't he wonder why you've kept this a secret? And hasn't he asked why I've never come to visit you—why we hardly ever call each other?"

"Not really."

Intrigued, Abby asked why.

"Well, he knows about your work, that it's very demanding and that you haven't been able to arrange a vacation yet. And since he doesn't have any idea that you're my twin..."

"Didn't he ever ask to see pictures?"

"Of course, but I said I'd accidentally left them at Giselle's. Not that it matters, since you look exactly like me." She cast Abby a sheepish glance, begging her forgiveness in an unspoken plea. "I guess I was afraid that if he met you, he might like you better than he liked me."

Nonplussed, Abby sat forward. "Tell me you're joking."

"Well—" she smiled mysteriously "—not completely."

"But he fell in love with *you!*"

"Let's be honest about something, Abby. Has any man ever been able to tell us apart? Nine times out of ten, Mom and Dad couldn't. When I met Max, I wanted him to love *me,* and only me."

Abby could understand that. Max Sutherland had set her heart racing the first time she'd looked at his photographs. In some he wore Western gear, in others he was dressed in sophisticated evening wear. He was six feet three inches of tough lean male. More rugged than handsome with dark hair and an aloof stance that must have made him irresistible to Kellie. How perfect they looked together.

Abby thought of Philippe. The physical differences between the two men could fill volumes, but at least Philippe had never intimidated her. She realized that was an odd observation, since she'd never even met her brother-in-law, only spoken to him briefly on two separate occasions. She still remembered his low distinctive voice.

Taking a deep breath, Abby said, "I recall the long discussions we used to have about our future husbands when we were teenagers. But we're grown women now, and Max loved you enough to marry you. You've lived together now for more than a year. He'll know the difference, believe me."

"He'd better." She winked. "I think at this point even Giselle would agree that this separation business has gone on long enough. I can't wait for the two people I love most in this world to meet each other."

"I've been looking forward to it, too. But I never thought it would be under false pretenses. Kellie, it's one thing for me to pretend to be you in your household and quite another to impersonate you in front of Max. I couldn't. In a lot of ways, you and I *aren't* alike. Not really."

"But the beauty is, only you and I are aware of those subtle differences. Like the fact that I'm the older sister and you have to do what I say." Kellie spoke in her superior voice. "Abby, what harm can there be?

"Even if the impossible happens and Max does get home before I do, phone me in Paris and I'll tell him the truth. When he's assured that I'm all right, he'll see the humor in our switching places. Can you think of a better way to introduce the two of you?"

Abby sighed, then shook her head. "No." She smiled slowly. "It's perfect. Kind of a tribute to all the stunts we pulled over the years. This has to be the ultimate switch." She'd never lost her sense of fun where their twin games were concerned. And she had to admit she was gratified that Kellie still felt the same way. The twin bond would always be there, something that separated them from everyone else on earth. That bond—and Kellie's refusal to take no for an answer— had worn down her objections.

"Good. Then it's settled." She jumped up from the couch. "You go lie down while I make a reservation for you."

Abby put her hands on her hips. "I don't have time to lie down. For one thing, I have to pack."

"No, you don't. You're impersonating me, remember? I put my bags in a locker at the airport. The only thing I refuse to share with you is my toothbrush."

They exchanged amused glances. "But the apartment... And I have to call my boss and explain everything."

"Leave that to me. I've arranged an overnight flight to Paris, and I don't need to be at the airport until six tomorrow evening. I'll have hours to set your affairs in order. I can't wait to get my hands on that fabulous blue crepe dress of yours. You don't mind, do you?" she asked with a quick grin. "From here on out, I'm Abby Clarke, Kellie Sutherland's little sister."

"Listen, Kellie..." Abby was starting to get nervous again. "We have to plan what you're going to say if Philippe should call tomorrow. I'm not expecting him to, but I suppose it could happen—he's due in next week."

"I was wondering when that question would pop up. Personally I'd like to tell him exactly where to go and send him there with my own two hands."

"I know." They smiled with perfect understanding.

"But it wouldn't be in character for you," Kellie admitted, "and he is the father of your baby, which gives him a few points. So I tell you what. I'll be a great deal more subtle than that. He'll never know what hit him."

"You're *hoping* he'll call!" Abby cried.

"Damn right I am. And if you're honest, you're hoping, too."

Abby's eyes filled. "Even knowing the truth, it's not easy to turn off my feelings."

Kellie eyed her for a long moment. "No, it isn't," she murmured, sounding far away. "So what do you have in the fridge? I'm starving."

Both of them were five foot nine and 120 pounds. They'd always been able to eat anything they wanted without worrying about putting on weight. "Not much."

"We could order a pizza, but since you're off salt, that's out."

"Don't be silly. Go ahead and order one. These days I'm lucky to keep down Coke and crackers. The doctor says this ought to pass in another month."

"Did he give you some medication for it?"

"Yes. I'll take it tonight."

"I wish I was pregnant!" Kellie blurted. "Not only would Max be ecstatic, but I could kiss PMS *au revoir*."

"And say *bonjour* to nausea," Abby groaned. The thought of pizza made her gag.

"Poor baby. Go lie down. As soon as I've eaten, I'll come in and we'll go over the mundane details of my everyday life, such as the fact that Max and I bank in West Yellowstone."

"How big did you say the ranch was?"

"Only four hundred acres, but he makes a good income from the timber. There are three hands who do the logging and manage the stable, but they live in West Yellowstone and take their orders from Jesse most of the time. You'll rarely see them, if ever. I'll give you all the details tonight."

Abby paused in the doorway to her bedroom. "You know as well as I do that, once I'm out there, this deception will last all of two minutes."

"Oh, please, little sister. You're a better actress than *I* am. Promise not to give us away until I get back?" Kellie was adamant.

"But I've never even been on a horse, and you've become an expert rider."

"So...you're too sick to ride right now, remember? You've got the flu."

Abby started to chuckle. "You're impossible."

"You mean I'm more adventurous. And you're already feeling better. I can tell."

Abby nodded and felt a surge of gratitude toward her sister. Only Kellie could lift her spirits like this. Only Kellie could revive her optimism and her sense of joy.

"Tell the truth now, Romulus. Who has more fun than we do?"

"Nobody, Remus."

"Hold that thought, *ma chère.*"

"I love you, Kellie."

"Love you, too, Abby."

"Don't ever let anything happen to you," they said at the same time.

CHAPTER TWO

"MAX? WHILE YOU WERE OUT, we had a delivery. Here's your mail."

A.J., Max's roommate, one of seven deputy marshals assigned to protect Ray Cass and his family, tossed a small bundle of letters onto the bed.

With shaving cream still on his face, Max walked the short distance from the bathroom to the bed and picked up the packet of letters. He removed the elastic band, then scanned the odd assortment of correspondence. Kellie would have kept the bills and paid them.

Grimacing when he didn't see what he was looking for, he tore everything into tiny scraps, flushed them down the toilet and went back to his shaving. When they were on a case, nothing that could be traced to them was ever left in the room.

A.J. poked his head in the door. "I'm going out for coffee. Want me to bring you some?"

"No, thanks. I'll be asleep."

"Right."

The door closed, leaving Max alone in the hotel room he and A.J. shared whenever they were off duty.

This week the two of them had been alternating their jobs as busboys at Mel's Family Restaurant, each taking four-hour shifts.

Mel's, located a couple of miles from the hotel in Oklahoma City, did a whopping business. So far, Max figured that every tourist leaving or entering town had come in, and any one of them could be a member of the East Coast mob out to kill Ray Cass. Ray, a secret-service plant who'd turned state's evidence against the mob leaders, had been forced to quit his job and assume a different identity. Now he and his family needed protection while they relocated to Oklahoma City and started a new life as owners of a restaurant.

Stripped down to his boxer shorts, Max turned out the lights and lay on top of the bed, tucking his hands behind his head, staring up at the ceiling.

Nothing from Kellie. Not one damn word. His gaze flicked to the phone on the table between the two queen-size beds, then away again. He could forget *that.* No phone calls unless there was an emergency.

He supposed not hearing from his wife in five weeks constituted something of an emergency, but not the kind the bureau would countenance breaking the rules for. The phones could be tapped. On any given case there were too many security leaks to do something that foolish.

An emergency at her end would be relayed to his boss in Billings, who in turn would make contact with the closest office here. Max had to assume that no news meant nothing had changed where Kellie was concerned.

He also had the gut feeling that their marriage was over.

His parents had managed to stay together almost forty years, yet he and Kellie had barely made it through their first—and they were already battle-worn.

If things had been different, he wouldn't have taken this assignment. In fact, if their *marriage* had been different, if it had been anything like the dreams he'd entertained after meeting Kellie Clarke, he would have given up his marshal's job by now and worked full-time on the ranch with her.

They'd met last summer, a little more than a year ago. Between witness-protection cases that often lasted months—which made longstanding relationships with women a virtual impossibility—he'd taken some needed time off. He'd spotted the long-legged red-head the second he'd walked into that cowboy bar in Jackson.

She'd noticed him, too. As if compelled by a mysterious force, they'd gravitated toward each other. By the end of the evening he was in love with her, and he knew he had to do something about it. What began as a vacation for both of them ended in marriage.

They were so happy in the beginning, so full of plans and dreams. He ached for children and assumed she did, too.

Lord. How could a man have been so wrong about a woman?

With a tormented sigh, Max turned on his stomach and buried his face in the pillow, his hand feeling automatically for the .357 Magnum hidden beneath.

Kellie. The most beautiful woman he'd ever laid eyes on. The first two months of their marriage had been heaven. Then, without being able to put his finger on it, he'd felt everything begin to change. *She* changed. All that promise of a glorious future seemed to vanish.

Something went out of their marriage, something elusive, and it had prevented her from giving herself to him anymore.

He didn't mean their lovemaking, although in the past six months even that hadn't been as satisfying. He'd bet his life she felt as unfulfilled as he did.

What really troubled him went soul-deep. Maybe that was the problem. She didn't like to share anything with him anymore—not thoughts or feelings or even everyday trivial events—and she closed up completely if he asked too many questions. She refused to talk about having a baby, yet she said she didn't want to go back to being a translator. He couldn't figure out what she wanted.

They no longer had the bond that had linked them in the very beginning.

She reminded Max of a beautiful gemstone, perfect to the naked eye, but upon closer inspection, flawed by the absence of that essential inner fire.

Maybe he was being unfair. Maybe it was there, but he wasn't the man to bring it out anymore. He just didn't know how to find it, how to release it again. He didn't know how to return to what he'd had. He felt utterly helpless.

Ever since their marriage had started to fail, he'd had difficulty thinking about anything else. Without Kellie's knowledge, he'd finally consulted a marriage counselor, who'd suggested Kellie could be suppressing something dreadful in her past, which would account for her inability to love him fully.

In desperation Max had gone to Kellie with the truth, telling her he'd sought professional help. He'd begged her to go to counseling with him to save their marriage. But it had been a grave mistake.

She'd scoffed at the notion and had erected a wall between them that was even higher than before. In a voice of ice she'd informed him that her life was an open book. She'd had an extremely happy childhood with her sister and loving parents. There were no dark unspeakable secrets.

Filled with conflicting emotions of pain and remorse—and anger, because he couldn't get through to her—he'd sublimated his feelings in work, taking extra assignments, volunteering for overtime. Anything to stave off the hurt.

From that point, everything had gone downhill. It was possible that by the time he finished this assignment and went home to the ranch, she'd be gone, back to New York or Paris, where she'd lived most of her life.

Apparently she and her younger sister, Abby, had been born in Europe, where their parents were stationed with the U.S. State Department, first in Brussels, then Paris. After their mother's death, their father had remarried—a Frenchwoman, Giselle, whom the girls adored.

When their father suffered a fatal heart attack, Giselle had cared for Kellie and her sister as best she could, but within three years, she'd married Paul, a man of her own nationality.

According to Kellie, although Giselle had tried her best to make a loving home for them, the girls could tell that their new stepfather didn't like them. He never made an effort to befriend them and seemed to resent his wife's devotion to them.

After two years, the contentiousness in the marriage became too volatile. The day arrived when their stepmother made arrangements for them to live and work in New York as diplomatic translators. Kellie was twenty-two by then.

Perhaps she hadn't gotten over the separation. During their marriage, she'd talked a lot about Giselle and had tried to keep a correspondence going. But the older woman had finally stopped writing. Kellie thought it was because of Paul's antipathy toward her and her sister.

She'd told Max that Giselle had never extended an invitation for the sisters to come and visit, which was totally unlike her. She'd also confided that she didn't dare phone Giselle, for fear her husband would answer and take his anger out on his wife.

Max flipped over onto his back once more, too restless to sleep. Maybe, he thought, those years living in Giselle's home had been anything but idyllic.

He nursed the growing fear that the counselor was right. Maybe Giselle's husband had abused, perhaps sexually abused, the girls. That would explain a lot of things. He wondered what Kellie's younger sister was like. Was she as withdrawn and unhappy? He didn't suppose he'd ever find out, since she'd refused all of Kellie's invitations to come for a visit.

Then again, maybe the answer was much simpler. Maybe the reality of living on the ranch after her years in the city had sent Kellie into culture shock. Maybe, despite what she'd once said, she hated the isolation, the lack of distractions.

She hadn't bothered to respond to the letter he'd sent her a month ago, the one begging for her to communicate with him before things went too far to be salvaged.

It appeared that no answer *was* the answer.

IDA WOOD RESTED the broom against the counter and reached for the kitchen phone. "Sutherland Ranch."

"Hi, Ida. It's Kellie. My husband hasn't decided to come home, by any chance, has he?"

Ida fought to control her temper, which had been getting the better of her since Max's wife had driven off who knew where yesterday and still hadn't come back. It was clear to Ida that Kellie Sutherland could do just fine without Max.

"No. There's been no word from him."

"I didn't think so. I just wanted you to know that I'll be home later, around five. My doctor in Rexburg says I've contracted the Asian flu. Apparently he's had to hospitalize several patients already. He's ordered me to bed. I might have to be down as long as two or three weeks. To be honest, bed sounds wonderful at this point. I shouldn't have fought it this long."

Ida blinked in surprise. She'd never known Max's wife to be sick before. "I'm sorry you're feeling that bad, Kellie. What can I do to help?"

"Maybe you could make sure we have some Coke and crackers on hand. Oh, how about some chicken broth and Popsicles, too. That's about all I can stomach right now."

"I'll see to it at once, but I was thinking of Max. He ought to be notified." No matter how strained the marriage had become, Ida knew Max would be angry if he wasn't told about this.

"If I get worse in the next couple of days, you can phone the marshal's office in Billings to get in touch with him."

The younger woman's calm acceptance of her suggestion alarmed Ida even more. "Kellie?"

"Yes, Ida?"

"Ought you to be driving if you're that sick?"

"I made it here in one piece and I'll take it slow on the way back. If I need a rest room, I'll pull into a gas station."

"Oh, dear. I don't like the sound of that. Max won't like it, either. Jesse would be happy to come for you."

"That won't be necessary, but thank you, anyway. I'll be home before you know it. Bye, Ida."

Ida replaced the receiver, hesitated a moment, then hurried to Max's study to look up the number of his supervisor.

Max's wife was an enigma. After he'd brought her home from the honeymoon, Ida had taken to her at once. Everyone got along like a house afire. Then Ida woke up one day and found a different woman living on Max's ranch. The new Kellie started acting withdrawn, uncommunicative. Sometimes even unpleasant. They all gave her a wide berth.

Ida pondered the changes and couldn't account for them. It was no wonder Max kept volunteering for more assignments.

But something about Kellie's phone call didn't feel right to her. For Max's wife to admit to any vulnerability seemed out of character—which must mean Kellie was a lot sicker than she was letting on. And that scared Ida.

AFTER GOING OFF DUTY Max always headed for the shower, shedding his busboy uniform on the way. As he tossed his shirt over a chair, he noticed a white envelope with his name on it propped against his pillow.

The small flare of hope that Kellie had decided to write withered and died when he realized there was no stamp or postmark. This had come from the marshal's office.

He reached for it and pulled out the note. *Max, it* began, *our office received word from Billings that your wife is ill with the Asian flu, although she hasn't been hospitalized. This, according to your housekeeper. Knew you'd want to be told.*

Max felt his stomach clench. The message had come from Ida, not Kellie. Even sick, she didn't want him or need him, although she'd never put it in so many words. *She didn't have to.*

As for Ida, she'd been with Max for ten years now and would never worry him with news of this kind unless she thought it was urgent.

If you want to fly home, the note continued, *let us know and we'll make the arrangements and send out a replacement. Please inform us of your intentions.*

What shook Max was his own hesitation to go to Kellie. That, more than anything, told him just how estranged they'd become.

He tossed the note onto the bed and took his shower. Part of him wanted to leave for Montana right now, as any dutiful husband would. Another part held back because of the cool reception he'd get. Hell— who was he kidding? There'd be no reception.

Kellie didn't fight or raise her voice. She just withdrew to a place he couldn't enter. Nothing chilled his blood faster.

After his shave he threw on a bathrobe and called room service. While he waited for his dinner to arrive he wrote out a brief message: Ida, please keep me informed of Kellie's illness. If she gets any worse, let me know and I'll fly home immediately. Max.

When one of the deputies planted at the hotel delivered Max's tray, Max handed him the reply to take back to the office on his next run, then shut the door.

Alone once more, he carried the tray to the table. He'd been hungry when he'd gone off duty, but as he stared at the club sandwich and fries now, he felt nauseated.

What had he done? *What kind of husband was he?*

"HELLO?"

"Kellie? Thank heaven I caught you before you left for the airport." No matter how much Kellie had filled her in on her routine at the ranch, Abby kept thinking of new questions that hadn't occurred to her the day before.

"Abby! Are you calling from the ranch?"

"No. Not yet. I'm in West Yellowstone at a gas station—a place called Larsen's. I must have missed the turnoff. Already several people have recognized me and waved. I don't dare ask anyone for directions. Give them to me again."

"I told you you'd come across the Hebgen Lake road so fast you might miss it! Leave town the same way you came in. It'll be a dirt road on your right about eight miles out. The sign's not very big, but it's there. After you leave the trees you'll be in a big open area and you'll see a bunch of cows grazing. It's right in there."

"I remember the cows. Okay. I'll find it."

"Any problems driving the Blazer?"

"None at all. I can't figure out why I was worried about handling a four-wheel drive."

"That's good. How's the morning sickness?"

"What is this? Twenty Questions?" Abby grumbled. "I think the pills helped me until I got on that small plane in Salt Lake for the flight to Idaho Falls. What a ride. I lost my lunch."

"How are you now?"

"Shaky, but I'll make it."

"Be sure and get your blood pressure checked every week at the clinic in West Yellowstone. It's by the museum."

"Kellie, can we change the subject? The pictures you sent me don't do this place justice. It's *beautiful* here."

"Mmm."

"It's so peaceful. After New York, I'd forgotten spots like this existed. You're a lucky woman to be able to live out here with a man like Max."

"Don't I know it!"

"Did you talk to my boss—Monsieur Gide? Did he get angry?"

"Of course not. I think the man must be in love with you, because he sounded crushed when I told him you were pregnant. After I explained about the seriousness of your condition, he couldn't have been nicer. He asked me to convey his congratulations and his sympathy."

"You're kidding!"

"No. He's waiving the two week notice clause in your contract. And, he's advancing you a month's salary on top of what he still owes you as his way of thanking you for the superb job you've done for him."

Abby's eyes closed in gratitude, not only for Monsieur Gide's generosity, but for her sister's diplomacy in handling him. "Thanks, Kellie. I owe you."

"Just play your part until I get back."

"I'm afraid my voice is going to give me away."

"Nonsense. We worked a whole year for the same man once, and he never suspected anything."

"But Max—"

"How many times do I have to tell you? You won't have to deal with Max. Anyway, the two times you actually spoke to him on the phone were too brief for him to form an opinion.

"Relax, Abby. Think how much fun it'll be when everyone sees me walk through the front door and discovers there are two of us. We'll have to break into our 'Heckle-and-Jeckle' routine."

"Please, no. Anything but that."

"How about Pete and Repete?"

"That's worse," Abby said, aware that her sister was putting on a performance right now. Why?

"Then how about Tweedle Dum and Tweedle Dee? I think Giselle still has our costumes for that one."

"Even if you could find them, we'd never fit into them now."

"Speak for yourself. I'm not eating for two."

"That's what's worrying me. I noticed you didn't touch your breakfast. In fact, you looked pale. Maybe you really do have the flu and you shouldn't go anywhere for a few days."

"Do you think I'd be flying to Europe if I had a virus? I told you. I've got female problems. The wrong kind," she joked, but Abby wasn't laughing.

"Promise me you'll keep in touch, Kellie. Call me from Paris and tell me what you've found out about Giselle."

"I will. Now go home and put your feet up. Oh, before I forget. I have a laptop computer under my bed. It's fun to fiddle around with."

"More fun than Max?" Abby asked deliberately.

"That, little sister, is classified information."

"Do you realize that you hardly ever talk about him to me? Why is that, Kellie?"

"Because there's nothing to tell. Bye."

"Kellie! You can't say something like that and then just hang up. Kellie—" The dial tone sounded in her ear.

Abby frowned and replaced the receiver. Since yesterday evening, her sister's gaiety had sounded forced. There'd been little or no mention of Max. A new intensity about everything her twin said and did disturbed Abby more than she wanted to admit. She couldn't dispel her suspicion that Kellie was on the edge, and that her tension had nothing to do with her alleged "female" problems or their stepmother's precarious situation.

Something serious was plaguing Kellie. Maybe it had to do with Max or more specifically, Max's absence. Three months seemed a long time to be separated from the man you loved.

Now that she thought about Kellie's answer to her question about being apart from Max, it seemed a little too pat. Perhaps Kellie was having difficulty coming to grips with Max's job, after all, and was afraid to admit it.

Witness protection was one of the most hazardous professions in the world, and regardless of the fact that Max Sutherland could take care of himself—as well as anyone else, for that matter—he was still mortal.

In all likelihood Kellie was suffering in silence. Did Max know how she felt? *Did he care?* The negative thought sprang unbidden into her mind.

Much as she hated to consider the idea, Abby supposed it was possible the couple was having marital problems. Her sister had given up her career to marry the man she loved. What a strange irony that she, Abby, had ended up getting pregnant first. In the beginning Kellie had confided that she could hardly wait to have Max's baby.

Trying to shrug off her nagging uneasiness, Abby slipped her sister's bandeau around her head to keep the hair out of her eyes and walked to the car.

She felt hot and sticky. According to Kellie, West Yellowstone was having one of the warmest Julys on record. Not even the drive through the forest had given her much relief. She was anxious to get to the ranch and lie down before she collapsed.

While she backtracked to the dirt road, she scanned the surrounding grassy meadows and dark forests, where her sister probably went horseback riding. It occurred to Abby that, for a woman without the companionship of a husband or children, even such beauty could grow old in a hurry.

Deep in thought, she almost drove past the lake road again and had to brake hard to make the turn. The jolt dislodged a pair of sunglasses and gloves stashed above the sun visor.

They fell in her lap, and she slowed to a stop to put them back. The glasses could have been Kellie's or Max's, but the well-worn leather gloves with the sheepskin lining probably belonged to her brother-in-law.

On impulse she slid her hand inside one of them, the first tangible evidence of a man she'd seen only in photographs. He had long fingers, no doubt lean and strong like the rest of his body. Until now he hadn't seemed real to her, even though they'd said hello to each other on the phone a couple of times.

Kellie's "little sister" probably didn't seem real to him either, especially without any photographs for proof. Would Max be as understanding as his wife had predicted when he discovered that she and Kellie were a matched pair?

Since yesterday, Abby had revised her opinion about several things. If there was tension in their marriage, and she was pretty sure there was, Abby figured he would have to be an exceptional husband to find the humor in a year-long deception like Kellie's. He might legitimately feel that she'd betrayed him—and their marriage—by hiding such an important truth about herself. Especially if he found out while Abby was in his home, impersonating his wife. Her twin.

In theory, Giselle's suggestion that the sisters go their separate ways for a while had sounded like a wise plan. But no one had stopped to think about the results. This wasn't a game they were playing. They were grown women living a lie!

The trouble was, if she broke her promise to Kellie and revealed her true identity to Jesse and Ida, her sister might never forgive her. All Abby could do was pray the older couple would detect the differences immediately so the charade could end.

Putting the car in gear once more, Abby watched carefully for the long curve in the road her sister had talked about. As she rounded the bend, she caught sight of Max's ranch house on the left, set back against a slope beyond which a ridge of mountains began. She sucked in her breath at the simple beauty of his home, a low sprawling structure built entirely of logs, yet modern in design, surrounded by green meadow.

She remembered that Kellie had told her his property bordered federal-reserve land, which the government allowed people to lease for a ninety-nine-year period.

But Max's four hundred acres had been deeded down through the family by his great-grandfather, who'd invested all his savings from working the Anaconda mines years earlier. Kellie explained that in today's market, his private property—small as it was in comparison to other kinds of working ranches—would be worth a fortune because of its prime location. Not that Max would ever consider parting with it.

Abby saw the sign for the Sutherland ranch, and stopped at the security gate, which opened onto a long drive leading to the house. She reached into Kellie's purse for the remote control.

It wasn't there!

After sorting through everything several times, she came to the conclusion that at some point in the past twelve hours it had fallen out of the purse. Maybe at the airport in Salt Lake or a highway rest stop or... In any event, it was lost.

While she clung to the steering wheel contemplating what to do next, she saw a half-ton Ford pickup coming from the direction of the ranch house. It traveled fast enough to throw up dust, then came to an abrupt halt at the gate.

A wiry-looking man in his late sixties, dressed in jeans and a long-sleeved plaid shirt, jumped to the ground and beckoned her to get out. From Kellie's description, he had to be Jesse Wood, Ida's husband, the man who managed Max's ranch.

Feeling as if she were wearing a sign that said Fraud, Abby opened her door and climbed out, but she was a little light-headed from an attack of nerves and an empty stomach.

He rushed toward her. "Kellie! It's a good thing you phoned Ida at that last stop and told her about losing the remote control."

Abby moaned at the close call. Kellie should have mentioned this to her. Abby was afraid this was only the beginning of many near slips. And there'd be no more help from Kellie, who was on a plane to Europe by now. Abby was on her own.

"Sick as you are, you don't need another complication. Here—use mine. I'll get you a new one when I go into town." He reached through the bars of the gate and handed her the device, unaware he was addressing a complete stranger.

"Thanks, J-Jesse. I feel foolish," she stammered, unable to look him in the eye. This was never going to work. She hated deceiving him. *Oh, Kellie. Why did I let you talk me into this?*

"Not at all. If you don't mind my saying, you look even paler than you did the other day when you came in from riding." *Jesse noticed Kellie's pallor, too.* "If I'd known you were going to see a doctor, I'd have driven you. Hurry on up to the house. Ida's got everything ready for you."

"I'm sorry to have put both of you out." Abby shivered, wondering how long she'd be able to live with the deception.

"You want to know the truth?" he said with what she presumed was mock gruffness. "There are a lot of people around here who like to be needed, and that's a fact. Don't you forget it!" He wagged his finger at her, then looked away embarrassed as if he'd said too much.

Shaken by his words and what they implied about Kellie's behavior, Abby watched him climb into his truck and start to back up.

Kellie, Kellie. What's going on? Who have you been shutting out? Max?

Emotionally exhausted by so many unanswered questions—not to mention Philippe's duplicity and her own high-risk pregnancy—Abby could hardly bring herself to get back into the Blazer and carry on with this farce. But if she continued to stand there, leaning against the gate as she tried to make sense of the puzzling bits and pieces, Jesse would surely come looking for her.

The remote control worked easily and the gate swung inward, allowing her to pass through. She slowed down long enough to press the remote again, then heard a clink as the gate closed.

The noise reverberated through her body. It seemed to taunt her with the knowledge that, by crossing the line onto her brother-in-law's property, she had just committed herself to Kellie's plan. There was no going back.

She and her sister had talked until late the night before, but neither of them could possibly have anticipated every detail, every contingency—like where Kellie usually parked the Blazer when she drove up to the house. Abby had the option of pulling in behind Jesse's truck at the side of the house near the garage, or parking on the graveled circle in front.

In a split-second decision she opted for the circle. Jesse was already out of his truck and rushing toward her. She opened her door and climbed down. Taking the initiative, she said, "I'm sorry, Jesse, but I don't think I've got the strength to drive anymore, let alone bring in my bags." It was the truth. The events and emotions of the past twenty-four hours had taken their toll. All Abby wanted to do was lie down.

"Max ought to be here."

"No!" she cried in alarm before she realized her reaction sounded too extreme. "He's better off where he is. It wouldn't do for both of us to be down with the flu at the same time."

Jesse shook his head, muttering that he still didn't like it. Abby, on the other hand, was anxious to change the subject and be left alone.

Kellie had drilled her on the layout of the house, which she knew by heart. But she needn't have worried, because a brown-haired trim-looking woman about Jesse's age ran out the front door and put an arm around Abby's shoulders.

"You look ready to faint, Kellie. Come on. Let's get you to your room."

With surprising strength the housekeeper ushered her through the main foyer to a hallway that led to the rear of the sprawling house. The warmth and serenity of this place reached out to Abby like a living thing. Jesse followed them into the spacious master bedroom, where he set her luggage down on the velvety blue carpet. She could see her sister's taste reflected in the decor; her own favorite color scheme was blue and white, too.

She didn't have to be concerned about opening the wrong drawer of the walnut double dresser to locate her sister's lingerie. Ida had anticipated her needs. A simple white nightgown lay at the foot of the bed, which had been turned down to reveal pale blue sheets and a comforter the same color as the carpet.

"I'll put the car away," Jesse said, and left the two of them alone.

Ida helped Abby remove her headband and clothes, then handed her the nightgown. "You get yourself ready for bed while I bring you something to eat."

"I—I'm not hungry, but a Coke sounds good. Do we have any?"

"Jesse ran into town and stocked up on everything right after you called. I'll get you one."

Abby tried not to let on how surprised she was by Kellie's last-minute emergency phone call to the ranch. "Thank you, Ida. If you don't know it by now, you and Jesse are angels," she said, wishing with all her heart that she could tell them the truth.

As if she'd done it a thousand times before, Abby walked toward the bathroom at the other end of the room. When she got there, she hurried inside and shut the door, then slumped against it, weak from the strain of living a lie.

Ida doesn't have a clue. Kellie would be overjoyed if she knew how well their deception was working. But Abby had never felt less like celebrating. Ida and Jesse were obviously devoted to Max and her sister. They didn't deserve this, even if Kellie only meant it in fun.

Abby's gaze flicked to the toiletries. Except for Max's personal items, this could have been her own bathroom, right down to the baking-soda toothpaste and unscented body lotion.

The switch was too easy. She had a premonition that it was going to blow up in their faces. . . .

CHAPTER THREE

KELLIE APPROACHED the hotel concierge, who eyed her with frank appreciation.

"*Oui,* mademoiselle?"

"In the next few minutes, a Monsieur Philippe Moreau will be asking for me," responded Kellie in flawless French. "Please tell him to join me for an aperitif in the dining room."

"Very good, mademoiselle."

Because she had no idea what Abby's lover looked like, Kellie decided to sit at the most visible table in the hotel restaurant and let him find *her.*

Before leaving New York, Kellie had phoned the overseas operator to get the number of Moreau Textiles in Nice and had ended up talking to the famous Georges.

She explained that she'd been unable to reach Philippe at his mother's house in Cap D'Agde, but that she was still anxious to speak to him. Would Georges please try to get in touch with Philippe and inform him that she was flying to Paris for an indefinite period? Philippe could phone her at the Hotel Beau Rivage.

Georges couldn't have been more accommodating. He assured her he would contact his employer right away.

He must have been as good as his word. Kellie had flown in from New York this morning, and as soon as she'd arrived at the hotel, the concierge had given her a message from Philippe. It said that he was taking the late-afternoon flight to Paris and would meet her at the Beau Rivage around eight.

Kellie glanced at her watch. It was almost eight now. She summoned a waiter and ordered a glass of chilled white wine, then sat back and sipped it while she waited.

There was poetic justice in what she was about to do. What pleased her most was that Monsieur Moreau had no idea he'd fallen from grace.

"*Mignonne . . .*"

Kellie let out a slight gasp as she felt a pair of hands land on her shoulders and squeeze gently. It had been too long since she and Max had made love. For a brief moment Philippe Moreau's touch had triggered heart-stopping memories.

Once she'd recovered her composure, she lifted her head and presented her cheek; he kissed her formally, then sat down opposite her.

At first glance she could see he *did* bear a superficial resemblance to Louis Jourdan, especially around the eyes. Kellie had no problem understanding why her sister had become enamored of him. Some men were their most appealing in middle age.

"Chérie—" he reached for her free hand "—I had no idea you were this anxious to see me. When Georges told me your plans, I rearranged everything so we could be together. How long can you stay?"

"Only a few days."

His fingers caressed hers. "Then we're wasting time," he whispered. "Let's go upstairs to your room where we can be alone."

"I can't tonight, Philippe."

He flashed her a coaxing smile. "You're teasing me."

"I wouldn't tease you about something like that."

He kissed the back of her hand. "I don't know you like this. So. . . so serious. I ache for you. We've been apart too long as it is."

Kellie had no doubt he meant what he said. "I'm sorry if you misunderstood my actions. I honestly didn't expect you to fly here. I only wanted to talk to you." She swallowed a little more wine. "In many ways, you remind me of my father, and I need him right now. At least I need his advice."

Philippe sat as still as a stone, but Kellie could tell her remark had done its damage to his pride. For a moment, she actually had it in her heart to feel sorry for him—but the moment passed.

"I came to Paris to see Giselle. But if her husband thinks I'm trying to contact her, he won't let her meet me. I don't know how to alert her that I'm here without his finding out. Obviously I can't go near the house. Do you have a suggestion?"

Philippe acted like a man suffering from shell shock, his reactions slow. At last he said, "No. I've told you before that I think it wise to leave that situation alone."

"I can't. It's a matter of life and death."

"You don't know that."

She nodded her head and met his gaze without flinching. "I do. Kellie agrees with me."

"Even if you managed to talk to your stepmother and she admitted he abused her, then what?"

Kellie had thought long and hard about it. "I would urge her to get away from him and seek legal counsel. When my sister and I had no one to turn to, she was there for us. Now I'd like to return the favor—before it's too late."

A shadow crossed his face. "Something is different about you tonight, Abby. I knew that you worried about your stepmother, but I didn't realize it had reached the crisis stage."

"That's because I love her and there's been no word from her in months. In many ways she was a better parent to Kellie and me than our natural mother. Don't misunderstand, Philippe. I loved my real mother, but she lived a hectic social life and didn't have a lot of time for us."

"I didn't know," he muttered.

"I've never discussed it because it sounds so disloyal. The truth is, Giselle gave us her all when we needed her. I can't bear to think of her suffering."

She leaned forward and put a hand on his sleeve. "You know what I'm talking about. Part of my great admiration for you stems from your devotion to *your* mother." Kellie watched him swallow hard. "If you thought her life was threatened in some way, you'd move heaven and earth to protect her. Could I do any less for Giselle?"

She gave him a shrewd glance, then drove the point home. "Please don't stay in Paris for my sake, Philippe. Go back to Cap D'Agde and enjoy the rest of your vacation with your mother. She needs you. As it is, I feel guilty that you cut your visit with her short to come all this way when it wasn't necessary."

The man staring at her seemed to have aged ten years. He was caught in a trap of his own making, smothered by his lies.

She noted a betraying movement as he started to reach for her hand, then thought the better of it and stood up. "My advice, chérie, is to leave things alone. You could end up getting hurt."

Kellie finished the last of her wine. "More than I've been hurt by her unnatural silence?" She smiled at him sadly. "No, I don't think so. But thanks just the same for the warning."

She could tell he wanted to say more but feared further rejection. Finally he simply stood up and bade her goodbye.

"Give your mother my love," Kellie said as he turned and walked away.

"I'LL BE SAYING good-night now. Is there anything else I can get for you?"

Since Abby's arrival yesterday, Ida must have asked that question every hour on the hour. To make matters worse, Abby had thrown up before breakfast because she'd forgotten to take a pill the night before. Pretending to be her sister had been too much of a strain. This morning she'd paid the price, which meant she'd been forced to put off touring the house until another day.

Unfortunately Ida had chosen the wrong moment to bring Abby some tea and toast, and she heard her being sick in the bathroom. Since then, the housekeeper's attention had bordered on the effusive, increasing Abby's guilt.

The Woods were an absolute treasure, displaying a concern and devotion that moved Abby to tears. What a blessing to be surrounded by such wonderful people!

"You've spoiled and pampered me all day long, Ida. Thanks to you, I don't need a thing. I'm ready to sleep."

"Even so, I think the doctor should have hospitalized you. You haven't eaten any solid food for days now. Max won't know you if you keep this up."

Abby rolled onto her side away from Ida so the older woman wouldn't see how those words had affected her.

Max won't know you... Well, that was true enough, and the reminder, however unintentional, increased her guilt. More important, though, was a new worry—just how long had Kellie gone without an appetite? And why? "The doctor assured me the sickness will pass," she managed to reply.

"I still say it isn't good for you and Max to be separated when you're this ill," the other woman grumbled.

"Ida, everyone's under the weather now and again. Max and I knew there'd be times like this," Abby improvised.

"If you ask me, there've been too many of them. You can hate me if you want for speaking my mind."

"I could never hate you, Ida," Abby said in mild exasperation. "Good night."

"If you need me, just call and I'll come."

To Abby's relief, the housekeeper muttered a goodnight, turned off the lights and left the room.

Heartsick for her sister and brother-in-law, Abby closed her eyes, but the tears crept around her lashes, anyway. Too late it dawned on her that Kellie had come to New York seeking comfort.

And did I give her that comfort? Oh, no. Instead, she'd dumped all her troubles on her sister, never giving Kellie the chance to unburden herself about her marriage, which was clearly in serious trouble.

No wonder Kellie had decided to fly to Paris. She needed someone to confide in, and when her sister wasn't available, she'd gone to their stepmother. Abby prayed Kellie would be able to see Giselle without dangerous repercussions.

All afternoon and evening she'd been listening for the phone to ring, ready to pick up the extension on the bedside table in case her sister happened to call, but it remained silent. Now Abby was doubly anxious.

The more she thought about it, the more she decided she couldn't wait for Kellie to act. She would place a call to her hotel in Paris right now and get the truth out of her sister. It was seven in the morning there, the perfect time to reach her. If possible, she'd talk her into coming home.

Abby could always tell the Woods that she'd asked her sister to fly out for a visit because she missed her and wanted her company. No one would ever have to know that they'd changed places for a little while. No one would be hurt.

She leaned over and turned on the lamp, then got out of bed and padded across the carpet to the dresser. Kellie had written her hotel number on a piece of paper, which Abby had put in her purse, along with her morning-sickness medicine.

She took a pill from the bottle and swallowed it with a sip of Coke Ida had left on the table. Then she got back into bed, picked up the receiver and punched in the number. While she waited for the call to go through, she turned off the light and lay against the pillows, determined to get to the bottom of everything.

MAX CLIMBED OUT of the Jeep and pulled his duffel bag from the rear seat. "Thanks, Hap. I owe you."

"Yeah, yeah." The airplane mechanic from the West Yellowstone airport flashed him a lopsided grin.

"Go home and get some shut-eye."

Hap nodded. "It might be a good idea if you took your own advice."

"Right," Max muttered, unable to remember the last time he'd had a decent night's sleep. Thoughts of his floundering marriage disturbed him until he ended up pacing the floor. A.J. couldn't get rid of him fast enough.

Max waved the other man off, then let himself inside the gate. Since he hadn't told anyone his plans, no lights were on to welcome him home. In any event it was too late. By now Jesse and Ida were asleep.

As for Kellie . . . A knot twisted in his gut, the same knot he'd been living with for months. But it was much worse tonight because he knew he was coming home to a sick wife. The thought of anything happening to her made him break out in a cold sweat.

He hadn't been able to get Ida's message out of his mind; he could no longer concentrate on the job, which made him a danger to his colleagues and to the people he was supposed to be protecting.

He walked around to the back of the house and entered through the door off the deck, unwilling to announce his arrival just yet.

Leaving his bag in the darkened hallway, he made his way down the corridor to their bedroom, anxious to catch Kellie unawares—before she put up that impenetrable shield he despised.

Almost at the door, he came to a standstill when he heard her slightly husky voice speaking rapid unintelligible French. For some reason, he'd pictured her too ill to even pick up the receiver.

Of course she had every right to be on the phone at any hour of the day or night—particularly when he'd been away on this latest case almost six weeks. But he was in an irrational mood. The fact that she was speaking to one of her old friends—or to Giselle, perhaps—hurt like hell.

Tired of being the last person she wanted or needed, tired of being forced to behave like a stranger in his own home, he crossed over the threshold, which was his right, after all, and felt for the wall switch.

SURPRISED WHEN LIGHT suddenly flooded the room, Abby paused in her conversation with the hotel concierge and sat up in bed, wondering why Ida, who was always so considerate, hadn't bothered to knock or call out to her first.

When her gaze took in the man walking toward her, aggression in his every step, Abby went into shock.

Max! Dear God.

She could hear the concierge's voice but nothing made sense.

Max reached the side of the bed and took the receiver from her nerveless fingers, staring down at her from intelligent eyes that looked more black than gray.

"She'll have to call you back," he said into the phone in that low resonant voice she remembered. Then he hung up.

Too late Abby realized the sleeve of her sister's white nightgown had slipped down her arm, exposing her shoulder and part of a breast to his gaze.

Dry-mouthed because his eyes hadn't missed a detail of the picture she made, she shrank from him and clutched the sheet to cover herself.

He must have been wounded by the fear he saw in her eyes. A mirthless smile broke out on his hard-boned face, a face that looked as if he'd gone without sleep for a long time. "It's good to see you, too."

Abby winced at his sarcasm.

"I knew things were bad when you refused to answer my letters," he said in the coldest voice she'd ever heard, "but I had no idea you were terrified of me. It's hardly the reaction I'd hoped to see in my beloved wife."

Oh, Kellie! Your husband is in deep pain.

His agony cut through the layers of fear and confusion to Abby's soul. She couldn't allow the lie to continue. Kellie wouldn't like it, but with Max's unexpected arrival, the situation had altered drastically. Abby refused to hurt her brother-in-law any more than he was already hurting.

"Max..." She struggled to find the words, awed by his presence. He was a tall powerful man, dressed in a simple dark T-shirt and faded jeans that only enhanced his aura of command. "I—I'm not your wife."

His head reared back, his facial muscles taut. "At least that's honest," he bit out.

This was worse than any nightmare. "You don't understand. I'm Abby. Abby Clarke. Kellie's twin sister."

"Twin..."

"I—I know Kellie told you I was her little sister, and I am. But only by a few minutes."

Max heard what Kellie said and wondered if he was hallucinating. Too many sleepness nights had played havoc with his nervous system. Then again, she'd come down with the flu. Maybe she was feverish.

Without conscious thought he put out his hand to feel her forehead, but she jerked away from him. Her movement fueled his anger all over again because he couldn't bear to see that his touch was repulsive to her. He couldn't believe she was reacting like this, not when he still loved and desired her so desperately. He knew *his* feelings would never change.

With hands clenched at his sides he said, "Ida told me you were down with Asian flu. Seeing you like this makes me realize why she was alarmed enough to get word to me.

"Whether you like it or not, I'm glad I've come home. I'm staying up with you tonight, in case you need anything. If you feel better in the morning, we'll talk then."

"I'm not Kellie," she insisted forcefully, sitting up a little straighter, still holding the covers to her neck. She looked even paler than before. "I'm Abby, and if you'll be patient long enough for me to phone Kellie in Paris, you can talk to her yourself. She'll explain everything."

Max eyed the woman who was his wife but seemed a total stranger to him. What in hell had gone on while he was away? "You're not making sense, Kellie."

"That's because I'm Abby, and the reason I'm sick is . . . I'm pregnant."

Max's heart started to race. *What did you say?*

"I'm going to have a baby. My doctor told me to stay in bed as much as possible for the next few months because my blood pressure's high. Kellie said I could stay here and try to find a job I can do at home while she's in Europe visiting Giselle."

She kept on talking, but Max had heard only one thing: they were going to have a baby. He could hardly take it in. "Why didn't you write and tell me?" Taking another step toward her, he said, "You knew how much this would mean to me. Do you hate me so much?" His voice shook on the last few words.

"No, Max," she cried, heartsick at his pain. "You need to speak to Kellie. Then you'd understand." Her voice was a tormented whisper, her eyes haunted. "She said you wouldn't be home for another month. Sh-she thought it would be fun to fool Ida and Jesse by trading places for a short time, just like we used to fool our friends when we were younger. We never meant to harm anyone.''

Max's thoughts flew back to a time when he'd had to guard a witness who suffered from recurring bouts of malaria. Whenever the fever took over, the mercenary would babble bits and pieces of the horror going on in his subconscious. Kellie was talking in much the same way, and it sent a convulsive shudder through his body.

Leaning over the bed, he demanded, ''When are you due?''

She edged farther away from him. ''Max, please. Listen to me. *I am not your wife!* When I asked Kellie how you'd react if you came home unexpectedly and discovered what we'd done, she said you'd think it was... amusing.''

What the hell was she playing at? ''Stop it, Kellie. I want the truth, and I want it now.'' His chest heaved. ''Is this your twisted way of telling me I'm about to become a father? And the thought sickens you?''

Abby shook her head, terrified. ''No, Max. I swear that everything I've told you is the truth. Let me get Kellie on the phone and you'll have your proof.''

''Forget the phone,'' he thundered. ''Let's start by examining your body for the evidence, shall we? If I've made you pregnant, by damn I'll know it,'' he vowed with shocking ferocity.

''No!'' she screamed. ''Don't touch me!''

But Max's emotions were out of control. Ignoring her pleas, which only incited the pain and anger, he yanked the flimsy sleeves of her nightgown down her arms, pinning her in place against the headboard, exposing the upper part of her body to his gaze.

Heat swarmed her cheeks as he looked his fill, no doubt seeing the physical changes that had begun to appear since conception. Slowly his eyes lifted to hers. She saw a strange sharp light burning in them. "You *are* pregnant," he groaned.

Abby escaped his grasp long enough to cover herself again. "But it's not your child, Max." Her whole body shook, not just her voice. "It's..." She was about to say Philippe's name, then changed her mind because it might inflame him even more. "It's someone else's."

"Kellie! For the love of God, don't do this to us!" His voice throbbed with raw pain. "Whatever your problems, let's talk about them. Don't shut me out," he begged. "Not now. I've missed you. It's been too long." His hands shot to either side of her hot face and he lowered his mouth to hers.

"No, Max!" she shouted in pure panic, but he stifled her cry by deepening the kiss, his whole heart and soul reaching out to her.

Abby felt herself going under and knew she was going to have to fight for her life.

She worked her hands between them till they were flat against his chest. Then she shoved with all her might. He was a powerful man, but she'd caught him off guard, enough to make him loosen his grip so she could scramble off the bed.

"Max—" she was sobbing now, the tears coursing down her cheeks "—you'll be sorry if you touch me. I'm *Abby!*" she shouted. "Call the Beau Rivage in Paris. Kellie's staying there. When you walked in on me a minute ago, I was talking to the concierge at her hotel, urging him to wake her up so I could beg her to come home!"

"She's telling the truth, Max," Ida inserted commandingly from the doorway where she was standing next to Jesse.

Abby thanked God that the housekeeper had remained within calling distance during the night and had overheard them in time to intervene.

"This woman is not your wife," Jesse repeated like a judge pronouncing sentence. "We both knew there was something different about her the minute she arrived yesterday, but the mystery wasn't cleared up until we heard her shouting that she was Abby. Then it all made sense."

Ida's eyes fastened on Abby, her gaze more curious than accusing. "So you're the little sister. I'll be darned." She shook her head. "Did you ever see anything so amazing in your life, Max?"

CHAPTER FOUR

HER QUESTION HUNG in the air, but Max wasn't capable of responding. "Amazing" didn't begin to cover it.

"Fantastic" was the word that came to mind. Kellie made every other woman he'd ever met pale by comparison.

But now there was another woman walking around on those long elegant legs, a woman with eyes as green as Montana grass, a woman who was Kellie's mirror image.

And there was a picture he would never be able to erase from his mind, the picture of a pregnant woman who was so beautiful she took his breath away.

Good Lord.

He'd kissed his sister-in-law in passion.

He'd come close to making love to her.

He felt sick to his stomach.

Max had never hated anyone in his life. But he came close to hating Kellie for doing this to him. To them.

A man had a right to come home to his own bed, to expect his own wife to be in it.

How could he have known that the woman lying there wearing Kellie's white nightgown and looking just like Kellie *wasn't* Kellie?

She'd let a whole year go by and had never once explained that Abby was her twin.

Why had she kept it a secret from him? Why hadn't Abby come to visit them, let alone shown up for the wedding?

Max was an only child who'd have given anything for brothers and sisters. He couldn't conceive of Kellie denying her own sister—her *twin* sister.

From the little he knew about twins, they were supposed to be exceptionally close. So what had happened to Kellie and *her* twin?

His jaw hardened. Only a twisted mind could have engineered such an ugly joke. Correction. Two twisted minds.

For weren't identical twins created from one cell? Didn't they share everything, the good traits as well as the flaws? And Kellie was flawed all right. So was her sister, for entering into a deception that had almost caused him to commit an unforgivable act.

Not that he would ever have forced Kellie. He'd never resorted to force with any woman and despised men who did. What he'd hoped was that kissing her might have revived the passion she'd once felt for him.

In those few seconds when he'd thought he was going to be a father, emotions were aroused in him that he hadn't known existed—a sudden overwhelming need to love and protect her, to fight for the family they'd started. The thrill of knowing he was going to be a father had energized him so that he'd been deaf and blind to his sister-in-law's terror.

The sound of a door closing brought him back to the present. He lifted his head to discover himself alone once more with Kellie's double. Ida and Jesse had apparently decided to make themselves scarce.

He raked a hand through his hair, aware of a thread of unfathomable disappointment running alongside his pain. There was no baby on the way, and his wife was in Paris. It was clearly impossible for them to do anything about their travesty of a marriage with ten thousand miles between them.

She'd gone to Giselle's, after all. And she'd gone without him. It was the final straw. Their marriage really was over.

He hadn't wanted to believe it, not even when he'd spent night after sleepless night in that claustrophic hotel room agonizing over the failure of his marriage, wondering why she hadn't answered his letter....

"This is your room, your house," his sister-in-law said tremulously, reminding him she was still there. "I have no right to stay. If you'll give me a minute, I'll get dressed and Jesse can drive me into West Yellowstone for the night. Tomorrow I'll leave for New York. Please, Max. Let's just pretend that none of this ever took place."

"But it did, damn you!" He had the satisfaction of seeing her flinch. "Your pretending days are over, yours and Kellie's. So are mine. I left my assignment because I thought there was an emergency here. But it seems I walked in on some kind of grotesque joke.

"When you finally connect with your twin, tell her I've gone back to the job I left and that I expect her to be gone—permanently—from the ranch when I return in a month or so. Her attorney will know where to reach mine."

Max could see her shaking her head, her beautiful face drawn and sickly white, but he couldn't stop the flow of vitriol pouring out of him. The pain had been dammed up for too long.

"As for you, beloved sister-in-law, you're welcome to stay the allotted time and dress up in my wife's clothes to your heart's content. I can't help but feel sorry for that baby growing inside you. What a fine mother *you're* going to make."

HE LEFT as quietly and stealthily as he'd entered. Within minutes Abby heard the sound of an engine near the back of the ranch house. She listened at the window until she couldn't hear it anymore.

Max had gone.

Galvanized into action, Abby dashed to the phone and placed another call to the hotel in Paris. To her chagrin, a different voice answered. It meant explaining everything all over again.

But as soon as she mentioned Kellie Sutherland, the person on the other end told her to hold. There was a message, he said.

Abby gripped the receiver more tightly and waited. When her sister learned what had happened at the ranch tonight, she was going to be shattered. But it couldn't be helped. Abby agreed with Max. The lies had to end.

"Mademoiselle? Are you there?" he asked in French.

"Yes," she answered.

The man read the message: "Have located Giselle through a friend who arranged a meeting for us here at the hotel. No problem with Paul, who has no idea where she is. All is well, so stop worrying. Am checking out of hotel to spend time with her while we plan how she'll make the break with Paul. Will contact you later and tell you details. Take care of yourself. Remember you're eating for two now. Love you. Romulus."

The good news about Giselle hardly registered. Kellie needed to fly straight home and work things out with Max before he called his attorney.

"Did she leave a forwarding address or a number?"

"No, mademoiselle. I'm sorry."

"So am I," Abby said with an aching heart. "Thank you." She replaced the receiver and collapsed on the bed, sobbing.

"Abby?" At the sound of Ida's voice, Abby lifted her head. "May I come in?"

"Of course." She sat up and wiped her eyes, smoothing the hair away from her face.

Ida walked over to the bed and pulled up a chair to sit down. She leaned forward with her hands on her knees. "I know how devastated you must be. In the ten years I've worked for Max, I've never seen him this angry. But because I *have* known him that long, I can make you this promise. In time, his anger over the deception will pass."

"Maybe."

"He can't take any more pain right now."

"He has every right to despise me, Ida, but I can't bear for him to hate Kellie when she loves him so much."

"But does she?"

"Oh, yes."

"If that's true, why has she shut him out all these months? They were so in love in the beginning. Then, overnight, she changed. We all noticed it. She broke Max's heart."

Abby jumped off the bed, too agitated to sit still. She rubbed the back of her neck absently as bits and pieces of formerly unassociated information started to fall into place faster than she could assimilate them. "Not because she wanted to," Abby murmured with a flash of fresh insight.

"What do you mean?"

"I'm not sure what I mean." She paused for a long moment. "How do I explain a lifetime of being Kellie's twin, the two of us moving in and out of each other's thoughts without the need to speak?

"But this time it's different. This time she's been hiding something. Even from me," Abby's voice trailed off. "*That's* why she insisted I only call her once a month. She didn't want me to tap into her thoughts any more than she could possibly help. I should have caught on. I should have known," she moaned. "I'm frightened, Ida."

"You're frightening me," the older woman said in alarm. She, too, had risen to her feet.

The hairs stood up on Abby's arms. "I have the strangest feeling that she's been orchestrating something for a very long time." She whirled around, beseeching the housekeeper with her eyes. "When did you first notice the change in her?"

"Six or seven weeks after they'd returned from their honeymoon. I remember, because Max wanted to celebrate their two-month anniversary. He asked me to fix a special dinner and have it waiting for her when she came home from town.

"She'd taken a run into West Yellowstone to shop. But she didn't come home that night. Around ten she called from a friend's house and said she'd decided to sleep over and wouldn't be home until the following evening. The look on Max's face haunts me to this day."

"Who was her friend?"

"Carole Larsen. Max talked to her a few days after the incident. She said Kellie had acted perfectly natural with her. But Kellie left her house right after breakfast and didn't come home until that night. Max figures there were about fourteen hours unaccounted for. Kellie never did volunteer the information.''

Abby's hands tightened into fists. "Something happened between the time she left for town and the first time she called Max. Maybe—" Abby caught herself before she said it.

"You're white as a sheet."

Abby dashed to the bathroom, barely reaching it in time to be violently sick. The retching went on and on.

"You poor thing," Ida commiserated, wiping her brow with a damp cloth. "I realize you have morning sickness, but what made you so ill just now, honey? What is it?"

Abby leaned weakly back against the wall. Heaving a great sob, she said, "I don't know. But I have this premonition that something's terribly wrong—that Kellie's in desperate trouble."

"What kind?"

"I'm not sure." Abby groaned. "But I should have realized when she was so adamant about trading places that she was up to something. Dear God—why didn't I see it?"

"Because you've got enough worries of your own," the older woman said, patting Abby's arm.

"Still—" Abby shook her head in bewilderment "—she was determined to visit Giselle, but she didn't want Max to know about her plans. She didn't want to upset him, she said."

Ida looked more puzzled than ever. "If it meant that much to her, she should have asked Max to leave his job and go with her. He'd do anything for Kellie."

"Yes. I saw that tonight," Abby murmured, wondering how her sister could fling a love like Max's back in his face. It didn't make sense. And because it didn't, Abby was afraid.

"Ida . . . I don't have time to go into the complexities of Kellie's personality right now. All I know is I've got to find Max and convince him he has to track down her down tonight. Something's wrong, something she's not telling any of us. I can feel it." She took hold of Ida's arm for support. "Where did he go when he left? Do you know?"

"To our cabin near the lake. That's where he goes when he's upset. He'll stay there till morning, then drive into town and fly out."

"Is there a phone?"

"No. But Jesse can have him back here inside of ten minutes."

"I'll go with him. Tell him to get the car out while I wash my face and brush my teeth. Then I'll meet him in the drive."

"We'll all go. Max is in a bad way, and he shouldn't be on his own," Ida said, hurrying out of the bathroom.

Shortly after, Abby emerged and rummaged through Kellie's drawers for clothes. Within minutes she was ready. She raced outside, oblivious to the chilly night air and the weakness attacking her body.

"Please hurry, Jesse," she urged the foreman as she climbed in the back of the Blazer, pulling her sweatshirt over the waistband of jeans she could no longer fasten.

He nodded solemnly, revving the engine. They barreled down the drive to the gate, which swung open to let them through. As they flew over the ruts of the winding road that led into the forest, she clung to the armrest to keep from being jostled too much. Jesse could probably find the cabin blindfolded. Abby thanked providence he knew which of the half-dozen little side roads to take through the pines.

The land around this side of the lake was deeply forested. Abby didn't see the small rustic log cabin in the stand of quaking aspen until Jesse suddenly pulled to a stop behind Max's truck.

Before Jesse had even turned off the engine, Abby clambered from the car. She shouted Max's name, and without waiting for the others, started running to the back porch where she could see wood stacked to the roof.

To her relief the door opened and a fully dressed Max stood in the shadows, barring her entry, his expression grim. "What the hell is going on?"

Earlier Abby had been intimidated by his hostility. But right now, fear for Kellie overrode everything else, even the alcohol she could smell on his breath. Thank God he hadn't had enough time to drink himself into oblivion.

"Don't ask me how I know, but I'm convinced Kellie's in trouble, Max," Abby blurted. There was no time to lose. "Come back to the ranch with us and get on the phone. Use your police connections to contact the proper authorities in Paris and get them to trace her and Giselle."

"What are you talking about?" In the next instant his hands gripped her shoulders with unconscious strength, his eyes glittering dangerously. "You're interfering in something that's none of your business. For the record, she wants nothing from me, so get out of my life!" His fingers dug painfully into her skin before he shoved her away from him, but Abby was beyond noticing. She held her ground.

"That's what she wants you to believe. What she wants *all* of us to believe. Max, we don't have time for this," she half sobbed, uncaring of the tears that streamed down her cheeks. "If you love Kellie, then come with me before it's too late!"

He stared at her. "What do you mean, too late?" His complexion had turned ashen.

How was she going to get through to him?

"All these months, she's been acting a part," Abby said, desperate to convince him. "Don't you see? Think! She's systematically been pushing both of us away from her, the two people who love her most. But I'm only now beginning to see a pattern."

He shook his head, his expression tormented.

Abby swayed from light-headedness and fear. "You'll have to trust me, because I'm running on instincts and feelings. Kellie and I share a bond closer than you could possibly imagine.

"It's hard to describe, but we've always been connected on a level that...that requires no explanations." She took a deep breath. "When we were seven and I was in downtown Brussels with my mother, I knew the very second Kellie came down with appendicitis because I got the same pain in my side. When Mother and I got home, Daddy was just rushing her to the hospital. That night, an emergency appendectomy was performed on me, as well."

Though Max's features had frozen into an expressionless mask, she was pretty sure he was listening.

"Kellie knew the moment my bike collided with a car on my way home from school and I was taken to the hospital with a concussion. She told my parents I was hurt long before someone from the hospital called to inform them that I'd been brought in.

"We both had disturbing dreams about our mother dying two days before she passed away. She was supposed to have lived out the rest of the year, but didn't. Kellie and I have shared dozens of experiences like that.

"We can read each other's minds and feel what the other's thinking even when we're miles apart. Identical twins do that all the time, and I'm telling you, if Kellie has turned her back on you, it isn't because she wanted to."

"Be more explicit," Max demanded in a gravelly voice.

She shuddered from some unnamed emotion. "I wish I could. All I can tell you is that for reasons known only to herself, she's been manipulating both of us. That's why she didn't prevent you from going out on this long case. It explains why she hasn't invited me to come out to the ranch for a visit. She hasn't dared let me come around for fear I'd tune in to her thoughts."

"So what are you saying? Do you sense she's in danger?"

"Maybe. The fact that she's gone to see Giselle despite your warnings, despite the fact that I couldn't accompany her, makes me wonder if maybe this has something to do with Paul Beliveau."

A muscle worked in his jaw. "You think this is a police matter? That he could be blackmailing her?"

Abby swallowed hard. "I don't know. Ida told me about the change in her that time she went into town and didn't come back until the next night. Perhaps she called their house, or he made contact with her and threatened her in some way."

"She's making sense, Max. Listen to her," Jesse urged.

Max's narrowed gaze darted from his foreman to Ida. "You believe her?" he lashed out bitterly, the peaceful sound of crickets mocking the violence of his mood.

Ida nodded slowly. "Kellie changed overnight from a contented loving wife into a stranger. Only something...earthshaking could have caused such a drastic reversal.''

"You're her whole world, Max," Abby whispered, her eyes awash with fresh tears. "If she has a flaw, it's loving you too much. I know exactly how her mind works. Pushing both of us away from her has been cruel, but it's been *her* way of coping with something terrible. Something she couldn't bring herself to tell us..."

An animal's savage cry somewhere in the forest made Abby shiver, and she suddenly found herself chilled clear through.

She could feel her brother-in-law's disbelief, his pain. If only she had the means to take it away. His face, his entire body, looked stricken, making him appear older, almost ill.

"Max." She put a tentative hand on his arm. "Please use your influence to have Kellie traced. She left a message for me at the hotel—that she'd found Giselle and everything's fine. But maybe she lied. Maybe she needs us and she's hoping we'll find her."

Her words seemed to give him a jolt; she saw his head rear back.

"You love her, and she loves you," Abby said urgently. "Each second we stand here trying to analyze her bizarre behavior, we're losing precious time." Abby didn't dare tell Max that she could feel Kellie slipping farther and farther away from them.

He didn't respond. Afraid she hadn't gotten through to him, after all, Abby refused to waste another second and ran toward the Blazer. Jesse and Ida were close on her heels. Once they were back at the ranch, she'd call the French authorities for help.

As Abby opened the door of the Blazer and climbed inside, she heard the truck's engine. She lay back against the seat in relief; so Max *had* decided to follow them home.

They drove in silence, Abby deep in her own tortured thoughts. Ten minutes later, they'd reached the house. Ida flicked on the lights and showed Abby into Max's den, a cozy hideaway off the living room.

A large pine desk with a computer and telephone and a bookcase sat near the fireplace. She glanced around at the couches and overstuffed chairs upholstered in red-and-green plaid, and the fabric lamp shades in a tiny red print. They added life and warmth to the room with its rustic pine walls and floor. Everywhere she looked, Abby could see her sister's touch.

Kellie had felt compelled to walk away from all this. Why?

Abby watched Max enter the study with Jesse, his eyes shadowed with anxiety. He strode to his desk and put a hand on the receiver but didn't immediately pick it up.

"Kellie could have met another man that day in West Yellowstone," he said.

Abby closed her eyes. No wonder Max was in so much pain. He was afraid Kellie might have been unfaithful to him. "She could never be interested in anyone else," Abby said. "Don't you know how much she loves you?"

His jaws clenched. "You can ask me that when she's been lying to me for ten months? How do I know *you're* not lying to protect her?"

The tension hovered between them. "You don't."

After an interminable pause he said, "What if you're wrong about your instincts?" The contempt in his voice shook her, but she met his fierce gaze without flinching.

"I pray to God I am. If so, Kellie needs to come home and explain herself. To both of us."

Silence.

Then, in an abrupt movement, he shoved paper and pencil to the end of the desk. "I'll need Giselle's home phone number and the number of the hotel in Paris."

Under other circumstances his icy tone would have intimidated Abby, but right now she was intent on reaching her sister. Nothing else mattered.

She hurried to the desk and wrote down the number she knew by heart. "That's Giselle's phone. I'll have to run to the bedroom to get the hotel number."

When she returned, she found Max on the phone at his desk, rapping out dictates and information about Kellie. After a few minutes he turned in Abby's direction. Covering the mouthpiece, he said, "Describe your stepmother to me."

"She's five-one, about a hundred pounds, short black hair in a pixie cut, amber eyes. She dresses with style, and she's what Kellie and I call a *jolie laide*—not beautiful but still attractive. She's petite and feminine. Very French.''

Max quoted Abby's description of Giselle to the person on the other end of the line. After another brief exchange, he replaced the receiver and got to his feet, his face almost gray with strain.

''Do you think we'll hear back tonight?''

His glance captured hers. After a weighty pause he said, ''No.''

The finality of his reply sent her spirits plummeting. Disappointed by his answer, Abby didn't know how she was going to make it through the rest of the night. The premonition that her beloved sister was in trouble was growing stronger with every passing minute.

As if it had just occurred to him that she was pregnant, Max's gaze dropped to her stomach, which was still fairly flat, although her waist had started to thicken a bit.

''If you're suffering from high blood pressure, you ought to be in bed. I suggest we all try to salvage what's left of the night.''

Abby was surprised that, despite his anguish, he'd still managed to remember what she'd told him about her high-risk pregnancy. She started to say that she'd move to the guest room, but Max preempted her.

''I'll sleep on the pull-out couch in here. Whenever I'm working on a case, I prefer to stay in here where I have access to my desk.''

"I'll get you some bedding," Ida offered. Jesse muttered his good-nights to Abby and Max, then followed his wife from the study.

Abby hesitated to leave her brother-in-law alone, but realized there were no words that would comfort him. Nothing short of Kellie's return—the Kellie he'd fallen in love with—could do that.

She left him and hurried to the master bedroom, where she could give in to her own pain without anyone hearing her.

CHAPTER FIVE

"*Bonjour, Philippe.*"

As he came down the stairs, Philippe nodded to the aging housekeeper who was arranging flowers in a vase. "Good morning, Vivige. You're up earlier than usual on this beautiful August morning."

"Yes. Because Delphine is expecting her sewing group at eleven and wants everything to look beautiful."

Philippe smiled. "You and the staff have always kept our château in perfect condition, and I know that hasn't been an easy task."

"Thank you. Delphine told me to tell you she is out in the garden supervising the cutting of the flowers. Rose has your breakfast ready in the *petit salon.*"

"Tell her thank-you, but I'm not hungry this morning."

Vivige stopped what she was doing and put her hands on her ample hips. "You haven't eaten breakfast once since you came home from Paris, and that was over two weeks ago. When you were a little boy and didn't eat your food, it meant you were sick or unhappy or both." She shook a finger at him.

"I'm not a boy anymore, Vivige. If you must know, I'm nursing an ulcer." Which was the truth, but not the whole truth. Far from it.

His last meeting with Abby had devastated him. Not only had she intimated that their affair was over, she'd implied he was too old for her. That he'd served as a kind of father figure. Dear God.

"Ah—" Vivige clapped her hands to her cheeks "—too much worry over Delphine. Too much business all the time. You work too hard and too many hours. No vacations, because you are afraid to leave Delphine alone too long. What you need to do is take a summer off from all your cares. Delphine could use the sea air.

"Why not cruise the Greek Islands? You haven't done that since your dear mother, God rest her soul, went with you five years ago." She crossed herself.

Vivige's devotion to Philippe's family would never cease to amaze him. But the mention of his mother reminded him of the colossal lie he'd told Abby. A lie that had slowly been eating him alive. He was sure it had contributed to his ulcer.

"I'll think about your suggestion," he murmured. "But in the meantime, not a word to Delphine. She must know nothing about my ulcer or she'll worry, and that could bring on added complications."

Vivige looked offended. "I would never say anything to upset her."

"I know that, Vivige. And I appreciate the care you give her. If I haven't told you before, I'll tell you now. If and when the day comes that you need help, I will give you the same care and attention you've always given my family."

Her dark eyes filled. "You were always such a good boy, Philippe. You are such a good man, so devoted to your family, your children. Not many men would stay faithful to a wife in a wheelchair. It's no wonder Delphine adores you."

Philippe muttered a thank-you and averted his eyes, attacked by a stomach pain he could no longer distinguish from guilt.

After the birth of their second child, Delphine's spine had started to disintegrate. In the beginning, it had torn him apart to think of anyone as lovely as his wife being forced to waste away.

As she required more drugs to dull the pain, the intimacy they'd shared grew less and less frequent. Seven years ago, it became impossible for her to make love. From that time on, they'd simply kissed and held each other at night, and he'd immersed himself in work.

But in the past two years, her condition had deteriorated enough that she seemed content with a tender kiss before bedtime. And she now needed to sleep alone, so Philippe had moved to the adjoining bedroom.

Not until Abby came into his life had he been tempted to sleep with another woman. When he recognized what was happening to him, he'd fought it, but not hard enough. Once he'd told the lie about his mother still being alive, he couldn't take it back without losing Abby. His warm, giving, beautiful Abby.

She believed he was a divorced man, an honorable man who loved his mother and children. She would despise him for deceiving her, for allowing her to unwittingly enter into an adulterous relationship. He'd taken advantage of her innocence. But he'd done it because he was in love with her, and—until their last meeting—he'd been on the verge of asking Delphine for a divorce in order to marry her.

Yet because he loved Delphine and always would, part of him felt relief that Abby had broken off their relationship before she could discover the truth, before he could hurt Delphine. Since Abby had said goodbye to him, he'd been able to wait on his wife without suffering the constant guilt that had been destroying his health and his peace of mind.

But Abby had inflicted a cruel wound that was still festering. She'd made him feel like a doddering old fool, made him feel every one of his fifty years. He hadn't realized she'd been looking for someone to replace the father she'd lost. He hadn't seen himself in that role. Anything but.

Now he had an ulcer, which completed the picture of a middle-aged man turning silver at the temples and going downhill with the speed of an Olympic skier.

Still, he ached for Abby and the closeness they'd shared. How long would he be tortured by her memory?

"Vivige? Tell Delphine I've gone to the office, but I'll come home early and we'll have dinner together on the terrace."

"Very well."

"Has Georges phoned?"

"No. I thought he was on a well-deserved month's vacation."

"He is, but it's unlike him not to check in from time to time."

She made a sound of disgust. "You drive him as hard as you drive yourself. It's long past time he went off with his friends and enjoyed himself. You should do the same!"

Ignoring her admonishment, he asked, "Are there any other calls I should know about?"

"No. Oh— Someone did ring for you about two weeks ago. A young woman with a Parisian accent."

Parisian? Philippe's skin went clammy. Could it have been Abby? But no. Only Georges knew his private phone number. He would never give it to anyone without Philippe's express permission.

Vivige continued with her explanation, unaware of Philippe's distress. "I told her you weren't here and suggested she speak to Delphine, who was out in the garden with one of the grandchildren. The caller thought Delphine was your mother. When I told her Delphine was your wife, that your mother had passed on five years ago, she hung up. Evidently she had the wrong number."

Dear God. Abby *had* called him!

Suddenly that nightmarish scene at the Beau Rivage when she'd broken his heart, when she'd rejected him and told him to go home to his mother, made perfect sense. Everything she'd said to him had been a lie. And she'd done it because of her own distress, her own anger.

Emotion raged through his body, releasing adrenaline that intensified the acidity in his stomach. Careful to school his features so he gave nothing away, he turned to his housekeeper. "You're probably right, Vivige. There are several Moreaus in the directory."

At last he had a reason for Georges's request for a month's vacation. His secretary had never taken so much time off before. Finally all the pieces of the puzzle were fitting into place—not the least of which was Georges's unusual silence.

An anger greater than Philippe had ever known consumed him. "Vivige, if Georges phones anytime in the next three weeks, tell him to call me at the office. There is something important I need to discuss with him."

"TRY TO RELAX, Mrs. Sutherland. I'll come back in a few minutes to take your blood pressure again."

Relax! If only she could.

"I-I'm not Mrs. Sutherland. I'm her twin, Abby Clarke," Abby corrected the nurse. The woman nodded and Abby's tear-swollen eyes following her exit from the cubicle. The second she disappeared, Max parted the curtain and stepped inside.

Not hearing any news of Kellie or Giselle had added new lines to his face. Each day his expression grew more haunted. Abby turned onto her side toward the wall, wishing he hadn't witnessed her dizzy spell. Because of that, he'd requested time off from his marshal's duties and had insisted on driving her to the clinic in West Yellowstone himself.

Her own grief over Kellie's silence was magnified a hundredfold every time she looked into his pain-filled eyes. Knowing she reminded him of his wife made everything that much worse. Abby was convinced that in many ways she and Max weren't good for each other. He shouldn't be worrying about her physical health on top of Kellie's disappearance. He had every right to resent her invasion of his privacy, every right to hate her for trading places with Kellie.

The pressures of his policing responsibilities, plus the constant problems of maintaining a ranch, were difficult enough. He didn't need a liability like Abby who'd arrived on his property from out of the blue, pregnant and jobless. It was now the end of August. Since mid-July she'd been eating his food, sleeping in his bed, receiving loving care from Ida and Jesse whose wages he paid.

So far he'd ignored her efforts to reimburse him. She felt like a parasite, which made her guilt all the more unbearable. She wanted to move to a motel in town, but Max wouldn't hear of it. In any event, she couldn't bring herself to step one foot outside the house for fear that today would be the day they'd hear from Kellie.

She knew Max suffered the same way. They were like two adversaries locked in mortal combat with no way out, every option for relief denied them as the struggle dragged on and on.

Max moved closer to her. "The nurse said your pressure is 140 over 90. Is that higher than it was before you left New York?"

"A little." But she was too distracted by her worries about Kellie to feel any alarm.

"That settles it. This town doesn't have a doctor. I'm driving you to Rexburg where you can be seen by an obstetrician."

"I don't need a doctor." Hot tears trickled from the corners of her eyes. *I need to hear from Kellie.*

"The nurse thinks you do," he returned, with more than a hint of steel in his tone.

"Not yet!" she cried, and sat up on the stretcher, dangling her legs over the edge. None of Kellie's clothes with buttons or zippers fit Abby anymore. She had resorted to wearing a pair of her sister's well-worn navy sweatpants. As soon as possible, she had to get to a store to buy some maternity clothes. "I'll visit one later on, after..."

"After we hear from my wife?" he said harshly. "Is that likely? Shall I remind you what the French Sûreté said?"

"Don't, Max." Her voice trembled. The waiting had become a living hell for both of them. There'd been no trace of Kellie or Giselle. When the French investigators caught up with Paul Beliveau, they got a sworn statement from him saying that almost six weeks ago his wife had gone to the bakery around the corner and never come back.

"It's possible they've gone into hiding so Paul can't find them. Maybe they're someplace without a phone," she theorized in an attempt to take the dreadful bleakness from Max's eyes.

She knew what he was thinking—that Kellie had gone off with another man. If Abby didn't know her sister as well as she did, she might have come to the same conclusion. But her initial premonition that Kellie was in trouble had only grown stronger.

In truth, Abby was terrified to tell Max what her senses were picking up, afraid that if she spoke her fears aloud, they might come true.

"Excuse me," the nurse said, entering the cubicle again. "Let's get another reading."

While she fastened the cuff around Abby's upper arm and pumped the bulb, Abby noticed that Max had positioned himself so he could read the numbers over the woman's shoulder.

There was a stillness about him that unnerved Abby. Anyone watching them would think *he* was the anxious husband and father. For the first time in weeks, Philippe's image flashed into her mind. She couldn't help wondering if he would have displayed this same kind of concern—almost a possessiveness. Abby found it touching and, under other circumstances, would have welcomed it.

"It's still 140 over 90," Max announced, his voice as sober as ever.

The nurse undid the cuff. "You can sit up now, Ms. Clarke. I was just telling your brother-in-law that a twenty-seven-year-old woman without a weight problem shouldn't have a blood pressure reading this high. I don't mean to alarm you, but you really ought to consult a specialist right away to make sure all goes well with you and your baby."

"She will." Max's deep voice resounded in the cubicle.

"There's an excellent obstetrician at the hospital in Rexburg named Dr. Lyle Harvey. If you'd like, I'll phone his office now and alert them that you'll be coming in."

"Not today!" Abby blurted when she saw Max nod. "I—I'll go in the morning. I promise," she whispered when she saw his forbidding expression.

He put his hands on his hips. She could tell he was judging the sincerity of her promise. He knew she didn't want to leave the ranch in case there was word of Kellie.

She realized he didn't want to be away from the house, either. Again, she felt a surge of guilt because she was an unwanted burden at such a critical time. Finally she heard him mutter, "I'm going to hold you to that, Abby." He turned to the nurse. "Tell his office we'll be there at ten in the morning."

"DO YOU THINK more coffee is a good idea?"

Max put the mug to his lips, ignoring Ida's comment. She meant well, but right now he didn't need a lecture and wished she'd just go to bed.

"You haven't had a proper sleep in months and it's showing," she persisted.

"It's either coffee or the bottle, Ida."

"You've never been a drinker!"

"Too much longer without any news and..." He shrugged and took another swallow of the steaming coffee. "Jack Daniels is starting to look like a pretty good friend."

"You know you don't mean that. It's just your pain talking."

"You know a better way to relieve it?"

"Go to bed, Max. Jesse and I are going to take turns listening for the phone."

"The only reason I haven't drunk my way into a stupor by now is that I'm driving Abby to the hospital in the morning. We'll be leaving for Rexburg at seven-thirty. If there's any word, you can reach me on the car phone."

"I'm glad you've taken some time off. You're the only one who can make her see a doctor. She's cried herself to sleep every night since you got here. That can't be good for the baby."

Max slammed the empty cup down on the sink and heard it crack. He'd listened to those muffled tears until the sound threatened to rip his insides apart. Every time he looked at that beautiful face he loved to distraction, so white and pinched and so damn haunted, he felt ripped apart all over again.

In the twilight hours of the morning, when nothing seemed quite real and he'd finally managed to fall into a tortured sleep, his mind would fill with images of her body as he'd seen it that first night when he'd come home unannounced. He'd remember the changes that pregnancy had made. He'd remember the feel of her warm velvety mouth, the ecstasy of drawing her into his arms, knowing she was carrying his child.

Then he'd hear the screams. "I'm Abby, not Kellie!" And he'd come fully awake, his body drenched in sweat, his heart thumping mercilessly. And always afterward, he'd feel guilty because it was Abby he'd been dreaming about, when it was Kellie who had possession of his heart.

Kellie. Kellie. Forgive me. Where are you, darling? What's going on? Why are you keeping me in this torment?

He felt Ida's hand on his shoulder. "Every night Jesse and I beg the Lord to end your pain. We'll keep on praying, Max."

He patted her hand, but for the life of him he couldn't say a word.

Long after she'd joined Jesse in the other wing of the house, he locked up, turned off the lights and headed for his study. On impulse he went down the hall to the master bedroom. The door stood ajar. The lights were off and everything had stilled for the night. He listened, rubbing his jaw absently. For once he didn't hear her crying and presumed she'd fallen asleep out of sheer exhaustion.

Relieved because he knew she needed rest if her blood pressure was going to go down, he moved in the direction of the den and decided to tackle his ranch accounts.

Normally such an activity worked like the most potent sleeping pill, and heaven knew he needed sleep. Ida was right about that. He'd been running on nerves and caffeine for too long; he wasn't thinking clearly anymore.

He turned on the desk lamp, and the picture of Kellie was illuminated, the same picture he always carried in his mind. For countless minutes he stood there, studying her image, wondering how many more days or weeks or even months they'd have to wait for news.

An overwhelming despair gripped him. He flung himself into the swivel chair, lay back and rubbed his eyes with his palms.

That was when he heard Abby scream. A blood-curdling scream that sent a shaft of fear through his heart and had him leaping from the chair and racing out of the study toward the bedroom.

He flipped on the hall light and found she'd already made it halfway down the corridor, a ghostly figure in one of Kellie's silk nightgowns.

"Max!" she cried, and lunged for him like a frightened child needing comfort.

Without conscious thought, he caught her in his arms and held her close, trying to reassure her that she was safe. "Shh," he whispered, rubbing his hand over her hair. "You've had a bad dream, but you're awake now. You're all right. I'm here."

"No." She refused to be calmed and thrashed so wildly he had to use all his strength to subdue her. "It wasn't a dream. *Kellie's dead!*"

Her voice had sounded more like a wail, and he shuddered. "No, Abby. You've just imagined it."

"But you don't understand," she persisted in a hoarse stricken voice. "I haven't been asleep. While I was lying there, I felt her die. She's gone...."

Her mournful cry rent the air, then came the sobbing and the convulsions of her body, convulsions he felt to the very depths of his being.

"I can't bear it." She started to shiver. "I can't bear to lose her."

She clung to him, her nails digging into his back through the T-shirt. Then her body went limp and he caught her before she slipped to the floor.

"What's going on, Max?" Jesse called out in alarm. "We heard Abby screaming."

Max saw the two of them enter the hallway. "She just passed out on me."

His actions automatic, he carefully laid her down on the carpet and felt for a pulse. Though a little fast, it was strong. Encouraged by the rise and fall of her chest, he lowered his head and put his cheek near her mouth. When he felt her breath at regular intervals, he heaved a sigh of relief.

"Bring me some water, Jesse."

"I'll be right back."

Ida drew closer. "She's been living on her nerves just like you. What happened? Jesse and I thought there must have been an intruder in her room."

Max couldn't bring himself to repeat Abby's words. Her traumatic outburst defied logic. The hell of it was, she sounded so convincing, he halfway believed her and felt a strange sense of dread.

"She had a bad dream. It made her faint."

"The poor, poor dear."

In his line of work, Max faced life-threatening crises every time he reported for duty. Meticulous training had taught him to handle the most precarious situations. But what had happened just now went beyond his realm of experience.

"Here you are."

Max took the glass from Jesse and tossed the water in Abby's face. Almost immediately she gasped and her eyelids fluttered open.

"Max..." She focused all her attention on him, her eyes still as haunted and full of anguish as ever. "What happened?"

"You fainted. Just lie quiet for a minute," he urged in soothing tones, chafing one of her hands.

Ida and Jesse stood close by. Abby's gaze darted to them and her eyes filled with tears. She raised herself on one elbow. "Did Max tell you?" she asked, her expression one of intense pain.

Ida leaned over her. "Tell us what, honey?"

Her chin quivered. *"Kellie's gone."*

The chilling words reverberated in Max's heart. He bent closer and wiped the tears from her chalk-white face with his hands. "You don't know that, Abby."

"I *do*," she insisted before she shuddered again, convulsively, and broke into another bout of weeping.

Moved by her grief, he cradled her in his arms and rocked her, trying to console her, trying to take some comfort for himself. "Shh..." he whispered, and stood up with her gathered to his chest. "This time your instincts are wrong. I'm sure of it. No more talk now, Abby. I'm putting you to bed, and I'm going to stay with you for the rest of the night."

"That's right, honey. You go with Max and do as he says." Jesse patted her arm. "A good night's sleep, and everything'll look different in the morning."

Ida whispered, "We'll be on hand if you need anything."

Max nodded and carried Abby back to the bedroom. Without letting go of her, he sat down on the bed. Propping his back against the headboard, he extended his legs and drew the quilts around them so her shoulders were covered.

The temperature in the house felt comfortable enough, but she needed warmth. *She needed a doctor.*

He glanced at the clock. Ten after three. If she didn't fall asleep by three-thirty, he wouldn't wait until daylight to drive her to the hospital in Rexburg. He'd simply bundle her in the Blazer and take off.

The wave of tears finally subsided. Just when he thought she'd dropped off, he heard, "Y-you think I'm hysterical, don't you?" The question floated in the air.

To his consternation she sounded wide awake. He sucked in his breath. "No," he answered truthfully. "What I believe is that you've been under too much strain and it's finally caught up with you."

"I'm so sorry for the pain I've caused you," she whispered in a shaky voice. She pulled out of his arms, shifting to the other side of the bed.

He didn't try to stop her. It had felt natural holding her, smelling the familiar sweet fragrance of her skin and hair. *Far too natural.* He knew every line and curve of his wife's body. In the darkness, he could well believe Kellie was in his arms again.

Disturbed by that thought, he levered himself off the bed. "There's nothing to apologize for, Abby." His voice was rough, barely controlled. "I think we can both agree that we're long past the point of accusations or recriminations. Whatever Kellie's playing at, we'll find out soon enough. Right now your baby is our number-one priority. You need sleep and lots of it. Good night."

CHAPTER SIX

FROM HIS PRIVATE SUITE on the third floor of the
Moreau Textiles building in Nice—a building that had
been in his family for several generations—Philippe
buzzed his receptionist.

"Sophie? I heard Georges was back. Did you see
him come in?"

"No, monsieur. He was already here when I arrived. Do you want me to give him a message?"

"That won't be necessary. Thank you, Sophie."

Philippe checked his watch. Five to twelve. Although none of his employees were expected to be on
the job before eight-thirty in the morning, Georges
was notorious for arriving as early as six. He used the
extra time to get paperwork out of the way. Otherwise, the demands of his schedule made it impossible.

Now that he'd returned from his extended vacation, no doubt he'd wanted to plunge into the back-
log awaiting him. But Philippe, who'd arrived at
seven, had expected Georges to report to him before
he did anything else—if only to talk about his trip and
find out what had been going on at the office while
he'd been away.

The fact that his private secretary had done neither and the day was already half-gone confirmed Philippe's suspicions. Georges was avoiding him on purpose. And he hadn't sent one card or made one phone call for the entire month.

He pressed the button of Georges's extension. "Welcome back, Georges."

"Philippe. I wasn't aware you'd come in yet."

Liar. Philippe swallowed a retort and fought to control his anger. "How were the fjords?"

"Magnificent."

Georges's paucity of words angered him further; seconds later, he could feel his stomach burn. "Meet me at our usual table in the dining room of the Hotel de la Grande Corniche in ten minutes. There are things we must discuss."

After a slight hesitation he heard, "Could we lunch there at the same time tomorrow? I need to clear my desk before I set foot outside the office today."

"I'm afraid this won't wait. Since you'd prefer to stay in, I'll have Annette bring us some lunch and we'll meet in my office. I expect to see you in five minutes."

Before Georges could refuse him a second time, Philippe hung up, gave instructions to one of the typists, then got up from his desk.

He stood at the window that overlooked the Promenade des Anglais, where the hot blue of the Mediterranean and the white sails of the ocean-going yachts dazzled the eye. He couldn't believe it was the first of

September. His turmoil had been so great he hadn't noticed that summer had already come and gone.

The view from his vantage point—reputed to be one of the most beautiful in the world—mocked the storm raging inside him. Torn apart by guilt and by a desire that was closer to need, he knew he couldn't go on this way much longer. Both conditions, equally intense and relentless, were ruining his physical health. As for his emotional well-being, it didn't exist.

A familiar tap on the door alerted him and he turned in time to see his private secretary enter the office. Georges was impeccably groomed, as always, and wearing a conservative business suit.

He'd been with Philippe twenty years. Though he'd turned sixty-six his last birthday, he had the kind of face and slight-of-build body that never seemed to age. Even his hair had stayed the same dark blond, hiding most of the gray. Philippe urged him to sit.

Out of courtesy, they exchanged a few pleasantries. Georges patiently answered Philippe's questions about his trip, but the camaraderie between them was gone. In no mood to continue the farce, Philippe decided to come straight to the point.

Sitting on a corner of his desk, he leaned toward Georges and looked him in the eye. "You gave Abby my private home number, didn't you."

"Yes."

His bald reply, given without hesitation, told Philippe the older man was ready and waiting for him.

Philippe's chest constricted, making it difficult to breathe.

"In all the years we've worked together, I've never known you to commit one disloyal act. You've been a family friend. Why the betrayal now?"

Georges removed his tortoiseshell glasses and rubbed the bridge of his nose. "Because Delphine doesn't deserve to be treated this way."

Philippe blinked in surprise. Good Lord! How blind he'd been. "I had no idea your feelings about my wife ran so deep."

"I've loved her from the first night the two of you invited me to your home for dinner. But then, as now, I could see *you're* the one she lives for." His quiet admission held a weight of bitterness.

Stunned, Philippe stared at the man he thought he knew so well. Georges had never married. To Philippe's knowledge, his secretary had never been interested in women. He'd assumed the older man led a different life-style altogether. His confession explained why he'd risked his job and their friendship.

Philippe got to his feet. "I have no choice but to let you go."

Georges nodded. "I knew our association would be severed when I gave Mademoiselle Clarke your phone number. But I'd do it again if I thought it would prevent Delphine from getting hurt."

Philippe's body tautened. "By breaking faith with me, you've managed to inflict a great deal of pain.

Abby didn't deserve to find out the truth in such a cruel way.''

"You deceive yourself, Philippe. You allowed her to think you were free. What you've done is unconscionable."

Philippe groaned inwardly but didn't try to silence Georges, who was only telling him what he already knew. What he'd castigated himself for a hundred times ever since he'd first met Abby.

"I like Mademoiselle Clarke. Not only is she beautiful, young and healthy, she's an innocent victim whose future and childbearing years are still ahead of her. She deserves better than the few hours you manage to give her.

"Delphine is the mother of your children, trapped in an unhealthy body through no fault of her own. She has no future to speak of—only heartbreak when she learns what you've been doing on your *business* trips to New York. It won't be long before Simone and Charles hear the gossip about their father. You're a fool, Philippe."

Though Philippe cringed, he agreed with Georges. He could even think of some arguments, some reproofs, his secretary hadn't touched on yet. With deep sadness, he watched the man who'd served him so faithfully rise from the chair and start toward the door.

"Georges, before you walk out of here, rest assured that your future is secure. I'm turning over more stock to you. I'll be generous. I think you already know that you'll be virtually impossible to replace."

Georges paused in his tracks. "I hope so. Up to now you've led a charmed life. It's time you suffered for the consequences of your actions."

"Then it should please you to learn I've developed a nasty ulcer."

The older man turned, his frown visible despite the distance that separated them. "Pleased? You think I'm pleased to hear such news?" he demanded with uncharacteristic emotion. "How can I be pleased to watch the man I've admired and loved like a son destroy himself and his family?" He shook his head. "Ours is a decadent society. I had hoped you were better than that." Georges sighed and left the room.

IDA SWEPT THE MATS on the front porch, anxiously awaiting Max and Abby's return from Rexburg. She'd had their dinner ready for more than an hour and told Jesse to go ahead and eat without them.

Like Kellie, who'd been so easy to love in the early days of her marriage, Abby had worked her way into Ida's heart. She couldn't help worrying about the young woman's health, particularly with a high-risk pregnancy and no word from Kellie.

That fainting spell had scared the daylights out of her and Jesse. Although Max had handled it well, Ida knew he'd been shaken when Abby collapsed. Losing consciousness like that could mean she'd developed complications of some kind. Worrying about her sister dying, of all things, had done it to her. Ida got chills just thinking about it.

"Ida?"

The minute she heard Jesse's frantic voice, she dropped the broom and ran inside the house. "Jesse? What is it?"

"Get on the phone in the study!" he shouted from the direction of the kitchen. "It's Kellie's stepmother. Quick!"

Losing no time, Ida dashed through the living room to the den and picked up the receiver. "I'm here, Jesse."

"My wife's on the line now," Ida heard her husband explain to the Frenchwoman. "Go ahead."

"Maybe it is better that Max and Abby hear this from you," she said in excellent English with a charming French accent. "She loved both of you very, very much."

Loved?

Ida sat down in Max's swivel chair, afraid her legs wouldn't support her.

"I am grieved to have to tell you that my dearest Kellie, who has been suffering from an inoperable brain tumor and has fought so valiantly for life, gave up the struggle this morning. She died at the hospital a few minutes before ten."

"No!" Ida cried, horrified, and heard her husband's equally pained response. Her thoughts flew to Abby. She could still remember her mournful *Kellie's gone.*

"I can't believe it myself," the Frenchwoman said in a tremulous voice. "The immediate cause of death was a ruptured aneurysm—the wall of the artery feeding the tumor burst. At least there is comfort in knowing she died almost immediately and without pain."

Ida couldn't talk, could hardly breathe she was so shocked. Judging by the silence on Jesse's end, he was in the same state.

Finally they had an explanation. But it was going to kill Max. As for Abby...

"I would have phoned earlier, but just before she lost consciousness, she said she didn't want Max or Abby coming to Paris. She asked that I accompany her body to Montana to be buried."

Gripping the receiver more tightly, Ida murmured, "Yes. It'll be better for Abby if you come here." The poor thing was in no condition to go anywhere.

"Kellie was worried about Abby's high blood pressure. So I've worked out all the legalities to make the trip to the States as soon as possible. That way Max and Abby can see Kellie one last time and say their final goodbyes."

Tears rolled down Ida's face.

"My plane out of Salt Lake City will be arriving at the Idaho Falls airport at two o'clock tomorrow afternoon. Perhaps on your end you could contact a local mortuary to meet the plane, and we can all travel together from there."

"Of course." Jesse spoke now. Ida could hardly recognize his heartbroken voice. "We're thankful she was with you when the end came." Then he coughed, too choked up to talk more.

"It's true," Ida said, struggling to get hold of herself. "Kellie loved you. She always talked about you."

"My two girls are very precious to me." The woman's voice cracked with emotion. Ida wished she had the power to comfort her.

"Abby's going to need you," Jesse interjected, clearing his throat.

"I need her, too." After a brief pause she said, "And we're all going to have to help Kellie's husband."

Ida's thought exactly. She reeled as the ghastly news really sank in.

"Thanks for letting us know." Jesse took over again. "We'll find a way to break the news to Abby and Max."

"God...help you." Giselle's voice faltered, and Ida surmised that Abby's stepmother had finally lost her composure. Who could blame her?

"We'll meet you at the plane," Jesse assured her.

Ida heard the click on both ends. By the time she'd put down the receiver, she felt Jesse's arms go around her waist. No words were spoken as he rested his chin on her shoulder and wept like a baby.

"Oh, Jesse..."

She turned to him and they clung to each other, her tears wetting his flannel shirt.

Neither she nor her husband were aware of any sounds around them until they heard Max's deep voice.

"What's going on?"

Jesse's eyes sent Ida's a message of pleading before he reached for her hand. Together they turned to face Abby and Max, who'd paused at the threshold of the study door.

Abby was the first to break the dreadful silence. "You've had news. M-my sister's dead, isn't she." It was a statement, not a question.

Max's arm went around Abby's shoulder and drew her close. Then he stared straight at Jesse. "Say what you have to say," he demanded flatly.

"I think it would be wise if you both sat down," Jesse muttered.

"I don't want to sit down!" Abby cried. "Please!" she begged.

Ida watched the blood drain from Max's face. "For the love of God," he said, "don't keep us in suspense."

Jesse's gaze flicked to Ida's for support. Taking a fortifying breath, he said, "Abby, honey—you knew the truth before the rest of us."

Abby let out a moan, then swayed against Max, whose eyes looked like black holes in the paleness of his face. "Are you telling me Kellie's dead?" he shouted.

Ida nodded, feeling her heart break in two at the anguish on his face. "She passed away in a Paris hos-

pital a little before ten this morning, their time,'' Ida
began, relating every detail Giselle had told them.

Quickly, before Max lost all composure, Jesse said,
"Giselle's bringing her body here for burial. We're to
contact a funeral home and meet her plane in Idaho
Falls at two o'clock tomorrow afternoon.''

His chest heaving, Max let go of Abby. She crossed
to the love seat and curled up there, releasing such
painful sounds of grief, Ida didn't think she could
stand it.

Like a man who'd just survived a devastating
earthquake, Max seemed to stagger. "Look after
Abby. I've got to get out of here for a while.'' He left
the room on a run.

Ida put her hand on Jesse's arm, knowing her husband wanted to follow Max out the door. In a soft
voice she said, "He needs time alone, Jesse. Later on
you can comfort him. Abby's the one who needs our
help right now.''

HOURS LATER, the first violent paroxysm of tears finally subsided. Realizing she'd been left alone in the
study, Abby sat up on the love seat and pushed the
hair out of her eyes. She'd cried so much they were
swollen half-shut.

On shaky legs, she stood and wandered over to
Max's desk. His favorite framed photo of Kellie was
propped near the phone. Abby reached for it.

The eight-by-ten picture showed her sister sitting on
the top crossbar of a boundary fence, dressed in a

Western shirt, jeans and cowboy boots that accentuated her long shapely legs. Her red-gold hair tumbled about her shoulders in bewitching disarray. There was a smile on her face and love in her eyes for the man behind the camera. Obviously he taken this picture before Kellie had learned about the tumor.

Abby tried to imagine what it must have been like for her sister to have been issued a death sentence. The horror of it made Abby fall apart all over again.

As if it burned her fingers, she put the photograph back on the desk and, in despair, sank to the floor, burying her face in her hands.

Mentally she cataloged Kellie's bizarre behavior over the last year, starting with her insistence that they limit their phone calls to one a month.

Because of her unwavering loyalty to her sister, Abby had never wanted to admit that she'd been hurt by Kellie's rules. Kellie had never once invited Abby to the ranch, never once entertained the possibility that she and Max might fly to New York City so they could meet.

Though Abby now had a partial explanation for her sister's damaging actions, the pain didn't stop.

Kellie was gone. She would never see Abby's baby. She would never have a baby of her own. Abby's child would never know this wonderful aunt. There'd be no more talks or laughter. No more sharing. No more togetherness.

With fresh insight Abby realized that her sister had endured this same agonizing torment, knowing her days were numbered, waiting for death, which would sever the bond they'd shared from birth.

Like an astronaut stranded in outer space, cut off from his life-support system to float endlessly in the void, Abby felt totally disconnected from her life. Kellie had been the center of her universe. Now she was gone, and nothing else mattered.

"Abby? It's almost midnight. Won't you at least go into the bedroom and lie down?" Ida suggested gently.

"No." Abby shook her head. "That was Kellie's room. I couldn't go in there again." She hardly recognized her own voice.

"All right. Then we'll get it ready for Giselle and move you to the guest bedroom. You need to rest."

"I'll never be able to rest. My sister's dead. Kellie's dead."

"I know, honey, I know. Cry it out. Let it all go."

When Abby felt Ida's arms go around her, she broke down again, sobbing. "I w-wish *I* were dead."

"I know," the older woman murmured compassionately.

"Why did it have to happen?"

"I have to believe it was God's will."

"There is no God, Ida. If there was, Kellie would still be alive. She's been taken from me. I can't believe it. I can't believe I'll never see her again."

"You *will* see her again. Just not in this life."

Anger stirred in Abby's breast. She pulled away from Ida. "This one's not worth living without her."

SLOWLY MAX GREW conscious of the gentle sound of water lapping against the inboard's hull, the slight rocking motion. For a moment he didn't know how or why he'd come to be there in the boat. He lay stretched out across the padded seats in the clothes he'd been wearing yesterday, exposed to the cold and damp. Snow had blanketed the mountain peaks already, and it was time for heavier clothing. He hardly noticed.

He turned over onto his back and opened his red-rimmed eyes. Through his blurry vision he could detect a faint lavender light in the eastern sky. Dawn was approaching.

Then he remembered.

Kellie was dead.

Once again pain consumed him. Like a battering ram, it bludgeoned its way through his body, tramping over his heart and soul till he wondered how he could still be breathing.

Last night he'd taken the boat and come out on the lake, where he could vent his grief in privacy. He'd dropped anchor in a bay far from human habitation, and here he railed against God, against Abby who was still alive, against Kellie who'd kept her secret from him. She'd denied them precious time they could have spent together, ten precious months they could have shared until the end came.

Why had she pushed him away? Why couldn't she have turned to him, her own husband? Did it mean there was something lacking in him?

It was a question for which there would never be an answer. He'd agonized over it until the nearly full bottle of whiskey he'd taken from Jesse's cabin was finished. At some point he'd passed out.

Just then the sound of a motor broke into his tortured thoughts, disturbing the stillness. It told him he was no longer alone. Though it was the second week of September and tourist season was pretty well over, some of the local fishermen were out for their morning catch.

The ripples from the other boat's wake rocked Max's twenty-one-foot inboard, almost throwing him to the floor. The hangover that had left him with a blinding headache had also rendered him sluggish and dizzy.

He growled out a stream of curses and struggled to his feet. As soon as he'd buried Kellie, he planned to take more time off from his marshal's duties to climb to the Coffin Lakes. Only a grizzly would dare to disturb him up there in air so thin it hurt to breathe. That was what he wanted. To hurt so damn bad he couldn't feel anything else.

But until then, he had responsibilities that couldn't be put off. He had to meet Giselle's plane and make funeral arrangements. Yet deep in his gut he dreaded returning to the house.

Why did Kellie have to have a twin? Was this God's way of punishing him for something he'd done wrong? Something he'd failed to do? If so, He couldn't have found a better way to exact retribution.

Every time Max looked at Abby he was reminded of his wife. He'd loved Kellie to the depths of his soul. They'd still been like honeymooners that day she'd driven into West Yellowstone.

But when she'd finally returned, a different person inhabited that beautiful face and body. The transformation had turned his life into a living hell.

When a man buried his wife, he had a right to pray for relief from the pain, for forgetfulness. How in God's name could he forget anything about Kellie when her mirror image was living in his house, eating his food, sleeping in his bed? His bed . . .

Tortured beyond endurance, he pulled up the anchor with quick jerky movements. Then he stepped to the front of the boat and turned on the ignition.

With the engine in neutral, he got some aspirin from the first-aid kit and swallowed them dry. And he found himself wondering why the tumor hadn't taken Abby, instead. She and Kellie shared everything else, he reasoned with a bitter anger that was growing out of control.

In a swift motion he pushed the throttle, and the boat took off across the water at full speed. He stood at the wheel, filled with uncharitable thoughts about the woman whose pregnancy was another painful reminder of the sons and daughters he'd never father now that Kellie was gone.

But as he rounded the point and entered the bay where he could see the dock he and Jesse had built years ago, another thought intruded, one that sent a shudder of alarm through his body.

Was it possible that Abby had a brain tumor like Kellie's and didn't know it?

Maybe her fainting spell had been a symptom of the very condition that had proved fatal to Kellie. Since his wife hadn't wanted to tell him anything about her illness, he had no idea what symptoms had driven her to seek a doctor in the first place. For that matter, he didn't even know the *name* of the doctor who'd first diagnosed her.

Since there were no doctors in West Yellowstone, he had to assume she'd gone to a specialist in another city close by. Otherwise she wouldn't have had time to get back to Carole's house on the night of their two-month anniversary.

The mere thought of that night stabbed him all over again. But this time there was an accompanying anger, which was doing a hell of a job of destroying every good memory of her.

Once more his black thoughts shifted to Abby. Dr. Harvey in Rexburg couldn't account for her high blood pressure. He hadn't found any protein in her urine to suggest toxemia and was forced to conclude it was pregnancy-induced hypertension. He'd ordered a salt-free diet and plenty of bed rest.

But it was more than possible that Abby was a walking time bomb, just like Kellie. Snatches of conversation with his sister-in-law flashed into his mind, and his fingers tightened on the wheel.

Abby had mentioned that she and Kellie had gotten appendicitis at the same time. In fact, according to Abby, their medical histories read as though they were one and the same person. Not only did two identical molars require fillings at exactly the same time, they came down with chicken pox on the same night, developed swimmer's ear at the beach one summer in the same ear on the same day and started their periods at the age of thirteen on the same day.

Joined as they were genetically, he had to assume that Abby would suffer his wife's fate, as well, and soon!

Max grimaced and gunned the engine, throwing up a huge wake. When he reached the pier, his headache had become a dull throb. He leapt from the boat, secured it, then headed for his truck at a run. He had to find Jesse.

Ten minutes later he screeched to a halt at the side of the house and jumped down from the cab. To his relief, Jesse had already come outside and was walking rapidly toward him. When the older man reached him, they hugged hard.

"Ida was getting worried about you," Jesse said in a husky voice and clapped Max on the back. "She went ahead and contacted a mortuary in Idaho Falls—Hazen Brothers. They'll be there to meet the plane. Is that all right with you?"

Max nodded. "I'm grateful to you."

"Look, Max, I figured you were down at the lake, that you'd had a hell of a night. Better not let anyone

see you looking like this. Let's go back to my cabin so
you can have a shower and shave."

"You're reading my mind, Jesse. And on the way I
need to discuss something vital with you." They
headed for Max's truck.

"What's wrong?" Jesse asked after they drove
through the gate onto the forest road.

"It's about Abby."

The older man's expression sobered. "She cried all
night and refuses to eat or drink. I don't know how
she's going to make it through a funeral. If she keeps
this up, she'll lose the baby. I tell you, I'm worried."

"So am I," Max said in a solemn voice, "but for an
entirely different reason."

CHAPTER SEVEN

"GISELLE!"

At the sound of Abby's voice, the diminutive woman with her cap of short dark hair stepped off the plane and started running toward Abby.

"Mon ange." My angel. Giselle had always called her that. They met halfway and reached for each other.

"Giselle..." Abby's voice broke as she crushed her stepmother in her arms, needing her desperately.

The older woman still wore the same sweet perfume. It brought back a host of memories of the three of them, some so poignant Abby began sobbing and couldn't stop.

"From the look of you, I think you must have been crying for a long time, eh?" Giselle murmured. "Remember that your sister has gone to be with your mother and father. She is at peace. You have to think about the little one now. You have to think about Max and how all this is affecting him. Men don't know what to do with a woman who cries all the time."

Her gentle rebuke brought Abby up short. She fought for control and lifted her head to look at the woman she loved. "What about Paul?"

Giselle's black eyes glistened with moisture. "He is a sick man who will never get better without counseling. I'm afraid such an eventuality will not happen. I stopped writing and phoning you girls because I didn't want to make it your problem. However, your sister's arrival forced me to make a decision, and I left him. But I'll explain all that later. Introduce me to Max. I want to meet the man who made Kellie too happy."

Abby paused in the act of wiping her eyes. "Too happy?"

"It is only my opinion, *naturellement*, but I think it is possible she couldn't bear to let him love her once she learned of the tumor. It would be too painful a reminder of all she was going to miss."

"But that doesn't make sense, Giselle."

The Frenchwoman's expressive brows lifted in speculation. "Perhaps it did to her. You know how her mind worked better than anyone. Do you have another explanation?"

"No," Abby whispered. "But still..."

"You don't think you would have done the same thing if you'd been in her place?"

"No. I know myself too well. I'm too selfish, too cowardly to be alone. Kellie was always the brave one." Abby's voice shook and tears started again. "I—I hoped she'd told you the truth about everything."

"*Non*. She concentrated on me and my problem. In fact, I knew nothing about her condition until she ended up in the hospital after suffering a severe dizzy spell in my hotel room. When the attending physician called for a neurosurgeon, she was forced to tell me the truth.

"It all happened so fast I am still in shock. We only had a few minutes before she lapsed into a coma and died. She asked that I bring her back to you and Max, which is exactly what I've done. Now, let's not keep him waiting any longer."

As they walked, Abby held on to her stepmother's arm. "When you can't give Max a reasonable explanation for Kellie's behavior, it'll break his heart."

In her mind, Abby could still see his chiseled profile, with the gaunt features and hollowed cheeks—the way he'd looked during the mostly silent drive to Idaho Falls earlier in the day. Once, when he'd turned to ask her a question, she'd gasped at the bleakness in his eyes. His wintry expression expressed every emotion she was feeling, from anguish to rage.

"*Non, non, mon ange.* If I'm not mistaken, Kellie broke her husband's heart when she first started keeping her secret. But that was her decision. Now it's a fait accompli, and you and Max must get on with your lives."

Everything Giselle said made sense. But it didn't lessen the overwhelming emptiness Abby was feeling. Her existence seemed futile now, because Kellie was no longer alive. Somehow, in some childish way, Abby had hoped that seeing Giselle would make the pain go away. She'd always been able to put the world right for Abby before.

"I want you to think about something else while I'm here," the Frenchwoman continued. "When I go back to Paris, I'd like to take you with me. Thanks to your wonderful father, I have enough money in investments to get myself an apartment and live comfortably. You and I could be together again.

"Kellie told me about the man who lied to you, the father of the child you carry. He is not worthy of you. I want to help you raise the baby until the right man comes into your life and marries you. In the meantime, it will bring me the greatest joy to be a grandmother, *mon ange*. And I believe it will help you."

Moved to tears by her generosity, Abby hugged Giselle tightly. But she didn't respond to her stepmother's suggestion. She couldn't think beyond the moment, not when she could see Max walking toward them. It meant that Kellie's body had been taken away in the hearse. He and the Woods were ready to go. All Abby wanted to do was drive to the mortuary and be with her sister.

"Max," Abby said when he reached them, "this is Giselle Beliveau. Giselle, Max Sutherland, Kellie's husband."

Max took Giselle's hand in both of his and held it for a long moment. The gesture was too much for Abby, who had to look away while she fought tears.

"I've wanted to meet you for a long time," he said quietly. "Kellie adored you."

"She adored *you,*" Giselle responded with her characteristic frankness. Abby saw the way his hands clenched, as if he was barely holding on to his control. "I know you don't believe that, but it's true. Otherwise she would never have married you within weeks of meeting you. For her, it was the *coup de foudre*. Love at first sight."

Lines of bitterness and cynicism marred his attractive features, deepening the shadows beneath his eyes.

"As I told Abby," Giselle confided, "I think Kellie loved you too much." At that comment, his head reared back, but Giselle paid no heed. "In you she found the perfect love. But when she learned that her life was going to be cut short, I believe her fears took over. Perhaps she was afraid to be reminded of everything that would soon end. Your love became painful to her. And yet, I think, she was also afraid that you'd *stop* loving her—because she had an incurable condition and could no longer be the woman you'd married."

Abby could have predicted his grimace and wished Giselle would stop with her theories. Couldn't she see he didn't believe any of it? Neither did Abby. For the first time Abby wasn't able to fathom her sister's behavior.

"I am certain she preferred to let you think she no longer loved you. In her mind it was better that you retain the picture of her when she was whole, rather than take the risk of your seeing her ill and changed."

"Did she tell you that?" Abby heard Max demand in a deceptively soft tone.

"*Non*. Her greatest concern was that you be spared a long flight to France. She wanted to come home to you."

Abby couldn't take any more and knew Max couldn't, either. "Why don't we go?"

Max's gaze darted to Abby. "You shouldn't have been on your feet this long. Are you feeling ill?"

Since she'd fainted, he'd shown surprising concern over her well-being. "No. I'm just anxious to get to the mortuary."

He studied her face as if he didn't quite believe her, then turned to Giselle. "Jesse, my foreman, stowed your luggage in the back of the Blazer before he and Ida went on ahead. If you're ready, I'll drive you and Abby over in the car."

Giselle nodded and took Abby's arm as the three of them walked to the doors of the terminal. "What arrangements have you made?"

"We'll be holding graveside services at noon tomorrow at the cemetery in West Yellowstone," Max informed her. "After we visit the mortuary this afternoon, we'll drive back to the ranch. The flight must have been exhausting, and Abby should be in bed."

"That's hardly your problem, Max. I'm not a child," Abby snapped. "You're talking about going home, and we haven't even seen Kellie yet. I may decide to stay here overnight."

"No. That's exactly what you won't do," he stated with the kind of authority she imagined he wielded as a deputy marshal. "I'm thinking about your baby. If you don't start taking care of yourself, you'll be in trouble.''

How dared he dictate to her! ''Do you think anything matters to me anymore? No one understands.'' Her voice trailed off, and she hastened to move away from Giselle and Max. But she only made it a few steps before she began sobbing again. It didn't quite drown out the whispering she could hear behind her.

''If she wants to spend more time with her sister, I'll stay at a hotel with her tonight, Max. We'll drive to West Yellowstone tomorrow morning in the mortuary limousine.''

''I appreciate the offer, but for reasons I don't wish to go into right now, that wouldn't be a good idea. Abby's health is at risk. She needs to be home where we can look after her.''

Abby couldn't stand to hear any more and ran all the way through the terminal to the car.

''MR. SUTHERLAND?''

Max had been talking to Jesse about when would be the best time to tell Abby he'd made a doctor's appointment for her. But at the sound of his name being called, he broke off and turned toward the director.

''If you'd like to follow me, I'll show you where we've put your wife.''

The moment had come.

Everything seemed unreal to Max. He couldn't quite grasp the fact that he was about to see Kellie again in these strange surroundings.

He left an inconsolable Abby, who was sitting on a couch between Ida and Giselle, and went out the door after the other man.

The funeral home had several viewing rooms. At the end of the hall he saw a sign with Kellie's name on it and a chilling sensation entered his heart. Inside the flower-filled room, the mingled floral scents assailed him. It added a bittersweet finality to the nightmare he'd been living.

A phone call to the marshal's office had let his boss know about Kellie, and it seemed everyone in the department had phoned or sent flowers to express sympathy. As well, word had traveled fast to friends and acquaintances in West Yellowstone and the surrounding areas.

His eyes went immediately to the casket in the corner of the room.

Kellie.

Max felt like a man sinking in quicksand. With feelings of reluctance and dread, he walked the remaining steps to reach her.

Because of his work, the sight of a dead person was not a new experience for him. But this was his Kellie.

A great heaving sob escaped him.

No longer aware of time passing, he stared down at the woman who'd stolen his heart, then shattered it.

Without her spirit animating her body, he had difficulty recognizing her. Death had robbed her red hair of its luster, and those incredible green eyes were closed to him forever.

Kellie. Darling Kellie. Why did you choose to suffer alone? Didn't you know how much I loved you? Why did you leave me so long ago? Why didn't you help me? Prepare me?

Sorrow for what her actions had denied them filled him. Tears pricked his lids again, needing release. Later, after having given in to his grief, he leaned over and brushed his mouth across her cold lips one last time.

Goodbye, my love.

He touched her clasped hands briefly, then turned sharply away and strode from the room.

Abby stood outside the door, waiting. When he saw her, his heart missed a beat and he came to a complete standstill.

Though her drenched green eyes gazed up at him out of a face made translucent by grief, she was vibrantly alive and warm to the touch.

An anger bordering on rage swept through him. He didn't want to look into those eyes; he didn't want to be haunted by those exquisite features. He didn't want to be tantalized by the red-gold sheen of her hair. He didn't want to feel this longing to lose himself in her scent.

When he saw her lips quiver, he had an insane desire to kiss them into stillness. But they were the wrong lips. She was the wrong twin.

He moved past her.

She called his name but he didn't answer. He couldn't. Right now he needed to get as far away from his sister-in-law as possible.

ABBY FELT as if her heart had just been torn from her body. When she'd seen the grief on Max's face, all she'd wanted to do was comfort him for a moment. But one flash of those angry gray eyes and she'd glimpsed a side of her brother-in-law that almost immobilized her.

She shouldn't have waited outside the door. She should have stayed in the reception room with Giselle and the Woods. Maybe Max felt violated because he thought she'd been watching him. He didn't know her well enough to realize she would never intrude on his privacy.

She'd wanted to be near Kellie, even if that meant standing outside the door. Giselle and the Woods had been doing everything in their power to offer comfort, but Abby had wanted to be alone, and there was little privacy in the small funeral home. She hadn't known where else to go except the empty hallway.

With a new weight added to her heart, she entered the viewing room. From the doorway, she glimpsed Kellie's hair and profile and received the shock of her life to see her sister lying so still.

Nothing seemed real to her. Not her sister, nor this claustrophobic room where the heavy perfume from the flowers made her feel nauseated.

"Remus—" her voice shook "—why did you do this to us? You've never been cruel in your whole life. What were you thinking of? I *hate* what you've done. I can't forgive you. I'm not going to cry any more tears over you. Do you hear me?"

Wild with pain, Abby spun on her heel and fled the room.

Bypassing the lounge, she hurried outside, gasping for air that wasn't tainted with the sickening scent of flowers.

"Come on, Abby. Just a few more steps," Max said in his deep voice, materializing seemingly out of nowhere. He slipped a strong arm around her waist and escorted her to his car, parked in the funeral-home lot.

Thankful for the support, she sank against his side, too weak to protest. After he'd helped her in and shut the door, he went around the car, slid behind the wheel and started the engine.

"Wait. What about Giselle?"

"I asked her to drive back to the ranch with Ida and Jesse."

She swung her head around to face him. "Why?"

"I'll tell you on the way," he murmured, his expression unyielding.

"Tell me what? Stop treating me like a child."

She heard his sharp intake of breath. "This isn't easy for me, but it has to be said."

"If you're worried that I might want to stay around Kellie until tomorrow, you don't have to be. That wasn't the Kellie I remember."

"Nor I," he whispered with so much emotion she could hardly bear it.

"I wish I hadn't looked at her."

"We *had* to look at her," he said. "Otherwise we'd never have believed she was really gone."

"I still don't."

"Abby—"

She cut him off. "I wasn't eavesdropping on you earlier. I want you to know that."

"Did I accuse you?"

"No." But she'd never forget the fierce expression in his eyes.

"Abby, listen to me. Before we left the ranch today, I made an appointment for you to see Dr. Harvey."

"You what?"

"When we reach Rexburg, we're going to stop at the hospital. That's why I sent Giselle on ahead. She's already suffering jet lag, and I have no idea how long your appointment's going to take."

Clenching her teeth, she said, "In case you've forgotten, I just saw him two days ago, and I resent the way you're trying to take over my life. I'll decide when I need to consult my doctor. If this is how you treated Kel—"

Too late she caught herself, mortified to have even thought such a thing, let alone said it. "I—I'm sorry," she stammered. "I didn't mean that. To tell you the truth, I hate imposing on you, adding to your burdens. Kellie put us in an untenable situation and—"

"It's a good thing she did." His solemn voice sounded several registers lower. "Otherwise we might have gone along not realizing that your unexplained high blood pressure, your fainting spell, could be symptoms of..." His voice seemed to fail him. "That you might have a brain tumor, too."

Abby blinked, and a gasp escaped her lips. Not because she was frightened of dying, particularly, but because for once in her life she hadn't related Kellie's condition to herself. She'd been too busy dealing with the realities of her pregnancy and how she was going to support her baby to think about much else. She was stunned that it had taken Max to point it out to her. Max, who even at the height of his loss, had come to a conclusion that made perfect sense.

"I'm sorry to have been so blunt," he said. "This has frightened the hell out of me, too, but for obvious reasons it had to said."

"Don't apologize. It should have occurred to me the minute we heard the news."

"If the doctor discovers a tumor, I'm not going to let you die without a fight. Kellie cheated me out of the chance to make a difference. That won't happen again," he vowed.

"Her brain tumor was inoperable," Abby reminded him in a small voice. "Most likely mine's in the last stages, just like Kellie's, which means I don't have any time left and there's nothing anyone can do."

"How the hell can you sit there and say a thing like that when you don't have the faintest idea if a doctor could help you or not! We're talking about your *life*, Abby! *And your baby's!*" he thundered, then floored the accelerator.

Abby flinched from his anger as they flew down the highway toward Rexburg. According to the road sign it was only twenty-six miles away.

Like a drowning victim, her life flashed before her. Suddenly she cried, "That's why Kellie wanted me to trade places with her! She was afraid we shared a fatal condition. When she found out I was pregnant, she didn't want me to be alone when the end came, and she knew you wouldn't turn me away."

If the forbidding expression on his face was anything to go by, Abby was certain he'd come to the same conclusion. "I'm sorry she put you in such an awful position," she said. "Maybe in a few days or weeks you'll be rid of me and—"

"If you ever say that again . . ."

Abby swallowed hard and looked away, frightened by the savagery of his tone.

"I'm not sure what in hell was going on in my wife's mind," he said in a less threatening voice a few minutes later, "but if she believed that you suffered from the same tumor, I find it unconscionable that she didn't contact you the second she was diagnosed, so you could get to a neurosurgeon right away."

The same thought had just entered Abby's mind, but she didn't want to admit it; she loved Kellie too much and hated being disloyal to her. Then another idea occurred to her, one more palatable, and she grasped at it.

"Maybe she wanted to spare me months of needless suffering."

She saw his jaw harden. "Maybe. We'll never know." He shook his head. "Whatever was in Kellie's mind, whatever secrets, went with her."

"If we could learn the name of her doc—"

"A private investigator has begun making inquiries for me." He anticipated her thoughts faster than she could voice them. "It may be some time before he turns up any information. But none of that matters right now. You and the baby are my prime concern."

The baby. Oh, God, the baby.

CHAPTER EIGHT

"COME IN, ABBY. Mr. Sutherland. Take a seat. I've been expecting you."

Max shook Dr. Harvey's hand. "We appreciate you fitting Abby in on such short notice."

Max had a way of taking over that came so naturally to him he probably wasn't even aware of it. If it wasn't for the fact that she felt weak and light-headed, Abby would have said something, even if it meant embarrassing him in front of this compassionate doctor.

"Abby, I take it your brother-in-law has confided his fears to you?"

She nodded jerkily.

The doctor frowned and sat down at his desk. "I took the liberty of discussing your case with Dr. Marsh, the neurosurgeon on staff here. As soon as we've finished talking, you're to go to his office in the east wing."

He paused for a moment. "If in the last fifteen months you've had no medical problems prior to your pregnancy—problems you might have forgotten to tell me about when I took your medical history—then I would have difficulty believing that you suffer from a brain tumor."

"Thank God!"

Abby was shaken by the depth of emotion in Max's voice.

"Please don't misunderstand me, Mr. Sutherland. There's a probability factor here that says Abby *could* share her sister's condition. But it may not be as advanced, or it may be in such a position that it hasn't started to affect her yet. That's Dr. Marsh's department. Unfortunately a CT scan is out because the radiation could harm the baby."

Abby shuddered, not only at the doctor's comments, but because that awful bleakness had darkened Max's eyes again. She'd been nothing but a liability since the night he'd come home to the ranch and found *her,* instead of Kellie.

The doctor switched his gaze to Abby. "Dr. Marsh and I have been going back and forth on the advisability of subjecting you to an MRI. We don't know what effect, if any, it might have on the baby. But you're almost at seventeen weeks now. So far, everything looks fine and we anticipate no problem."

"Forget the baby," Max broke in. "If Abby does have a tumor, and it's operable or treatable with chemotherapy, then we need to act *now.*"

The doctor's glance flicked back to Abby. "I tend to agree with you. How do you feel about it, Abby?"

But she could recognize no feelings apart from numbing grief, despair and dark hopelessness. Slowly she shook her head. "No."

"You don't mean that." Max's voice sounded as if it had come from some hidden depth.

She sucked in her breath. "Max, I'm thankful for your concern. You've been wonderful to me when you had no reason to be. I'm sorry Kellie forced you to feel a totally unwarranted responsibility for me. But this is my problem, not yours. If you don't mind, I'd like to talk to the doctor alone. Please don't be offended."

She felt his anger and sensed a tautening of his body before he rose to his feet and left the room. His careful closing of the door let her know he was barely holding on to his control.

Abby sat forward in her chair.

"Doctor," she began in a tremulous voice, "because Kellie and I have shared identical medical histories since the day we were born, the tumor is probably there. It's probably inoperable, which means I don't have long to live."

He pursed his lips. "We won't know anything until we take a look."

"It'll be a waste of time. I'd like to be free to attend my sister's graveside services tomorrow, then fly back to New York and close up my apartment. After that I'll leave for Paris to spend time with my stepmother. She was with Kellie at the end, and she'll know what to do for me. I want to be buried in France, next to my parents."

He took his time before answering. "I can understand your reasoning and I sympathize with it. However, you have to consider the possibility that no tumor exists. You haven't suffered from headaches. There's been no hearing loss or blurred vision."

"But my blood pressure is up and you really don't know why."

"We do if you've shown that symptom only since conception."

"When I went for a checkup in New York, I hadn't been to a doctor in two years. I have no way of knowing whether or not my blood pressure was normal prior to that visit."

He tapped his pencil. "You're fighting this because you're frightened of learning the truth. I don't blame you."

Abby shook her head. "Dr. Harvey, you don't understand. I already know the truth. Kellie and I have lived a connected life, sharing everything. It would be abnormal if we didn't die in exactly the same way. If I can be thankful for one thing," she said shakily, "it's that my baby will die with me and be spared the same fate."

His frown deepened and he got to his feet, putting his hands in his pockets. "That's not the kind of talk I want to hear. My instincts as a doctor tell me you're not dying of a brain tumor. I'd like you to have the MRI to confirm my belief."

"It won't, you know."

"The one thing I've learned in my many years of medical practice is that you should never make assumptions about anything. There are too many variables that have to be considered if you're going to see the whole picture."

"Not in my case."

His smile was kind. "I realize you and your sister have led a unique existence. But let's suppose for a moment that you *don't* share her fatal condition."

Abby knew he was trying to give her hope, but he didn't understand. No one had ever understood except Kellie, and she was gone.

"Considering your high blood pressure, I don't want you flying anywhere, and I don't want you living with a potential time bomb for the rest of your pregnancy. It would be better to find out now, as your brother-in-law has suggested, so that your mind will allow your body to relax—which will decrease the chance of toxemia. But that's a decision for you to make after you've talked to Dr. Marsh."

He walked over to the door and opened it in time for her to catch sight of Max. Unreasonably, it irritated Abby that he was still around. But what really upset her was to see him talking to the nurse as if he was Abby's husband and had every right to discuss her case.

Dr. Harvey patted her shoulder. "When you're through with Dr. Marsh, come back to see me."

"We'll do that," Max answered for her. He'd ended his conversation with the other woman and approached Abby.

She walked past the three of them without saying anything. Max had engineered this visit, had insisted on staying with her to make certain she kept her appointment with the neurosurgeon. If she'd been alone, she told herself bleakly, she'd have left the hospital and never looked back.

Max cupped her elbow. "He's down this hall and around the corner. The nurse tells me the test only takes a half hour and there's no discomfort. They'll have the results to Dr. Harvey within another hour. While we wait, we can have dinner in the cafeteria."

"I'm not hungry." She walked faster.

His grip held firm. "I am."

"Then *you* eat and stop worrying about me."

"That would be impossible," he murmured with infuriating calm. "Here we are." Before she could protest, he opened the door to Dr. Marsh's office and ushered her inside.

If there hadn't been several patients in the reception room, Abby would have pulled her arm away. As it was, she had great difficulty controlling her temper.

"I'm Abby Clarke," she announced to the receptionist before Max could take over.

"Oh, yes. We just received your chart. You're to go on back. Second door on the left."

Abby whirled around to face Max. "There's no need for you to wait."

"Nevertheless I'm staying," he stated matter-of-factly. "In fact, I plan to talk to Dr. Marsh before the test. Shall we?"

Forced to contain her resentment at his interference, she purposely walked ahead of him so he couldn't take her arm.

They entered another office much like the one she'd just left. Since the doctor had to fit her in between his other appointments, Abby figured there'd be a long wait. But she was wrong.

No sooner had they sat down than a slim immaculately dressed man who appeared to be in his late fifties walked in carrying her chart. He introduced himself, shook hands with both of them and propped himself against the edge of his desk.

"Dr. Harvey and I have discussed your situation at length, Ms. Clarke, and based on your office visit of the other day, we both doubt you have a tumor. But we think it wise of Mr. Sutherland to bring you in for a picture, just to be safe."

"If you find one, it will be inoperable like Kellie's. So I don't see the point."

"It's true that you and your sister have similar medical histories. But case studies on identical twins have revealed that when it comes to the major organs of the body, such as the brain or the heart, one twin may manifest a serious condition which is nonexistent in the other."

"I have no reason to disbelieve you, Doctor, but I don't feel those statistics apply to Kellie and me."

"Because you've never come up against any major illness before."

"If she doesn't have a tumor, then what, in your opinion, caused her fainting spell?" Max asked while Abby was still pondering his comment.

The doctor's gaze focused on Abby. "Medical science can't explain the extraordinary ESP shared by twins, but we do know it exists. According to this history, you *felt* your sister die. If I were a twin and had lived through your experience, I'm not at all sure that the pain and shock, combined with your high anxiety level, wouldn't have made me faint, too.

"But let's see what the test has to say. I'll ask Mary to show you to the MRI center. Mr. Sutherland, you're welcome to accompany her as far as the waiting room."

With a feeling of inevitability, she heard Max take the doctor up on his offer.

Damn him and his sense of duty.

They'd just come from the mortuary. Max shouldn't have to be dealing with anything but his own grief.

Damn you, Kellie. Damn you for leaving us in this mess.

MAX SAT DOWN to wait and rested his head against the wall, exhausted. It seemed as if he'd just closed his eyes when he heard someone say, "Mr. Sutherland. The doctor asked me to wake you. Your sister-in-law is waiting in Dr. Harvey's office."

Coming to with a start, Max flicked a glance at his watch. Almost an hour and a half had gone by. The test results must be in.

Surprised he'd actually slept, he got to his feet and strode swiftly through the corridors, anxiety forming a knot in his stomach. For some reason he had yet to understand, the safety of the baby, of Abby, had come to mean everything to him. He couldn't account for his feelings, for the staggering sense of loss he experienced whenever he thought of losing them, too. It didn't make sense.

As he entered the office his eyes sought out Abby, but she refused to meet his gaze. Her complexion was much paler than before.

He turned to the doctor. "What's the verdict?" he demanded without preamble.

Dr. Harvey smiled. "It's exactly as I thought. Abby shows no sign of a tumor."

"Thank God." His relief was exquisite. Max felt as if he could breathe again. But when he realized Abby wasn't saying anything, his gaze flashed to hers.

"What's wrong, Abby? This means you'll be able to have your baby. You'll be able to raise your child."

"It's not quite that simple, is it?" the doctor answered for her. He turned to Max. "I have no doubts she'll deliver a fine healthy infant, provided she takes care of herself.

"But because of the stress, I'm afraid her blood pressure is even higher than it was the other day. I'm recommending that as soon as the graveside services are over tomorrow, she go straight to bed and stay there, no ifs ands or buts."

"I'll make sure of it," Max decreed, ignoring the furious look on her face.

"Good. I expect to see you back here one week from today, Abby. Check with the receptionist and she'll make the appointment. Remember, no salt."

When Abby didn't respond, Max said, "From here on out I'll go over all the menus with my house-keeper."

They said their goodbyes, and Max walked her to reception. When the appointment was made he ushered her outside. The air had turned colder since their arrival earlier in the day.

"The heater should warm you up in a minute or two," he murmured, driving off the hospital grounds onto the main street. They hadn't gone far when he saw a grocery store and pulled into the parking lot. "I'm going in to buy us something to eat and drink. Is there anything you'd like?"

"No, thank you." She continued to stare out her side of the window, as still and remote as a statue.

"I'll be right back."

Without wasting any time he hurried into the store, heaped grapes, apples and bananas into a sack, found some fruit drinks without sodium and checked out at the counter inside of a few minutes. Abby made no comment when he returned to the car.

After they'd been traveling a while he said, "You have to eat something. Doctor's orders. Otherwise you'll make yourself so sick you won't be able to get through tomorrow's services." He'd purposely mentioned the funeral to jolt her.

Much to his relief, she eventually plucked a few green grapes from the bunch and started to eat them.

Alarmed and angered by her silence, he said, "Abby, don't close up on me! This is exactly what Kellie did—to both of us—and you know how much pain she caused. Don't make the same mistake. Talk to me, dammit!"

"What do you want me to say?" She turned accusing eyes on him. "That I enjoy the way you've taken over my life?"

"Is that what I've done?" he asked, making an effort to restrain his temper. "Would you have bothered to see a doctor or get your blood pressure checked on your own?"

"Whether I would have or not is none of your business. After the services are over, I'm leaving for New York."

"The hell you are! Dr. Harvey has ordered permanent bed rest."

"First I have to close up my apartment in New York. Then I'm leaving for Paris."

Paris? "Do you honestly believe the man who made you pregnant is going to divorce his wife and marry you, after all?" He knew he was being cruel, but he couldn't help it.

"No." Her voice wavered, tugging at his heart. "My decision has nothing to do with him." In truth, Philippe rarely figured in her thoughts.

"Then what are you saying?"

"Giselle has asked me to come and live with her."

His hands tightened on the steering wheel. "That's out of the question. She's just left her husband, and she'll be forced to deal with Paul Beliveau when she gets back to Paris. Her life will be in turmoil for a long time, no matter what she chooses to do with the rest of it. That's hardly a peaceful atmosphere for you.

"Maybe later, after the baby's born and you're back to normal, when things have settled down for her one way or the other, you could go for a visit. But right now you're not traveling anywhere. The doctor has definitely ruled out flying until your blood pressure returns to normal."

He heard a sharp intake of breath before she said, "I don't particularly care what the doctor says. It's my life."

"Not anymore, it isn't," Max ground out. "You're carrying a child who happens to be my niece or nephew. This baby was important enough to Kellie that she got you to the ranch where she knew we'd take care of you. Are you willing to throw it back in her face? Is that cavalier attitude the way you plan to honor your sister's memory?" He drove the point home, disregarding the cruelty of his words.

"How dare you say that to me!"

"I dare because you're not thinking clearly right now. Don't you know how blessed you are *not* to have that tumor? You've been given a chance to bear your child!"

"You mean I've been given a chance to bear the child you always wanted with Kellie! Why don't you just come out and say it? You can't stand it that I'm alive, instead of her!"

He was silent for a moment. "That may have been true at the height of my pain," he said in complete honesty, "but it's no longer the case. What do you want, Abby? To make this into a Greek tragedy? Don't you give a damn about anyone but yourself?"

"Let me out of the car!"

"Forget it. If you have a death wish, there's no way I'm letting you carry it out. We have to bury Kellie tomorrow, and then you're going to go to bed and stay there."

"You can't make me!"

"Try me."

"I hate you. I can't imagine what Kellie saw in you."

"Obviously not enough."

"Dear God, Max. I didn't mean that." She felt as though she'd just snapped out of a trance, an evil spell of hopelessness and despair. "I don't know what's the matter with me, what I'm saying."

She knew she'd been dreadful to him, but the words seemed to pour out of her without volition. She had no right to treat him like this. He was a man who'd suffered, too. An exceptional man, one who'd been wonderful to her.

All she'd done in return was take out her anger on him. She wiped her eyes and averted her face, humiliated by her uncharacteristic behavior.

"Let's agree that neither of us is at our best and let it go at that," he muttered. "Now I suggest you start eating and drinking, or I'll pull over to the side of the highway and force it down your throat."

"...AND SO, WE DEDICATE the grave of our dearly departed, Kellie Clarke Sutherland, asking God's blessing to protect it from the elements until that glorious day when all will rise triumphant from the tomb and unite in the glory of our resurrected Lord. Amen."

A large group had assembled. So many people Abby didn't know, including the pastor who conducted Sunday services at the Chapel of the Pines in West Yellowstone and had married Kellie and Max.

Carole Larsen, a close friend of Kellie's whom Abby liked on sight, was the first to lay a rose on top of the pale blue coffin Max had picked out. Pale blue had been Kellie's favorite color.

One by one, everybody paid tribute. After Ida and Jesse said their goodbyes, Giselle took her turn. Then it came time for Abby to place her rose. She was trembling so hard, Max had to help her take the last few steps.

"Remus," she whispered, still in shock that her sister's body lay inside. "You promised nothing would ever happen to you. You lied to me. What am I going to do without you?" Suddenly the tears she'd been holding back wouldn't stop.

"Abby..." Max's compassion-filled voice resonated to her soul. She felt his arm go around her waist as he started to lead her away from the casket.

"No. Not yet."

"They have to finish, Abby. Then we'll come back," he whispered urgently.

"We can't let her go in that cold dark ground. I can't bear it. Daddy always called her his sunshine girl."

"She's with your parents now. The sun's shining there, I promise. She's happy."

"How do you know?" she cried in a mournful tone, clutching at the lapels of his suit.

When she looked up at him, his gray eyes mirrored her agony. They were the last things she remembered seeing before everything went black.

"Hɪ!"

Philippe nodded to the young T-shirted man who opened the superintendent's door.

"If you're here about a vacancy," the young man said, "I can tell you right now that the only apartment available was taken a week ago."

"*Non, non.* I am looking for someone. Abby Clarke."

"You mean the knockout redhead with the great legs."

Philippe cleared his throat. "Yes. Does that mean she still lives here?"

"That's right."

"I haven't been able to reach her by phone."

"She's out of town."

"Do you know how I can contact her?"

"Are you a relative?"

Much as he wanted to lie, Philippe didn't dare. There'd been enough lies. He would never know if word had already reached Delphine about his relationship with Abby. It would be exactly like his wife to say nothing and suffer the hurt in silence.

"*Non.* She's a very close friend."

"Then I can't give you any information. But if you want to leave me a letter, I'll see that it gets forwarded with her mail."

Philippe shook his head. "That's all right. Do you have any idea when she might be coming home?"

"Nope. If she asks, who shall I tell her was looking for her?"

"It doesn't matter. Thank you for your time."

"Sure."

The door closed in Philippe's face.

He hadn't come to New York on business; Abby was the only reason he'd decided to make this quick trip. Georges's painful rebuke, coupled with his own self-loathing, had left him lying awake nights until his conscience drove him to do something about the pain he'd caused her.

He wanted to apologize, to explain. To beg her forgiveness. *To see her one last time,* a voice nagged.

And then what?

Unless he divorced his wife, whom he still loved, he had no right to ask anything of Abby, no right even to see her again.

There was no solution without heartbreak, he realized sadly as he propelled himself down the steps to the waiting taxi.

She'd probably be back in her apartment the next time he flew to New York on business. Maybe by then he would have decided that it was better to leave well enough alone. But as the taxi merged into the heavy traffic, his disappointment at not seeing her grew so acute he had to admit that he was nowhere near ready to cut her out of his life.

EVERY TIME the door of her hospital room opened, Abby was afraid it was Max. When Giselle swept in, Abby felt her tension leave.

"Mon ange—" she cried with motherly concern. "You're still being fed through an IV? I was hoping you would try to eat something today."

Abby turned her head toward the window to avoid her stepmother's scrutiny. "I'm not hungry."

"But you *must* eat!" She sounded scandalized. "You're too thin and the baby needs nourishment. How can I leave you like this?"

"Leave?" Abby's heart pounded in alarm and she raised herself up in the hospital bed to grasp her stepmother's hand. "But you've only been here two weeks. You can't go!"

Giselle lifted the hand and pressed it to her cheek. "I don't want to go, but my visa expires in three days. You see, I didn't have enough time to get a passport. After Kellie died, if it hadn't been for the help of a government official who was a friend of your father's, I wouldn't have been able to make all the plans and fly here so quickly."

Because her thoughts had been focused on her sister, Abby hadn't realized that Giselle's flight to Montana had had to be specially arranged. Abby had taken Giselle's presence for granted; still, she couldn't believe her stepmother was on the verge of leaving. "Let me go back with you."

"There's nothing I would love more, but right now you have to stay in bed and gather your strength. All this rest has been good for you. I know, because your blood pressure has been dropping. I am elated about that. Now, if you would only start to eat, I could go home content. Don't you realize how worried Max is?"

"Max has nothing to do with my life!"

There she went again, saying things about Max she didn't mean. But she couldn't seem to stop herself.

"It isn't like you to be rude to anyone," Giselle reminded her in a gentle rebuke. "Why do you insist on his staying away?"

Abby was saved from responding as Dr. Meyers, a psychiatrist consulting on her case, came into the room. He asked Giselle to excuse them while he talked to his patient alone. Abby dreaded seeing him almost as much as she did Max.

"I'll be outside when you're through, *ma chére.*" Giselle leaned over to kiss Abby's cheek, then slipped out of the room.

Dr. Meyers was such a tall man that when he sat down on the bedside chair, Abby had the impression he was still standing.

"I read over a transcript of the conversation you had with Dr. Harvey the day you came in for your MRI, and I discovered something that needs clarification."

She had no choice but to listen.

"Abby, are you hoping you'll lose the baby because you're afraid it will grow up to have a tumor and die—like your sister?"

She was so astounded by the astuteness of his question she couldn't say anything and averted her eyes.

"It won't happen, Abby. The type and location of your sister's tumor was too rare to occur again in several million births. Your baby is a product of you and the father, not your sister. So far, all the tests we've run indicate that you're carrying a normal healthy baby."

His words brought such exquisite relief Abby couldn't hold back the tears. "Y-you make me feel so ashamed.'' She almost choked getting the words out. ''Please don't tell anyone what I . . . what I said.''

''I've sworn an oath not to. But I'll make you a deal. You start to eat something, and we'll forget this conversation ever took place.''

''I promise.''

''One more thing. Don't you think it's time you stopped punishing your brother-in-law?''

His question brought her up short, his reading of her thoughts and actions seemed uncanny. She knew she'd said hurtful things to Max, things she could never take back. He didn't deserve any of it.

Hot tears trickled down her cheeks. ''I'm so ashamed of myself, Dr. Meyers. I don't know why I've been treating him so horribly.''

''It's very simple. There's a part of you that blames him for taking Kellie away from you in the first place. You've admitted that the long separation from your sister drove you to become intimate with Philippe.

''It stands to reason that Max posed a threat to the closeness you and Kellie once shared. In an indirect way, you've blamed him for your troubled pregnancy because it prevented you from being with your sister when the end came.''

Abby hid her face in her hands. ''You're right. But there's more to it than that. I feel guilty whenever I'm around him.''

''Because you think he hates you for being alive, instead of Kellie?''

"Yes!" she cried. "How did you know?" A sob racked her body. "Everytime he does something nice for me, I can't bear it, because I know deep down he resents me. You don't know how he looked at me, how he spoke to me the night he came home and found out I was Kellie's twin. It was ghastly."

"I don't doubt it," the doctor murmured.

"That's why I'd rather stay in the hospital. I'm afraid to go back to the ranch and be a . . . liability."

"I don't blame you for feeling that way. What you've just told me makes perfect sense."

She lifted her ravaged face. "It does?"

"Yes. Given the circumstances, I'm quite certain that at one point he did hate the fact that you were alive and his wife was dead."

"He said as much," she admitted, devastated.

"And because you're an intuitive person, you probably picked up on those feelings even before he expressed them. Your natural reaction was to put up a defense.

"What you need to remember is that his anger was natural and normal, just as yours was. But those are transitory emotions. They don't last.

"Let me tell you something about grief. After the shock and the despair and the pain comes the anger. It's a necessary step in the healing process. Already I can tell you're letting go of the worst of it. Today you've made real progress—you've admitted your feelings to me. In time, both you and your brother-in-law will accept what has happened and get on with your lives."

"Has Max confided this to you?"

"No. He didn't have to."

"Doctor, how can I make amends to him?"

"If you would talk to him as you're talking to me right now, it would help him heal. The man has been in hell. He lost his wife, a woman from whom he was estranged for almost a year without ever knowing why. You're all the family he has left, the one person who understands what he's going through and could give him the kind of comfort he needs.

"Instead, for the past two weeks you've refused to see him or even talk to him on the phone. Your love for your sister is so self-contained you forget that other people are hurting, too. He has nowhere to go to work this all out. Of course he *will* work it out, given time. But you can speed up that process."

Abby could hardly swallow for the lump in her throat. "You make me sound like a monster."

"Not a monster. Rather, a human being who has shared a unique relationship with her twin. I don't know what that feels like, but case studies have proved your bonds go deeper than other sibling relationships.

"I've talked to your stepmother. Apparently she's tried to help you and your sister learn how to live separate lives and find your own individuality. You've made a start in that direction, and the baby you're expecting is going to change your focus again.

"The question is, do you want this child enough to do all you can to safeguard its welfare?" He got up from the chair. "Think about it, and give me your answer tomorrow."

CHAPTER NINE

WHEN THE PHONE RANG, Ida had just put the last dinner glass in the dishwasher. She reached for the wall phone. "Sutherland Ranch."

"Hello, Ida."

"Abby?" Ida couldn't believe it. This was the first time Abby had phoned since being hospitalized. Ida assumed she wanted to speak to Giselle, who was packing to go back to France the next day. "How are you, honey?"

"Since I went off the IV and started eating regular food, I'm beginning to feel better."

"That's the best news we've heard around here in a long, long time."

"Thank you, Ida. You and Jesse have been wonderful to me. Thank you for the beautiful flowers and the crossword puzzles, *and* the new nightgown and the books."

Ida could feel the younger woman's sincerity, and it brought tears to her eyes. She just wished that her gratitude had included Max. *He* was the one Ida and Giselle were starting to worry about now. Jesse was, too; he just didn't talk about it. "It was the least we could do."

"It was too much. More than I deserve after the way I've acted."

"Honey, you've been grieving. You should have seen the way I carried on after my mother died. Jesse almost left."

"Really?"

"If you don't believe me, ask him."

Ida's comment brought a faint chuckle, the first she'd ever heard from Abby. She wanted to hear Kellie's sister laugh again—the sooner, the better.

"Ida," Abby was saying in a serious voice, "Is Max there?"

Excitement made the housekeeper grip the receiver with both hands. "No. He's out issuing a bench warrant, but he's got a car phone. Shall I give you the number?"

There was a slight pause. "Do you think he'd mind my disturbing him?"

Ida would've liked to tell Abby Clarke a thing or two. But at this late stage, she was too grateful that the younger woman had broken her long silence; under no circumstances would she say anything that might jeopardize the precarious situation between Abby and Max.

"Not at all. Are you ready?"

"Yes."

Ida gave her the number. "If he doesn't answer right away, it means he stopped for a cup of coffee somewhere. Keep trying and you'll reach him."

"I will. Thank you. Like I told you the first day I came to the ranch, you and Jesse are angels. I'll see you soon."

As soon as an elated Ida hung up the receiver, she dashed outside to the garage, where Jesse was fixing the winch on the truck. She couldn't wait to tell him the good news.

MAX'S BLAZER followed the serpentine road through the pines until he spotted the turnoff for the Burton cabin. Long before he pulled alongside it, he saw Taylor, his neighbor, up on the roof making his annual repairs before the next storm blew in, bringing snow to the lower elevations.

Last year he'd fallen off, but that didn't stop him from going up there again. Max had never known a man who worked so hard—or had so much fun doing it.

As soon as he saw Max, the older man waved.

Max stopped the car and got out. "Don't you know when it's time to quit? A few more minutes and I'll have to turn on my headlights for you."

Taylor's laughter reverberated through the forest, disturbing a family of squirrels. "I'm not coming down till I finish. What brings you by? How are you, anyway?" he asked. "I thought maybe you'd take some time off to get away and go fishing or something."

Max had thought so, too. But he couldn't go anywhere, not with Abby on the brink of a breakdown, refusing to see anyone but Giselle, and Giselle leaving for Paris tomorrow. Lord. He dreaded morning and what it would do to Abby when her stepmother dropped in to kiss her goodbye. In the back of his mind lurked the growing fear that Abby might never leave the hospital.

He'd never be able to handle that. "I decided it's better to stay busy," he said.

"Now you're learning. So, what's up?"

"Your wife called the sheriff. She wants you to phone her in Salt Lake. I'm supposed to tell you it's not an emergency. Since I had business over at the Reardon dude ranch, I volunteered to pass the information along."

"Thanks, Max. As soon as I finish here, I'll get in the Jeep and drive to the phone."

"Want me to steady that thing you call a ladder while you come down?"

"No, thanks. I've got my work cut out for a while yet."

Max waved to him. "Take care, Taylor."

"You, too. When my wife comes up to help me close the place, we'll have you over for a lamb roast."

"I'll hold you to it," Max murmured, climbing into the Blazer. He backed down the dirt track to the forest road and started for the ranch, his thoughts so troubled he almost hit a porcupine who'd waddled into the middle of the road. He had to practically stand on the brake to miss it.

Shutting off the ignition, he waited for a minute, then tried starting the engine again. It wouldn't turn over. When he heard the car phone, he reached for it, cursing under his breath because his action appeared to have flooded the engine.

"Sutherland here."

"M—Max?" A husky female voice said tentatively.

His thoughts reeled. "Abby?"

"Yes. Do you mind? If I'm interrup—"

"Abby." He cut her off impatiently, feeling a surge of adrenaline. "Why would I mind? What's wrong? It must must be serious if you're trying to reach me."

She was the last person he would have expected to call, particularly on the car phone. Jesse or Ida must have given her the number. He raked an unsteady hand through his hair, fearing the worst. "Has something happened to you? To the baby?"

"No. The baby's fine. We're both fine. The reason I'm calling is to tell you that the doctor has taken me off the IV and—"

"That means you've started eating," he broke in, hardly able to believe what he was hearing.

"Yes. And provided I don't get out of the car, he says I can drive with you when you take Giselle to the airport tomorrow."

The change in her voice, in her attitude, stunned him. "When did he tell you that?"

"This evening when he made his rounds." She paused for breath. "He said he'd release me from the hospital in the morning, provided I go back to the ranch and stay there until after the baby's born. Do you think you could stand to put up with me that long?''

Her question seemed to remove a heavy weight he hadn't known he was carrying. "It's what I've wanted, Abby. We're family.''

"We are,'' she said in a shaky voice. "If you can forgive me for being such a basket case, I'd like us to start over and become friends.''

He could scarcely credit the change in her. "Amen to that.''

"Max . . . I realize we didn't meet under the best of circumstances, which is a shame because I wanted to get to know you the minute Kellie first told me about you. Did my sister ever admit that she phoned me from her motel room the night you two met at some cowboy bar in Jackson?''

A thickness tightened his throat. "No.''

"Well, she did. She woke me up at four in the morning to tell me she'd met the man she was going to marry.''

"It happened fast." For the first time in almost a year, it felt good to remember.

"You know, Kellie and I used to have this fantasy about two fiercely handsome desert sheiks, brothers of course, riding into our lives and sweeping us away to their tents in the Sahara. We would live side by side and raise our families and be ecstatically happy forever.

"It came as a great shock to both of us when the sheik who stormed her heart turned out to live in Montana. Not only that, he wore cowboy boots and brandished a .357 Magnum."

Max laughed out loud.

"Among other things, Kellie told me how much she loved to hear you laugh. I can see why. She said your eyes turn the most beautiful color—a molten silver."

He shook his head. "Do I dare ask what else you two talked about?"

"So you're intrigued. Well, she said, and I'm quoting, 'Romulus, I was standing at the bar listening to a great Western band, when this *god* walked in. I couldn't believe it. My ultimate fantasy in the flesh! I was so afraid he'd disappear, I started moving toward him so he couldn't miss me.'"

A deep chuckle rumbled out of Max. "She was impossible to miss."

"Obviously," Abby inserted in an amused voice he didn't recognize. In fact, he had difficulty connecting this warm outgoing woman with the Abby he'd taken to the emergency ward after her collapse two weeks ago.

"I'll let you in on another secret."

He was still smiling. "What's that?"

"She'd never been riding before she met you. So when you made a date to take her horseback riding at your stable the next day at ten, she arranged for a private lesson with a local stable at seven, so she wouldn't disappoint you."

He laughed again, delighted to learn that Kellie had gone to such lengths to please him.

"Since I've kept you on the phone too long already, I'll tell you one more secret and save the rest for another time."

"I'm all ears." He found he didn't want their conversation to end.

"She vowed that she would extract a marriage proposal from you within forty-eight hours of your horseback ride."

"Actually it took all of twenty-four. She underestimated her power over me."

"I'm so glad. She would have been devastated if you hadn't reciprocated her feelings. You were her *grande passion.*"

He took a steadying breath. "Thank you for sharing that with me. I didn't realize how much I needed to hear it."

"Oh, there's much more I could tell you," she said in a wry tone. "In future, when I catch you in a despondent mood, I'll remind you how much she loved you and quote you another chapter and verse."

Her words caught at his emotions, and for a moment he couldn't speak.

"What time shall I be ready in the morning?" she asked.

He cleared his throat. "Eight-thirty. We need to get Giselle to Idaho Falls by nine-thirty. Her plane leaves at ten-twenty. Abby...I realize you're going to miss her."

"Terribly. But there's always the telephone. I know you won't let me pay room and board, but I have enough money saved to take care of the phone bills. Let me at least do that."

"If it will make you feel better."

"It will. Good night, Max. See you in the morning."

"Good night."

In mild shock, he forgot where he was and didn't try to start the engine until a Jeep came barreling along the road flashing its lights, reminding him he was in the way.

On his third attempt, it turned over. He waved to the other driver and took off for the ranch, his mood drastically different from a half hour ago.

ABBY HUNG UP the receiver and lay on her side, having discovered that being almost five months pregnant made it impossible to sleep on her stomach anymore.

Though she'd phoned Max out of a sense of duty, she had to admit she'd felt much friendlier toward him by the time they'd said goodbye.

Dr. Marsh had been right. He'd intimated that she was probably the only person who could help her brother-in-law. With just a little effort on her part, she'd found that he'd spoken the truth; she'd heard it in Max's voice. The more she told him about the private things her sister had confided, the happier he sounded.

In a way, it gave some purpose to her life, knowing she could do something for him no one else was capable of doing—because no one else was privy to Kellie's secret thoughts and dreams.

Earlier in the day she'd had another appointment with Dr. Meyers, and the whole thrust of the session centered on the fact that she needed to keep busy, so busy that she wouldn't have time to brood about her loss. Since she'd been forbidden to get a job, that meant finding a hobby, something to give her pleasure and occupy her thoughts.

Kellie had done a lot of the bookkeeping and accounts for her husband. Abby liked working with figures, too. Maybe Max would be willing to show her what to do and let her take over Kellie's tasks. It would be a way to repay him and provide her with a constructive outlet. Best of all, it wouldn't affect her physical health.

"Hi, Abby." The nighttime nurse breezed into the room carrying some apple juice which she put on the bedside table. "I know you hate all these tests. One more blood-pressure check and I'll let you go to sleep."

Abby pushed the sleeve of her hospital gown to the shoulder while the nurse wrapped the cuff around her upper arm.

She seemed to take longer than usual and kept pumping. Alarmed, Abby worried that if the reading was too high, the doctor wouldn't release her tomorrow. To her surprise, she realized she was tired of the hospital, bored with her own company. She found herself looking forward to going back to the ranch. She missed Ida and Jesse. And if the truth be known, she missed Max. Desperately.

"Is it bad?"

The nurse finally unfastened the cuff and shook her head. "No. In fact, it's almost normal. That's why I took it again. Bed rest and no salt are the best remedies for high blood pressure. When you go home tomorrow, make sure you stay down as much as you can. I've enjoyed you as a patient, but until you deliver, I don't want to see you in here again," she said with mock severity.

"Don't worry. I've seen enough of the inside of this room to last me for the rest of my pregnancy. Thanks for everything, Leah."

As soon as she'd left, Abby got out of bed and walked to the closet. Always thoughtful and generous, Giselle had brought her a couple of maternity outfits from Paris, ones she and Kellie had picked out together before Kellie was rushed to the hospital.

Abby took them off the hangers and laid them on her bed. Since leaving New York, she'd had to dress in Kellie's clothes. For once, it would be nice to have something she could call her own, something that fit—and something that wasn't a hospital gown.

She loved the pleated dove-gray jumper with the gray-and-white silk print blouse, but her eye kept darting to the stunning leaf green dress with the full-length sleeves and square neck. Green was Giselle's favorite color on the twins, and in honor of her departure, Abby decided to wear it.

The style reminded her of a gown she and Kellie had oohed and ahhed over in a pre-Raphaelite painting of Gwynevere. No wonder her sister had chosen it. She would have looked gorgeous in it.

Abby rubbed the shimmery material between her fingers. It felt soft and utterly feminine.

A new dress required a new hairdo. Since coming to Montana, she hadn't cared about her looks and had worn her hair in a braid much of the time. As for makeup, she hadn't bothered. But this dress called for hair worn long and loose, the way she'd worn it in New York.

Her mind made up, she put the clothes back on their hangers and pulled on Kellie's quilted robe and slippers. With luck, she'd find someone at the nurses' station who could find her a curling iron and a hair dryer.

As PREDICTED, there was a snowstorm during the night—typical enough for mid-October in Montana. Max drove with more caution than usual, because he didn't want to upset Giselle; as a result, they arrived in Rexburg a little behind schedule. Since they'd left the forest, however, the snow had turned to drizzle, which meant he could make up some distance between here and Idaho Falls.

He drove to the hospital's main entrance, where someone on the nursing staff would be bringing Abby out in a wheelchair. Urging Giselle to stay put, he hurried inside with Kellie's lined raincoat over his arm.

"Max? I'm here."

At the sound of Abby's voice, Max paused in mid-stride and turned.

He wasn't prepared for the sight that awaited him.

Neither was his heart, which slammed against his ribs and started the pain all over again.

He knew she hadn't done it on purpose. She wasn't even wearing one of Kellie's outfits. But the glistening red-gold hair he loved so much flowed to her shoulders in exactly the same way. The same exquisite eyes mirrored the color of her dress, a dress that hinted at the breathtaking shape of her body beneath it.

The same seductive curve of her mouth made him tremble with desire.

He closed his eyes tightly, but nothing could blot out the memory of that mouth. The way it tasted, the way it responded to his kisses...

Since Abby's phone call last night, which had come as an olive branch of sorts, he'd had his first good night's sleep in months, maybe a year. He'd awakened this morning with a new sense of direction, something that had been missing from his life for too long.

But looking at her, he saw two women. One woman who, a summer night more than a year ago, had changed his world for all time. The other was the pregnant woman he'd found in his bed three months ago, a breathtaking woman who had somehow worked her way under his skin and was there to stay. And now, God help him, he didn't know what to do.

This was agony in a new dimension. And judging by the way her eyes suddenly clouded in pained confusion, he knew he'd ruined any chance for a fresh start.

"I didn't expect to find you ready and waiting." He could hear his own voice. It sounded aloof and unfamiliar even to him, but he couldn't seem to do anything about it.

Her face hardened into an expressionless mask. "Dr. Harvey wanted to get all the paperwork done before you arrived, so he came in early to release me."

"I'm glad. The weather's bad, so we're running late. You're going to need this." He steadied the chair while she stood up, then helped her on with the coat. "I'll find someone to wheel you out to the car."

IT WAS HAPPENING AGAIN and they hadn't even left the hospital.

Abby had explained to the psychiatrist, Dr. Meyers, how hard it was to ignore Max's pain whenever he looked at her. She could tell he wished Kellie was the one still alive. It was the same look he'd given her at the funeral home.

The doctor had counseled her not to react, promising that in time, this would happen with less and less frequency.

In theory, she knew he was right. After last night's phone conversation with Max, she'd been more optimistic about the future. But just now he'd made her want to crawl into a hole somewhere and vanish.

Out of the corner of her eye she watched him accompany a male nurse through the doors. The attractive younger man approached the wheelchair with a smile. "Good morning. I see you're ready to go." His appreciative glance swept over her. "I don't suppose you want to stay around here a little longer?" He winked.

He would've had to be blind not to notice she was pregnant, which made his harmless flirting ridiculous and brought a half smile to her lips. But apparently Max didn't find it amusing. A distinct frown formed on his face.

"We're in a hurry, so if you don't mind—"

"No, sir."

Abby lowered her eyes, imagining how well the "sir" must have gone over with Max, and felt herself being pushed through the hall and out the doors with the greatest dispatch. Thank heaven for Giselle, who managed to dispel a little of the gloom surrounding Max on the way to Idaho Falls.

Too soon they arrived at the airport. Abby got out of the car to embrace her stepmother, kissing her on either cheek. But her protruding stomach got in the way and both women laughed.

"The maternity clothes are very chic—like you. Thank you again, dear, dear Giselle."

"Mon plaisir, chérie." Without the slightest hesitation, Giselle patted Abby's stomach. "This is the

kind of weight gain I like to see." Her moist amber eyes played over Abby with motherly pride. "You look *magnifique.* Better than I'd dared hope."

"My blood pressure is down."

"Grace à Dieu." She crossed herself. "So, do not do anything to make it go back up, all right?"

"She won't," Max interjected in a voice that brooked no argument. "I'm going to see to it."

"Then I can leave without any worries. Thank you from the bottom of my heart for all you have done." Giselle stood on tiptoe to kiss both his cheeks, then turned to Abby once more.

"Mon ange, only four more months and we'll be together. I will have a bed waiting for our *petit enfant."*

Abby nodded and grasped her stepmother's hands. "Please don't let Paul know where you are," she said urgently. "I want your divorce to be free of problems."

"Do not worry. I have an excellent attorney, a friend of your father's. He won't let anything happen to me."

"Promise to call me as soon as you're back in your hotel in Paris."

She caressed Abby's cheek. "Of course. Phoning you will be my first priority."

Experiencing a sharp pang of loss, Abby reached for her stepmother and they clung one last time. Abby felt Max watching her. No doubt he expected her to become hysterical. She relished disappointing him and remained dry-eyed.

"I'm sorry, Giselle," Max finally intervened. "If you don't hurry, you'll miss your plane."

"You're right." The older woman sighed and stepped away from Abby. "Get back in the car. Go on." She gestured with her hands, leaving Abby no choice but to do her bidding.

Before Max shut the passenger door, Giselle leaned down and whispered, "When you get to the ranch, go to bed and stay there. I will pray for you."

"And I for you."

Max's gaze met Abby's over Giselle's shoulder. "I won't be long."

"That is true because as soon as I've checked in at the airline counter, I'm going to send him right back out. *A bientôt, chérie.*" Giselle blew her a kiss and started to walk away.

As Max picked up her bags, he turned to Abby. "If you get too cold, turn on the engine. I've left the keys in the ignition."

"I'll be fine."

She watched until they disappeared into the terminal. *I'm doing better, Max,* she said silently, brushing the tears away with the back of her hand.

WHILE THEY STOOD in the short line waiting for Giselle's turn at the counter, she confided to Max, "Dr. Meyers's therapy has been good for Abby. She has made definite progress. But now that she is out of the hospital, I worry she might suffer a relapse.''

Max stiffened. ''I won't let that happen.''

''Thank you for the care you are giving her. She is the light of my life. I know four more months must seem an eternity to you. But it will pass quickly and soon she'll deliver. I long for her to return home to France, where I can help her raise the baby. Send her to me as soon as she is able.''

''We'll see,'' Max muttered, more to himself than to her, and saw an uncomprehending look on Giselle's face.

''What do you mean?''

He moved her bags along. ''Only that neither you nor Abby knows what the future holds. We'll have to bide our time and see what happens.''

Her expressive brows lifted. ''I understand your concern. You have reservations about my husband, Paul. Let me assure you that I am taking steps to make certain he never comes near me again.

''I haven't told Abby yet, but as soon as I've concluded my business in Paris, I'm moving to Grasse in the south of France. *Naturellement* I'll have to be very careful with my money, but I have enough to rent a small villa there. The sun and the fresh air will make the place perfect for raising my grandchild.''

Deciding this wasn't the time or place to bring up disturbing arguments, Max said nothing. All too soon Giselle would find out what she was up against trying to divorce Paul Beliveau. It could take years....

According to Max's sources in Paris, the man wasn't stable and needed psychiatric counseling. Max had seen obsessive types like him before. In spite of protective efforts by the police and bodyguards, they managed to continue stalking their ex-wives. In some instances, they murdered them.

No way was he going to allow Abby and her baby anywhere near Giselle until he had positive proof that Paul Beliveau was no longer a threat.

"You are so quiet, Max."

Her comment reminded him that they were still in line. "I'm thinking that when Abby's time nears, you should be with her. I'll send you a ticket."

Giselle's eyes filled. "Bless you."

CHAPTER TEN

"AH, MONSIEUR MOREAU. What a great pleasure to see you in New York once again." Abby's former boss stood in the office doorway and greeted Philippe.

He shook the other man's hand. "Monsieur Gide."

"Come in and sit down."

He walked around his desk and seated himself in his chair opposite Philippe. "I take it you have need of our translating services. Since you were last here, we've lost Mademoiselle Clarke, but have added two new people to our staff, both of them with impeccable credentials. You will find their work excellent."

Philippe's heart lurched.

Abby was gone?

Earlier today, when he'd talked to the super of her apartment building for the second time, the cocky college student had told Philippe she was still on vacation.

Had he lied? Had Abby asked him to lie so Philippe couldn't trace her?

Struggling not to show any reaction, he said, "I have no doubt of it. Your company's reputation precedes you. I'll need someone full-time for the next three days, beginning at nine o'clock tomorrow morning. Is that possible?"

"Of course. Marc Chappuis is available. Shall I call him in?"

Philippe cleared his throat. "In a moment. But first I would like to know what happened to Mademoiselle Clarke. She did excellent work for me. I must admit that I am very disappointed she is no longer with you."

"Everyone says the same thing. She was always in great demand. Unfortunately, due to illness, she had to quit."

Illness?

Philippe stirred uneasily in his chair. His thoughts flitted to the nightmarish evening in the hotel dining room when she'd said goodbye to him. Now that he thought about it, she'd seemed a bit pale and fragile.

Mon Dieu. When she'd found out that he was married, that he'd deceived her, had the shock done something to her health?

He swallowed hard. "What kind of illness would cause her to give up a career she loved?"

Monsieur Gide eyed Philippe speculatively. "I'm not at liberty to divulge that kind of information, but I can tell you she had to quit on doctor's orders. As I said, you are not the first person to lament her absence."

Philippe could have pressed the other man to tell him what he wanted to know. But Monsieur Gide already suspected Philippe's question hadn't been asked out of professional interest alone.

He needed to be discreet.

Feigning a calm he didn't feel, he said, "It's never good to lose a valued employee. I know because I recently lost my private secretary, Georges, a man who'd been like a father to me for the past twenty years."

"Ah, that is serious. My condolences, monsieur."

"Thank you. Nevertheless, one has to go on. Therefore, I'd like to meet this Monsieur Chappuis. I'm negotiating some delicate export agreements that require a certain level of finesse."

"Marc has a firm business background. He won't disappoint you."

"Good. If it's convenient, I'll interview him now."

"Of course. Just a moment."

While Philippe waited, his mind leapt ahead. As soon as he left here, he would engage the services of a good private investigator who could find out if the super had been telling the truth.

Better yet, if he could locate Abby's twin sister, Philippe would learn everything he needed to know.

Her name was Kellie. To his recollection, she was married to a rancher in Montana who did some kind of police work. Philippe had never met her. If he could just remember her husband's last name. It started with an S. Something like Sommerfeld. No, that wasn't right. Summerb—

"Monsieur Moreau?"

Philippe's head jerked around in the direction of the door, and he rose to his feet, anxious to get this over with so he could find a detective to trace Abby's whereabouts. Money was no object.

ABBY HEARD the Blazer in the driveway and put down the booklet Dr. Harvey had given her on the importance of breast-feeding.

Max was home.

She glanced at her watch. It was only nine in the evening, the earliest he'd arrived at the house in ages. Her heart started hammering so hard she was afraid he would hear it.

More than six weeks had gone by since they'd seen Giselle off at the airport and driven back to the ranch. Abby had tried to make light conversation as she'd done on the phone the night before, but being with him in person made her feel less confident that he'd forgiven her.

Throughout October and into November, she rarely saw her brother-in-law. He'd gone out on a witness protection case, and the rest of the time he'd been busy with DEA warrants.

They'd occasionally exchanged a few words at odd hours, when she happened to see him returning from one of his assignments or heading out. They hadn't shared more than a dozen meals in that whole time. Abby was almost ready to beg him to stay home.

Ida didn't like the way he'd been driving himself, either. Abby had heard the housekeeper discussing his grueling work schedule with Jesse, who reminded his wife that this was Max's way of dealing with pain. He'd assured Ida it would pass.

Abby wasn't so sure.

Lately she'd noticed a subtle change in Max. When they met unexpectedly in a hallway or their gazes suddenly connected as he walked into a room, he no longer looked at her as if he wished her on the other side of the world. Instead, he seemed to look right through her.

Dr. Meyers had defined the stages of grieving. He'd said that men often had more difficulty than women overcoming their grief because they'd been trained from the cradle not to cry.

If that was true, then Abby pitied Max. He kept his sorrow bottled up. She, on the other hand, had cried so much it had put her in the hospital. Since then, she'd succumbed to several bouts of weeping, but they were growing less and less frequent. She was learning to exert more control on her emotions, in part because she feared that her excesses might hurt the baby.

Whenever Abby caught herself giving in to sorrow, she immediately plunged into a new project. She'd been hoping to help Max with the bookkeeping but hadn't had the opportunity—or the courage—to approach him yet. Her hesitation came from fear that her request would remind him of Kellie, or that it would seem as though she was trying to replace his wife. But Ida had recently gone into town to buy her some maternity tops and slacks and had brought home some yarn; she'd begun teaching Abby how to knit. So far, she'd helped her finish a pair of average-looking booties and now they'd moved on to a baby sweater.

February fourteenth was her due date. A Valentine baby. With Ida's assistance, she'd designed a pattern for the sleeves and neck, incorporating a band of pink and red valentines against a white background.

Of course, the baby wouldn't be able to wear it for a while, but ever since she'd felt it move, her baby had become real to her. She found herself thinking about all the adorable baby clothes she wanted to buy, but of course she didn't know if they should be for a boy or a girl.

"Abby?"

She blinked, unaware that Max had come into the study. She'd been lounging on the love seat in front of the fire, reading, planning, dreaming. She loved this room. *His* room.

"Max! You're home earlier than usual. Ida will be happy. She made stuffed pork chops for dinner."

"I ate in town." He sounded exhausted.

Abby watched him toss his gloves onto the desk and shrug off his sheepskin parka. His hair looked damp.

"Do you think it's going to snow again?"

"Maybe." His gaze wandered restlessly around the room until it came to the pamphlet lying beside her. "What are you reading?"

From out of nowhere a warm blush crept up her neck and face. "Some information on babies the doctor gave me."

"Let me see it."

"I—I don't really think—"

In seconds, he'd covered the distance between them and picked it up. Several moments passed before he lifted his head. "Are you going to nurse?"

Such a personal question coming from him threw her. She wasn't embarrassed, exactly. She wasn't sure *what* she was feeling. "If I can."

He frowned. "Is there a problem?"

"I don't think so. Some women have difficulty. My mother couldn't nurse Kellie or me because she didn't have enough milk. But I'm not anticipating any trouble, since I'm not expecting twins—thank heaven," she said with a little smile. Unexpectedly, he smiled back.

The sudden transformation made her breath catch, reminding her of the first time she'd seen her ruggedly handsome brother-in-law in a photograph. But up close in the firelight, the flesh-and-blood man was disturbingly attractive.

While he added another log to the fire, Abby swung her legs to the floor and stood up.

"Where are you going?" he asked. "Don't let me chase you away."

"After getting home from a hard day's work, a man has a right to his privacy."

There was a time he'd felt that way, but no longer. Lately he found that he craved Abby's company more and more. "I'll let you know when I require it." He

paused before asking, "Did you hear from Giselle yet?
Has Paul been served papers?"

"I presume he got them, but Giselle says the French
courts move slowly. Paul's attorney probably hasn't
had time to respond. She promised she'd call when she
had news."

As if on cue, the phone rang. In a few strides Max
reached the table and lifted the receiver. "Sutherland
here."

While he listened to the party on the other end, his
eyes narrowed on Abby. "Just a moment."

He handed her the receiver. "It's for you."

She placed her palm over the mouthpiece. "Who is
it?"

"The super of your apartment."

"You're kidding. It's almost midnight there." She
put the receiver to her ear.

"Hi, Sid."

"Hi! You told me to call if something important
came up."

"Yes?"

"I thought you'd better know that a man's been
around asking about you. He's come by three different times. Says he's a close friend, but he won't leave
his name. A couple of days ago, another guy phoned
me, also asking questions about you. But I didn't tell
him anything, either."

She couldn't imagine, unless— No, it wouldn't be
Philippe. If he'd wanted to get in touch with her, he

would have written her a letter weeks ago. And all her mail had been forwarded.

Philippe. Good heavens. She hadn't thought of him in ages!

Something had to be wrong with her if she could so easily forget the man who'd made her pregnant. The father of her baby. But just thinking about Max, let alone being in his company, drove thoughts of any other man right out of her mind. Since she'd arrived at the ranch, Max had been the one at her side, helping her every step of the way through her difficult pregnancy. She'd begun to think of him as the father.

In her heart of hearts, she *wanted* him to be the father of her baby.

Sid was still talking, and Abby forced her attention back to his words. Mystified about the strange men he'd mentioned, she gripped the receiver more tightly. "Can you describe the man you saw?"

Before she could hear Sid's response, Max had taken the phone from her. "What's going on?" he whispered, his gaze piercing hers.

"I don't know." She repeated what Sid had just told her.

Beliveau. Max thought.

Max put the phone to his ear. "This is Deputy Marshal Sutherland. I work out of the federal marshal's office in Billings, Montana. You can call information for the number to get verification.

"Ms. Clarke is my sister-in-law, and she's living under my protection. Now say what you have to say to *me,*" he said in a voice of steely authority. "Tell me about these men. The smallest detail could be vitally important."

"I wouldn't know about the guy on the phone," Sid replied, "but the other one is about five-ten, maybe in his early fifties. Brown hair going gray at the temples, well dressed, like he has a lot of money, and speaks with a heavy European accent."

"French?"

"I don't know."

Max grimaced. "What kind of car does he drive?"

"I haven't noticed."

"What have you told him? Try to remember your exact words. It's important."

"I said she was on vacation. If he wanted me to forward a message from him with her mail, I'd do it. That's all."

"But he didn't take you up on the offer?"

"No."

"What did you tell the man on the phone?"

"The same thing."

"What's your full name?"

"Sid Fink. I'm a college student, filling in for my father who's been sick this past year."

"Give me your phone number and the times you're available." Max wrote down the information. "If he should make another visit before I contact you again, play dumb. If you do anything different, he'll know you're on to him. If that other person calls, say nothing to him. Do you understand?"

"Yeah. Sounds like she's in danger."

"She could very well be," Max said gravely.

"She's one knockout babe. Every guy in the building has the hots for her. I don't think this character is going to give up."

"Just keep your eyes open and your mouth shut," Max said rudely. He couldn't help it, Sid's comments had irritated the hell out of him. "I'll be in touch."

He slammed down the phone, making Abby wince.

"That settles it. I'm leaving for New York in the morning."

"Why? What's wrong?"

"I have every reason to believe that Paul Beliveau has been stalking your apartment, trying to discover Giselle's whereabouts. And I don't think he's working alone."

"Dear God..." She put a hand to her throat.

"My feelings exactly. He's not about to let Giselle go without a struggle. The fact that she wants a divorce has probably exacerbated matters. I know his type all too well. It's no longer safe for you to keep that apartment. I'll have your furnishings put in storage."

"All right. Y-you've never trusted him, have you?"

"No."

She paced the floor. "Giselle shouldn't be alone."

"She has a high-powered attorney and friends in the right places. She also told me she's making arrangements to move to Grasse."

Abby was stunned by the news. "When did she tell you that?"

"At the airport. It's a good plan, one I hope she puts into effect as soon as possible. When she calls, let's keep this latest development confidential, in case I'm wrong and it's not Beliveau. There's no need to upset her unnecessarily."

Abby agreed.

In the silence that followed, she could almost hear what he was thinking, and it prompted her to say, "The only man I ever dated in New York was Philippe, and that was over a long time ago."

He stared at her, his eyes half-veiled. "What about the various men you've worked for, doing translations? How many of them wanted to see you on a more personal basis?"

"A few."

"Elaborate."

"I—I don't know." She looked away, unable to sustain his level gaze.

"That many," he muttered. "How about *all* of them?"

Color stained her cheeks. "Of course not all!"

A strange tension hovered between them. "Does a particular man come to mind, one who was persistent and didn't like being turned down?"

She shook her head. "No. Monsieur Gide has a reputable business to run. If a client were to step out of line, he'd refuse him service."

"So how did Philippe manage to accomplish what all the other hopefuls were denied?"

She detected an edge to his question; she didn't like where this was leading. "It's a moot point, isn't it? I've put that part of my life behind me."

"But has *he?*"

Her eyes met his. "I honestly don't know."

"Where does this Philippe live? What's his last name?"

"Moreau. He lives in Cap D'Agde, near Nice. He's the head of his family business, Moreau Textiles."

"Do you have his home phone number?"

After a brief pause she said, "I wrote it down in my address book, which I left in my dresser drawer in New York."

"You mean you don't know it by heart?" he baited her, feeling a rush of jealousy that overwhelmed him with its force and unex pectedness.

"I only ever called him once." The words came out in a whisper.

"What happened? Did his wife answer? Is that how you learned the truth?"

For the life of her, Abby couldn't bring herself to tell him how close he'd come to guessing the exact scenario. But her shamefaced expression clearly gave her away.

"The bastard!" he said in a low growling voice. "Then what happened?"

"I'd rather not talk about it."

"You don't have a choice if I'm going to find out who's been hanging around your apartment. Did you argue?"

"No." She smoothed the hair away from her temple. "After I learned the truth, I never wanted to see him again."

"When was the last time you saw him?"

"Two weeks before I left New York to fly here."

"So you disappeared on him."

"Yes."

"And he doesn't know why. That probably drove him crazy..." He gave her a speculative glance. "How long did you have a relationship with him?"

She hated having to tell all this to Max. It was humiliating to have to reveal what a naive little fool she'd been. "Six months." Her voice trembled, despite her attempt to sound matter-of-fact.

Max drew in his breath. "And if you hadn't learned about his wife?"

There was another long silence; she simply didn't know what to say. He paced the room, fists clenched, brow furrowed.

Nervous because he seemed so distraught, Abby said, "I think I'll go to bed."

"I was about to suggest the same thing. I'll say goodbye now. I'm leaving for the airport at dawn. After I've gone, don't answer the phone. Let Jesse or Ida screen every call. In case it is Beliveau or one of his cronies, don't speak to anyone until I tell you it's safe."

"I won't. How long will you be gone?" She tried to mask the wistfulness in her voice.

"After I leave New York, I have to transport a couple of prisoners across state lines. I should be back within two weeks."

She groaned inwardly. Two weeks sounded like two years. She started for the door. But as she reached it, a tremor of fear made her pause. She turned to look at Max, realizing how much she depended on him, how abiding his support had been despite his own loss. He always watched out for everyone else. But who watched out for him?

"Max?" His head came up, as if his thoughts had been faraway. He caught her gaze, giving her his full attention. "Will you be back for Thanksgiving?"

"I doubt it."

She couldn't bear to think of him gone for the holidays. "Be careful," she whispered.

Something flickered in the depths of his eyes. "That's my job."

"Just come back."

"I intend to."

As she left the room, Max stood by his desk, lost in thought. He couldn't remember the last time he'd heard those words said to him. It felt good to hear them. *Let's face it, Sutherland. It felt good because they came from Abby.*

The grandfather clock in the living room chimed eleven times, reminding him that if he expected to get any sleep tonight, he better make his plans.

After calling his boss to request some personal leave that was owed to him, he searched through his Rolodex for a phone number. Then he made a call.

When a familiar voice answered, Max gave a great sigh of relief and flung himself into the chair. "Rand? Did I get you out of bed?"

"I may be an old fogy, but I'm not headed for the rest home yet. Max Sutherland, as I live and breathe."

"So you haven't forgotten me."

"That would be pretty impossible after all the jobs we did together. In fact, you've been on my mind a lot lately. It's a damn shame about your wife. She was a real sweetheart, just like my Bess, God rest their souls."

Amen, Max thought. "Rand, what's your schedule like?"

"Nothing I couldn't change now that I've retired. What've you got?"

"How would you like to put on your private investigator's hat and fly out to New York with me in the morning?"

"Now you're talking, boy."

"I've got a job that pays the going rate. You're to close up an apartment and put everything in storage. Then you're going to sit there. It might be a few days or it might be a month."

"You mean I'm going to sit around an empty apartment?"

"I'll throw in a cot, TV and a phone. A microwave, too. You can live on frozen dinners."

"Who am I guarding?"

"No one. This isn't a feds' job. It's personal. I'll be paying your salary. On one of those days the apartment super is going to let a man into the building and send him up to you. You're going to keep him there and find out everything there is to know about him. I'll explain the details on the plane. Can you make it to West Yellowstone by six?"

"Just watch me."

"Thanks, Rand. This is important."

"I can hear it in your voice. I already feel sorry for the poor devil you're setting up."

"After the briefing, you'll change your mind."

ABBY LEFT THE CLINIC and walked carefully across the snow-covered street to Larsen's Drugstore. She wanted to buy a quart of chocolate-marshmallow ice cream, Jesse and Ida's favorite, to take home to them.

As she entered, she heard a female voice say, "It's Abby, isn't it?"

Immediately Abby turned toward the lunch counter and recognized Kellie's friend, Carole Larsen, a pretty blonde not much older than Abby. Apparently she and her husband owned the store and the gas station out front, the very one Abby had phoned from the first day she'd driven into West Yellowstone.

"Hello, Carole."

"I'm so glad you came in. I've wanted to visit you, but Max said you were in a bad way and had to stay in bed."

"Not anymore. I've just come from getting my blood pressure checked. It's stayed normal for quite a while. The nurse called my doctor in Idaho Falls, and he's given me permission to be up and around for a few hours every day. Of course, I still have to stay off salt."

"Oops, then I won't offer you a piece of our best apple pie. There's salt in the pastry. How about an apple?"

"I'd love one."

"Here."

Abby sat on one of the stools and bit into the crisp red fruit. Carole poured herself a cup of coffee, then propped her elbows on the counter in front of Abby. The only other customer sat at the far end of the counter eating a hamburger.

"For someone who's been through so much grief, you look absolutely terrific. Pregnancy agrees with you."

"Thank you."

"I miss your sister terribly. She had a vitality that was infectious."

Abby nodded in remembrance. "She was the light of my life—and of Max's," she said simply. In fact, Kellie had become Max's whole existence. Now it seemed Max was becoming Abby's.

"That's true. When you first walked in here, I thought I was seeing Kellie, but you're a lot different."

Abby was intrigued. "You think so?"

"I realize we hardly know each other, but yes."

"You're a very discerning person. People who've known us for years can't tell us apart."

"I'm not talking about the physical similarities. You seem more confident somehow."

No one had ever said that to her before. Abby stopped chewing. "Are we talking about *me*?"

Carole chuckled. "Yes. Kellie came across as very exciting and intense, but I think deep down it masked some insecurites. You're . . . well, forgive me for saying this, but you're more of an earth mother . . ."

Abby broke into laughter. "That I can believe." She patted her protruding stomach.

When Carole smiled, her blue eyes twinkled. "No, you know what I mean. You have a more mellow quality about you. I'm not explaining it very well. It's just something I sense about you, that you're more . . . grounded."

"I'm grounded, all right. Confined to home and bed for the next three months."

They both laughed again. Abby liked the feeling after so many months without any reason for laughter.

"How's the most gorgeous man this side of the continental divide? I haven't seen him in here lately."

Abby knew exactly who she was talking about. "I haven't seen him in over two weeks."

But she lived for his nightly phone calls.

Sometimes they talked for close to half an hour, mostly about the baby and how she was feeling. When he asked about Giselle, she let him know that there'd been no response from Paul Beliveau yet or from his attorney.

"What's he up to?" Carole asked.

"He's transporting prisoners. But if I had the right, I'd ask him to give it up and work full-time on his ranch."

"Really?"

Abby nodded. "What he does has to be incredibly dangerous. I hate it."

"That's interesting, because your sister found that aspect of his life fascinating."

"I know. She looked for adventure in everything, but I don't see anything remotely exciting about guarding other people's lives for a living."

"I agree with you, but I couldn't tell Kellie that."

"Why not?"

"Oh, because I felt that her attraction to the thrills really covered the same fears you have, only she couldn't talk about them. As I said, you're quite different."

Abby put the apple core on a napkin. "Thank you for being her friend and for being honest with me. Why don't you and your husband come over to the ranch one night next week and have dinner? I'll do the cooking and give Ida a rest."

"Do you think your doctor would approve?"

"Probably not." Abby had forgotten.

"I have an idea. Why don't we meet in town? We'll let someone else do all the work. At the Lasso Club they serve broiled trout that's out of this world. If you called ahead, I'm sure they'd cook yours without salt."

"I'd love that. I have no social life at the moment, so I'm free any night."

"Shall we say Wednesday at six-thirty? I'll give you a call sometime during the day to make sure we're still on."

"Sounds terrific. Maybe I'll get some Christmas shopping done that day, as well. It's going to be here before we know it."

"You're right. I'm still trying to think of something special for my husband."

"I know. I've got the same problem where Max is concerned."

"Let's both think on it. Maybe by the time we see each other, we'll have some ideas to share."

"That'll be wonderful."

Abby reached into her purse and put a dollar on the counter, but Carole threw it back at her.

Laughing, Abby left the store. She'd almost made it through the foot-deep snow to the Blazer when she realized she'd forgotten the ice cream and had to go back for it.

CHAPTER ELEVEN

"MONSIEUR MOREAU? There's an overseas call for you on line one."

Philippe checked his watch. Three o'clock. If this was the one he'd been waiting for, then it was nine in the morning New York time.

"Thank you, Sophie."

He picked up the receiver and turned toward the window, rubbing his stomach. "Monsieur Moreau here."

"It's René."

Philippe eyes closed tightly. "Yes. Go ahead."

"She's back from vacation, but there's no phone. Apparently the building super told her you've been anxious to see her, and she's asked him to let you in, so it looks like your problem is solved."

"Excellent work, René. I'll mail you another check."

"I guess there's no need for me to keep trying to find her sister."

"No. You've given me the information I want. Thank you."

"Call me again if you ever want help."

"Of course," Philippe responded, but he couldn't imagine needing a private investigator again.

As soon as the other man clicked off, Philippe buzzed Sophie. "Get me on the next flight to Paris and book me on the Concorde for the evening flight to New York."

"Is there a problem?"

"A small matter that can be cleared up in one day. I'll be back in plenty of time for my wife's anniversary."

"Very good, monsieur. I'll see to everything immediately."

Philippe had one more call to make. To Delphine.

MAX GRABBED a quick breakfast and ate it while he sped over snowy roads toward the Bismarck airport, anxious to be on his way back to West Yellowstone. Back home.

Yesterday, after he'd delivered the prisoners safely across the Montana state line to the Morton County jail in North Dakota, he'd called home, wishing he could have been there for Ida's Thanksgiving feast the day before.

Everyone had gotten on the phone, warming his heart with talk that made him ache for the ranch, for all of them. For Abby. The pride in her voice when she announced that she'd finally finished the baby's sweater made him break out in a broad grin.

While he'd been in New York he'd stopped at a children's boutique and bought a couple of little stretchy suits with feet, one white, the other pink, to match the hearts in the sweater. If the baby was a boy, then pink would do just fine for around the house. The thought made him chuckle. So did the clothes, which were so tiny he shook his head in disbelief. But the clerk had assured him they'd fit a newborn up to ten pounds in weight.

Abby's baby would be beautiful, a miniature duplicate of its mother. Secretly he hoped it would be a girl. He couldn't help wondering if she'd be born with red-gold hair and that same pale creamy skin, which the slightest blush turned a delicate rose color.

He'd seen Abby do it twice so far. Once two weeks ago, when he'd asked her what she was reading, and the first time when he'd pulled down the sleeves of her nightgown to—

Oh, Lord, what was happening to him?

Why couldn't he get the memory of that night out of his mind? He was starting to confuse their images. No, that wasn't true. Not anymore.

Kellie would always hold a place in his heart, but it was Abby's face and smile that haunted him now.

Suddenly the anticipation he felt at knowing she'd be waiting at the ranch, growing more beautiful as the baby grew, seemed a terrible betrayal of Kellie's memory. He stepped on the accelerator and hurtled down the highway at top speed. But he couldn't escape the guilt.

So deep was his turmoil he didn't realize the car phone had been ringing. He welcomed the intrusion and grabbed for it. "Sutherland here."

"My boy, we have a strike."

"Rand..." He reduced his speed.

"The super had a call from the same man who phoned him before inquiring about Abby. He told him Abby was back from vacation, but her phone wouldn't be working for a few more days. If he wanted to see her, though, all he had to do was ring the super's bell and Sid would let him in."

"How long ago?"

"Five minutes ago. I just hung up."

"I'm going to join you. I'll grab the next flight out of Bismarck."

"You do that. I'm getting sick of my own company."

Max chuckled. "I know what you mean. How'd it go moving Abby's stuff, by the way?"

"No problem. Your sister-in-law keeps a tidy home. I filled a suitcase with a few mementos and pictures I figured she wouldn't want put in storage. I hope I did it right."

"You did. I know how you work." Max held Rand McMullen in the highest esteem. "Were you able to find her address book?"

"Yes. Philippe Moreau's phone number was in there, just like she said." He paused. "I found something else between the pages."

"What?" Max demanded.

"A couple of photos. If I'm not mistaken, boy, one's of you. You're so dressed up I didn't recognize you."

Kellie had sent that picture. He was surprised Abby still had it. "What's the other?"

"A picture of a man matching the description the super gave us."

Moreau. He hated the name, and he'd developed a troubling curiosity for the man who'd broken down Abby's defenses, lying through his teeth all the way.

"What's he look like?" he asked in a gravelly voice.

"He reminds me of some French film star my wife used to be crazy about. Did you ever see the one about a Frenchman who sails to Polynesia and falls in love with an islander? In the end she jumps in this volcano to appease the gods?"

Max shook his head in exasperation. "No. It was probably before my time."

"Now, now. Let's not get testy. What I'm trying to tell you is that this guy looks a lot like that movie star. If I could just remember his name, you'd know him. He was even in one of the James Bond movies."

"Which one?"

"Don't remember. But he was the villain."

"You've got *that* right!" Max blurted with enough venom that it surprised even him.

"Seems to me it took place in an exotic part of the world."

"They all do, Rand."

"No, now wait a minute. I mean really exotic, like India."

Max blinked. He remembered that one. Louis Jourdan. "Are you talking about the guy in *Gigi*?" Kellie had loved that film.

"Yeah, that's him. I remember now. Lewis Jordan. But this guy's better looking."

He wished Rand would stop talking.

After everything Moreau had done to Abby, she still kept his picture. Did she love him so much?

With his thoughts in chaos, he seized upon another possible explanation, one that almost drove him over the edge. Maybe she was preserving it so her child would know what his or her natural father looked like.

Max had to tamp down his fury.

Philippe Moreau didn't deserve to be remembered. He didn't even know Abby was pregnant—and no doubt wouldn't care if he did. He hadn't been there to hold her in his arms when she fainted or wipe her face with cool water after she'd been sick to her stomach. He hadn't agonized day and night over her high blood pressure, hadn't gone out in a blizzard to get her grapes because she craved them.

He'd done nothing but take his pleasure whenever he damn well felt like it.

The thought of his hands on Abby's body...

"Max? You still with me, boy?"

"Yes. I'm pulling into the airport now. I'll see you when I see you. If that—" he paused before he could say something even Rand would question "—if that

Frenchman shows up before I get there, you know what to do.''

"I'm kind of looking forward to it. Oh, and while you're at it, pick me up a pizza with everything on it. I'm getting tired of vegetarian lasagna and Salisbury steak.''

WHILE JESSE PUT the Blazer away in the garage, Abby hurried into the house. "Ida?''

"I'm in the kitchen. What's the verdict?''

Abby took off Max's parka, the only thing she could find that halfway covered her, hung it in the closet, then removed her boots and padded into the kitchen in her stocking feet. "The baby's grown, I'm getting big, and my blood pressure's still close to normal. Dr. Harvey praised you for your care in preparing my meals. I'm doing better and better, and I owe it all to you and Jesse—and Max.'' She gave the older woman a hug, then went to the sink for a glass of water.

"I couldn't be happier for you, honey. Things have gotten so much better around here.''

Except that Abby yearned for Max to come home. Everything seemed more complete when he was in the house. "Did he happen to phone while we were gone?''

"Yes. Just a few minutes ago. He's still out on a case and won't be back for a while.''

"Oh.''

Disappointment flooded through her. He'd been gone so long. Now to miss his call... Talking to him had become the high point of her day, and she'd wanted to tell him about her visit to the doctor. She'd wanted to hear his voice.

She wanted *him*.

It was no use lying to herself any longer. *She was in love with him.* Terribly, desperately, in love.

She needed to pull herself together so Jesse and Ida wouldn't guess her guilty secret. Bending awkwardly, she rummaged in the refrigerator for an orange. She'd been craving them lately.

"Did I tell you I met Carole in town the other day?" she chatted as she put the peelings down the disposal.

Ida was stirring white sauce on the stove. "I think so. Carole's a lovely person." She shook her head. "They want a baby so badly. But from what Kellie told me, she's never been able to conceive."

"Oh, Ida!" Abby said in a stricken voice. "I wish I'd known."

"How could you?" she scoffed gently, removing the sauce pan from the burner.

"You're right." Abby put an orange section in her mouth. "She said something that really surprised me, though."

"What was that?"

"She intimated that she thought Kellie was more insecure than I am."

"She's right."

Abby was brought up short. "You think so, too? But Kellie was always the brave one."

"If that's true, why didn't she face Max straight on, instead of running away?" Ida placed her hands on Abby's shoulders. "I'm not criticizing her, mind you. If the same thing had happened to me, I don't honestly know what I would've done."

"Neither do I," Abby whispered.

"You know what I think? I think if it had been you, if you were the one who got sick, you would have told Max and shared every minute of the time you had left with him."

Tears came to Abby's eyes, the first she'd shed in weeks. "Why do you say that?"

"Because I saw what happened here the night Max came home and found you in his bed. That was a hellish situation, but you didn't run away. You made us drive right over to the cabin, and you forced Max to face the issue head-on."

Now Ida's eyes had filled. "That took more courage than I would've had. Max can be downright scary when he's mad, but you didn't cower in front of him. You faced him. Your pain was great, and it was awful to watch, but your love for your sister was greater."

"Ida's right," Jesse chimed in. Abby hadn't heard him come in. "You're a very strong, courageous woman. We all thought you might end up in that hospital bed for months. No one could've been more surprised than Max when you rallied so fast."

"It was all a sham, Jesse. Ask my psychiatrist. I was dying inside."

"Of course you were, but you didn't let it break you down. That's what we're talking about. Carole sees that strength. That's why she said what she did."

Embarrassed and humbled by their kind words, Abby muttered a thank-you and dried her eyes. Reaching for another orange section, she chewed it slowly and swallowed before she spoke again. "Carole and I are going to dinner at the Lasso Club on Wednesday night. She's bringing her husband. I thought I'd do some Christmas shopping in town first, then meet them there."

"Good." Ida nodded her approval. "Now that the doctor's given you permission to be up for part of the day, you need some entertainment besides two old fogies who fall asleep in the middle of a Scrabble game."

On a rush of emotion, Abby threw her arms around both of them. "I love you two. I don't know what I'd have done without you."

"The feeling's mutual." Jesse's voice came out sounding more like a croak. "Ida and I married too late in life to have kids. With you expecting the baby, we kind of feel like we're the grandparents or something."

"You are!" Abby cried, the tears brimming over. "Between you and Max and Giselle, my baby's going to have more love than any other child in the whole world."

Giselle.

Abby had almost forgotten that she was going to live with her stepmother when the baby was born.

Jesse and Ida didn't know that yet.

Somehow she didn't have the heart to tell them. Not now. Not after what they'd just confided to her.

Not after what she'd just admitted to herself. She could never live so far away from Max. Never.

"THIS PIZZA'S GOOD. They really know how to make them in New York. If I could get the recipe, I'd make a fortune back in Bozeman." Rand's gaze darted to Max. "Aren't you going to have any?"

"I ate earlier," Max lied, standing at the window where he could see the street ten stories below.

On normal stakeouts he felt a rush of adrenaline and usually craved food. Lots of it. But this was different. Personal. The thought of food nauseated him.

He'd grown impatient to meet the man who'd betrayed Abby.

"He might not come tonight, Max."

Max gritted his teeth. "He'll come."

"What makes you so sure?"

"Gut instinct."

The bastard was still panting after her, falling apart a little more each day because he knew what he was missing. Dying to touch her, to lose himself in her. Dying to feast his eyes on her...

Damn him. Damn the man.

THE TAXI DRIVER thanked Philippe for the big tip and drove off.

It was late. Twenty to ten. But due to landing-gear problems, his plane had been delayed, making his arrival in New York much later than originally scheduled.

But he had to see her. He couldn't go another day not knowing how she was. He couldn't handle the guilt.

He buzzed the super, and a moment later, the door opened.

"Hi. After the phone call I got this morning, I figured it might be you. I described you to Ms. Clarke, and she said you could go on up whenever."

"Thank you."

Philippe walked over to the door, waited for the click of the automatic lock and entered the lobby. He was hardly conscious of passing several people, hardly conscious of sharing the elevator with several more.

He rode to the tenth floor, thankful Abby had agreed to see him. She could have refused.

Always before, when he saw her after a separation, his heart would thud heavily and he'd feel an ache in his midsection. Tonight would be no different, but *she* would be different. That was what was killing him.

The hall was empty when he approached her door and gave three taps. She would recognize his knock.

The door swung open. "Yes?"

Philippe took a step back. Instead of seeing Abby standing in the entry, he was looking up into the cold gray eyes of a tall dark-haired man. A man considerably younger than himself—younger, stronger, incredibly fit....

He didn't have the wrong apartment, he was sure. What was going on?

"I'm looking for Abby Clarke."

"Come in."

Puzzled, Philippe stepped over the threshold and came to a standstill. The place was empty. Empty as a tomb. He heard the door close behind him.

"The super told me she was here."

"She was. But now she's gone."

"I'm afraid I don't understand."

"At the last minute she decided to move."

"Who are you?"

"Her brother-in-law."

Philippe had the sudden realization that he'd been set up. Then he remembered seeing a small photograph of Abby's sister and her husband, and he made the connection. He breathed with difficulty. "Then you know everything."

"That's right."

A chill ran down Philippe's spine, impressing on him that this forbidding relative could do real damage if provoked.

"I heard she's been ill. Too ill to continue her job."

"Right again."

"Look, Mr.— I don't recall your last name."

"Sutherland."

"Yes. I remember now." He cleared his throat. "She has every right to despise me. But she couldn't possibly despise me more than I despise myself. I'll go on paying for those lies for the rest of my life.

"Nevertheless, I'm worried about her. I haven't slept since Monsieur Gide told me she'd had to resign. Is she all right? Please. I have to know."

The eerie stillness surrounding the younger man froze Philippe in place. It was useless to appeal to him.

When he'd all but given up hope of a response, the man said, "She'll live, if that's what you're talking about."

Philippe crossed himself.

"Did she become ill because she found out I'm a married man?"

Something flickered in Sutherland's eyes. "No."

"Grace à Dieu." Philippe felt tears threaten. He hadn't cried since the day the doctors told him Delphine would never walk again.

He tried to find the right words, but finally gave up and stated the simple truth. "I love my wife. She was my childhood sweetheart, my dearest friend, the mother of my two children. When she became an invalid, I loved her more because she had such courage. I remained faithful to her all our married life—until I met Abby. Mademoiselle Clarke.

"Earlier this year, while I was here in New York, I asked for a translator, and into the room walked Abby. Something happened—something beyond my control."

Much as he hated to admit it, Max could understand those feelings. Something had happened to him when he first met Kellie—and when he first saw Abby lying in his bed.

"Until that moment I didn't think it was possible to love two women at the same time," Philippe murmured. He could hear his voice trembling. "I fought it for the first four months."

Max remembered she'd said they'd been seeing each other for six, which meant they'd been sleeping together for two. Long enough to get her pregnant. "What more do you want from her?"

It was the question Philippe had been asking himself over and over, like a litany.

"I've missed her. There's a void in my life without her. I'm prepared to divorce Delphine if Abby will marry me."

Max didn't move a muscle. He'd been wrong about Moreau. The bastard really loved Abby. He had no idea she was pregnant and he *still* wanted to marry her. *A new nightmare was beginning.* . . .

Philippe watched the other man pale. It could mean anything or nothing. He didn't suppose he'd ever know, but at least the truth was out. "You owe me nothing, monsieur, but I hope you will at least be honorable enough to convey my message to Abby. If she wants to get in touch with me, she knows how."

In a voice of ice Sutherland said, "That word— honorable—kind of got stuck in your throat, didn't it, Moreau?"

Philippe knew he deserved that. "If I don't hear from her, I can assume one of two things. Either you chose not to tell her we've met. Or you gave her my message and she chose not to have anything to do with me. No matter what happens, I'll never try to contact her again."

FOR LONG MINUTES after Philippe Moreau had left the apartment, Max stood in the semidarkness, desolate.

He finally heard footsteps on the hardwood floor and turned to face Rand. The two men stared at each other. Streams of unspoken messages flowed between them.

"You're going to have to do it, boy."

Max took a harsh breath. "He doesn't deserve her, Rand."

"He's the father of her child. He's prepared to marry her. I know what he did was wrong, but the man's in love, painfully so. Even I could feel it, and I was clear in the other room."

"He already has grown children."

"So do I, but I also have eyes in my head, and if a woman like Abby came along, I'd probably make a fool of myself, too."

"She's not the right woman for him. He has a wife."

"Come on, Max. Your sister-in-law is a raving beauty. Married or not, Philippe Moreau's no more immune to her than the next man. You heard him. His wife's been an invalid for years—and then he met

Abby. The point is, she fell for him, too. After all, she's pregnant with his child. Think abou—"

"Shut up, Rand."

"What's stuck in your craw, boy?"

"None of your damn business."

"You made it my business when you asked me to stake out the place."

"You did your job. You'll get your pay. Now let's get the hell out of here."

CAROLE'S HUSBAND, Mike, was a natural wit, and such a great impersonator Abby laughed all the way through dinner. She was still laughing when they dropped her off at the ranch later that night with several gifts she'd bought Jesse and Ida for Christmas. She still hadn't decided on anything for Max. Nothing seemed right, or special enough.

Because of a fresh snowstorm that was finally abating, Jesse had driven her into town. He'd given her the remote control so that when they brought her home, she'd be able to open the gate, allowing them to drive her right to the front door.

"Thank you for a marvelous evening. You'll have to come over for dinner during the Christmas holidays. Ida and Jesse won't believe your imitation of Alfred Hitchcock—they love those old films. I'll call you with a definite time, okay?"

"You're on."

Mike opened his door with the intention of coming around to help Abby. But suddenly light spilled onto the circular drive and a tall masculine figure started through the snow toward them.

Max.

Abby's pulse raced.

"When did you get back?" she asked the second he opened the passenger door.

Snowflakes played on his eyelashes while his gaze wandered over her face for a heart-stopping moment.

"Hap—one of the airport mechanics—dropped me off a few minutes ago. Now I know what happened to my parka. I was looking for it so I could snowblow the drive, but it's obviously been put to better use."

She searched his face, hoping he really didn't mind. "It's the only thing that even partway covers me anymore. We've been out to dinner," she said a trifle breathlessly. His gaze had dropped to her rounded stomach. "I hope you haven't been back long." Her voice trailed off.

Dear God, she thought. *What's wrong with me? What's happening to me?*

Suddenly she was aware of the silence. No one was saying anything. She averted her face because *his* was too close. He smelled too good. "I—I think I can make it on my own if you'd just help me down."

The next thing she knew, Max had lifted her from the seat of the cab and started carrying her toward the house, her hair splayed over his arm.

"Good night, you two," he called back to Carole and Mike. "Thanks for bringing our mother-to-be home safely. I owe you one."

But Mike followed them inside with Abby's packages. "We're coming to your place after Christmas," he said, leaving the packages on the hall table. Then he sketched a wave and headed for the door.

"I'll make a point of being here," Max replied, his eyes never leaving Abby's.

"Goodbye, Mike. Thank you again." Abby's voice sounded more like a whisper.

"Sure. See you soon."

Once Mike was gone, Max closed the door with his boot and made for the study, Abby still in his arms.

His nearness made her panic. "Where are Jesse and Ida?"

"According to their note, they went to a movie in town." His voice was low and husky. She felt his breath on her cheek and a slow languorous heat invaded her body.

No—this can't be happening. I love him—but he was Kellie's husband. This is wrong.

Her body didn't seem to understand and was reacting of its own volition. Even the baby sensed something, because there was a lot of movement.

Just before he lowered her to the couch, the baby gave her a good jab in the ribs and she gasped.

Max's eyes quickened. "Lord. I felt that."

"So did I," Abby groaned. "I knew I shouldn't have eaten so much dinner. There's no room. I appreciate you carrying me in from the truck, but I need to stand up so the baby will change positions."

The friction of her body sliding against the hardness of his sent a yielding feeling of delight through her system. She was helpless to deal with all these new emotions, these exciting new sensations. Her legs felt like rubber as he relieved her of the parka and tossed it onto the arm of the couch.

"I don't believe it," he murmured. She followed his gaze. The gray jumper was made of a thin fabric and moved as the baby moved. His eyes trapped hers. "Does it hurt?"

The heat from the fireplace and the pungent smell of a pine wreath on the mantel made her light-headed and breathless. "Mostly it's uncomfortable, especially when it goes on and on in one spot."

He wanted to feel it. She knew he did. But the thought of his hands on her body almost sent her into shock.

Because she *wanted* to feel his hands on her body.

Acting on a compulsion totally foreign to her, she reached for his right hand and placed it on the side of her stomach, where the baby's foot or arm was moving back and forth with maddening regularity.

She heard his sharp intake of breath, and suddenly she felt two strong masculine hands begin their slow exploration of her swollen belly, as if he, too, were compelled to do something beyond his control.

Her eyes closed and her breath caught while he went on touching her, examining, pressing gently where he felt the baby's little jabs.

"She knows I'm here," he murmured. "She's telling me I've made contact."

"She?"

"I have this feeling it's a girl."

Abby watched him through lowered lashes. The smile on his face, in his eyes, was so tender, so full of wonder, it moved her to tears.

"If it is a girl, she knows your voice," Abby murmured. "Sometimes when you come into a room and start talking, she moves."

"How do you know she's responding to me?"

"Because she doesn't do it for Jesse or Ida."

"Abby..."

His hands stilled on her stomach, as if he was in the throes of the same intense emotion that gripped her. But when she looked into his eyes, she saw pain.

How could she have forgotten even for an instant? *He wished she was Kellie.*

CHAPTER TWELVE

"ABBY." HE SAID HER NAME again, this time with an edge to it. "There's something I have to tell you. Maybe you should sit down."

She backed away from him, forcing his hands to drop to his sides. "You sound exactly like you did when you thought I had a brain tumor." Her voice shook as she said the words.

All the tenderness, the wonder, had vanished from his face. It had grown hard, and his eyes were dark pinpoints of light.

"Philippe Moreau came by your apartment while I was taking care of the move." When she didn't say anything, he added, "Apparently he's tried to see you on several occasions."

Abby hadn't thought of Philippe in ages. She felt nothing for him. Absolutely nothing. If ever she'd needed proof that theirs was not a love match, this was it. Her complete lack of feeling.

They'd only been lovers for the last two months of their relationship. Even though he'd used protection, she must have gotten pregnant the first time they'd made love—which had been an instructive experience, at best.

Philippe had been gentle and sweet during their lovemaking, but he'd always had to coax her. Theirs had never been a passionate affair like the one she knew Kellie had shared with Max.

Like the way she, Abby, fantasized it would be with Max.

She'd never known the meaning of desire until tonight. She'd felt it leap to dizzying life as Max picked her up in his arms and carried her into the house.

She'd never been on the verge of a faint when Philippe caressed her. Yet all she had to do was *think* about Max touching her, and her bones turned to liquid.

His brows met in a dark frown. "Why aren't you saying anything?"

"I'm thinking."

His chest heaved. "He's prepared to divorce Delphine and marry you. The man's a mess—over you."

Poor Philippe. He was deluding himself if he could call what they'd had love. Comfort, maybe, relief from loneliness, but never love. It was a little late in the day to atone for his lies. Poor Delphine.

"He must have said that because he knows I'm pregnant with his baby. Did you tell him?"

A bleakness entered his eyes. "No. He has no idea you're going to have a baby. He found out you had to quit your job because of illness. That's all he knows." After a pause he said in a strained voice, "My apologies for doubting his motives. He's offered you marriage."

The firelight flickered, casting dancing shadows over his tense expression. "He's very much in love with you, Abby, and he doesn't want to spend the rest of his life without you. But he won't try to contact you again. You'll have to go to him."

Abby turned away and walked over to the fire, staring into the flames.

Max's news changed everything.

Philippe's desire to marry her wasn't prompted by her pregnancy, but by what he thought was love for her. Incredible.

He was willing to give up Delphine, willing to face the condemnation of family and friends, in order to marry her. How foolish of him, when he already had everything a man could want and didn't realize it.

Even if Abby *had* been in love with him, she'd never have asked that of him, or of any man. She'd never be able to live with the breakup of another marriage on her conscience.

But she was carrying his child.

Now that she knew he wanted to marry her, she had a moral obligation to tell him the truth.

Now a new agony would begin, because he'd have to deal with the shocking news that he—the father of adult children—was going to be a father again. He'd have to tell Delphine. His children would find out.

How they would all hate her!

Abby felt sick. "Max—" she turned to him "—would you try to put yourself in Philippe's place for a minute? Then answer a question for me? Keep in mind that he has a wife, two grown children and several grandchildren.''

After a long silence he gave her an almost imperceptible nod.

''How would you want me to contact you so that I caused your family the least amount of embarrassment and pain?''

If she'd slapped him hard across the face, her question couldn't have hurt him more.

''No matter how you did it,'' he began in a thick voice, ''the result would be the same. But I'd probably prefer a simple telephone call at my office, provided I was alone at the time.''

He reached for his parka and shrugged into it. ''I've got some shoveling to do before Jesse and Ida get back. When you go into the kitchen you'll find a package on the table. It's for the baby. Something to match the sweater you made. You'll have to show the sweater to me later.''

After he'd gone outside, Abby dashed into the kitchen. She saw a box labeled The Pink and Blue Boutique. Her hands trembled as she took off the lid and folded back the tissue. Two little sleepers, one pink and one blue lay on the bottom. She lifted them out and buried her face in them, sobbing.

''WOULD YOU LOOK at that!'' Jesse whistled as they drove up the drive toward the garage. ''Max got back while we were out and he's done all the snowblowing. I confess I didn't feel much like doing it tonight.''

Ida gave him a kiss on the cheek and slid out her side of the Blazer. "While you put the car away, I'll go in and make some hot chocolate for all of us."

"How about whipping up some scones while you're at it?"

"After all that popcorn?"

"That was just an appetizer, honey."

She chuckled, then hurried along the path to the front door, looking forward to spending the rest of the evening with Max and Abby.

"Hi! We're home!"

She shut the door and took off her parka. When there was no answer, she slipped off her boots and hurried into the study. Still no sign of them. Maybe Abby hadn't come home from town yet.

They could be in the kitchen, but she doubted it. The house was too quiet. She headed in that direction to start making the hot chocolate, but got sidetracked when she saw two little sleepers lying in a box on the table.

Smiling, Ida picked them up. It was just like Max to do something so thoughtful. Where was he, anyway?

She put the sleepers back in the box and started heating the milk. With that accomplished, she left the kitchen and went down the hall to let Jesse in the back door.

On the way she heard crying and stopped dead in her tracks. It was like déjà vu—with Abby inside the bedroom, sobbing her heart out.

Ida thought those days had gone for good. Her heart sank to her feet.

What had happened here tonight?

Where was Max?

She went across to the master bedroom and poked her head inside. No sign of him.

With a growing sense of dread she ran down the hall and opened the back door.

"Jesse?" She raced along the path Max had cleared to the garage. "Honey?"

"I'm coming."

"No. Get back in the Blazer. Go find Max and talk to him."

"What are you talking about?"

"Abby's in there crying, and he's gone. Something's wrong."

"Which means he's gone to the cabin. When's it going to stop, Ida?"

She shuddered. "I don't know."

He let out a heartfelt sigh. "Don't bother with the scones. I have a feeling this is going to be an all-nighter."

WHERE WAS the Jack Daniels?

Max had gone through every cupboard in the cabin and come up empty. Tonight he had to have something strong enough to knock him out. Tomorrow he'd get his boss to send him on another witness-protection case. A long one.

Grabbing his parka, he slammed out the cabin door and waded through the snow to the truck. Bud kept his place over in West Yellowstone open until two; he wouldn't mind if Max passed out on his couch in the lounge.

He started to back up the truck and almost ran into his own Blazer coming straight at him.

Slamming on his brakes, he jerked his head out the window in time to see Jesse jump into the snow and run toward him. He moved fast for a man his age.

"Jesse! Get back in the Blazer. I'm on my way to town."

"Bud's will be closed before you get there."

"What did you do with your bourbon?"

Jesse scratched his head. "Well, now, as I recall, you finished it off a couple of months ago."

Max let loose a stream of invective that made Jesse whistle. "Someone's put a burr under *your* saddle. For starters, want to tell me why Abby's back at the house sobbing her heart out? Until tonight, she was doing just fine. Until tonight, you were several thousand miles away. It doesn't take Sherlock Holmes to figure out we've got mess on our hands."

"You don't know the half of it."

"I'd like to," Jesse said quietly. "'Course, you can tell me to drop dead if you want. I'll oblige you one of these days."

"Don't say that," Max thundered. "Not even in jest."

"You're as close to a son as I'm ever going to have. I love you. When you hurt, I hurt."

Max's eyes smarted. "I love you, too." He sighed. "Okay. Try this one on for size. The man who got Abby pregnant came to the apartment while I was in New York. He wants to divorce his wife and marry her."

Jesse frowned. "After the way he lied to her, Abby said she wasn't ever going to tell him about the baby. How'd he find out?"

"He didn't. Don't you understand? He wants to marry her because he can't live without her. You should have heard him." Max groaned in despair.

"Did you tell Abby that?"

He nodded.

"And?"

"She wanted my advice on the best way to get in touch with him without hurting his family."

"No wonder she's in such bad shape right now."

"What do you mean?"

"Try to see this from her point of view. She didn't know he was still married when she started dating him. She probably feels terrible for his wife and kids. And when they find out about the affair, they'll think the worst of her.

"But he *is* the father of her baby and he loves her. If he's prepared to divorce his wife to marry her, and she wants to get married because she loves him, then that'll open up a whole new set of problems. She'll have to share him with his other family. Of course, they'll resent her....

"Then there'll be the question of where they live, all those details that need to be worked out. Abby's got too much on her plate for..."

The more Jesse talked, the more the pain constricted Max's chest. He tried not to listen.

"Max, what is it? Why does it matter so much? It's her life to live. You've more than fulfilled any obligation Kellie imposed on you when you placed her sister in your care. No one could have done more than you have. Maybe it's time to let her go, to think about *your* needs."

"What in the hell are you talking about?"

"I thought you were too old for a lesson about the birds and the bees, but—" he shrugged "—I'm talking about finding yourself another woman, getting married, having a family."

Max raked both hands through his hair. "I tried that, remember?"

"And while it was good, you were happier than you've ever been in your life. You'll feel that again."

That's just it, Jesse. I already have felt it. Tonight—with my own sister-in-law! Kellie's sister. Kellie's twin. It was grotesque. Wrong. A betrayal of Kellie and, at the same time, a betrayal of Abby herself.

"I'm leaving in the morning, Jesse. I'm going to go out on another case. After that, I have some time coming."

"Rob Miller over in Colorado has been asking you to go cross-country skiing with him. Why don't you take him up on it?"

"Maybe I will."

Jesse eyed him for a long moment. "You going to be all right here tonight? You want company?"

"No. You go on back to Ida before you turn into an icicle."

Jesse smiled and patted his shoulder.

"Jesse?" he called as the older man turned to go back to the Blazer.

"Save it, Max. I already know what you're going to say. Good night."

"Good night."

"MOREAU TEXTILES. *Bonjour.*"

"*Bonjour, madame.* May I speak to Monsieur Philippe Moreau, please?" asked Abby in French. "I'm calling from Monsieur Gide's office in New York."

Abby wasn't calling from there, of course, but she assumed that when Philippe knew the reason for her phone call, he would forgive her for the lie.

The pain of watching Max drive off in the truck earlier had been so unbearable she couldn't have gone to sleep after that if her life had depended on it. Her watch said it was 3:10 a.m. Midmorning for Philippe, who didn't leave for lunch until one. Now would be as good a time as any to get this over with.

She should never have kept the news of her pregnancy from him. If she'd confronted him when she'd first learned of it, she wouldn't be facing this ordeal now. Every step she'd taken since the day Kellie showed up at her apartment had been the wrong one, and the person who'd suffered the most for it was Max.

Philippe should never have met Max, should never have involved him in their messy aff—

"Philippe Moreau here,"

"*Bonjour,* Philippe."

She heard him gasp.

"Don't say anything else," Abby said. "Are you alone? Can you talk?"

"Yes. For a moment only. It's Delphine's birthday. I was just leaving. *Mon Dieu,* Abby. Meeting your brother-in-law was an unforgettable experience. I never dreamed he would convey my message. My impression was that he wished me to the other end of the earth."

She gripped the receiver more tightly. "Your impression was correct," she murmured dryly. "However, Max is a very honorable man. He always tells the truth—even if it hurts."

"I deserved that, chérie."

"Philippe, since we don't have much time, I'll come right to the point. I'm not in love with you. I felt an attraction, but it never went deeper than that.

"I—I've met another man," she confessed, her eyes brimming over. "I'm in love with him. The kind of love that lasts forever. It's the kind of love you feel for Delphine and always will.''

The silence on his end was deafening.

"This man is the only one I want to marry, to spend the rest of my life with." She said the words aloud for the first time. It was heaven to say them.

"I haven't told you this to be cruel, Philippe. I'm only stating the truth. Which brings me to the second reason for this call.

"You lied to me. You made me commit adultery. But I have to take equal responsibility. I slept with you without any sort of commitment. It was a risk, and it had consequences.''

"What consequences?'' he whispered.

"I'm going to have your baby.''

"You're pregnant?'' His voice shook.

"Yes. I'm due in February. I've had a difficult pregnancy, which is the reason I had to quit my job with Monsieur Gide. Philippe, before you say anything else, please listen.

"You gave my baby life, but the man I love *saved* my life, which also saved my baby's life. This man is already more of a father to my baby than you will ever be, Philippe. H-he loves my baby.'' Abby's voice quavered. "He intends to be a big part of this child's life. I intend to let him.

"I've told you the truth. It was my moral obligation to do so. What you decide to do from now on is your affair. My advice would be to say nothing about this yet. When the baby's born, I'll inform you.

There's enough time between now and then for you to do some serious thinking."

"But what if our baby asks about me one day? What if I want to see the child?"

"Then we'll work it out. Naturally the baby will be told the truth as soon as he or she's old enough to understand. I would never keep our child from you. Just remember that this baby will never want for anything. There are a lot of people who love it. Doting grandparents, and a man who's already taken over a father's role.

"The baby deserves to have this man's complete attention and love all the days of its life, the way your children have had yours. Do you understand what I'm trying to say?"

"Yes, Abby, I—I do." His voice cracked painfully.

"You and I came together because we were both at a low point in our lives. We'd both suffered losses of a kind and found comfort in each other. Let's recognize it for what it really was.

"Be honest with yourself. You loved Delphine in the beginning. You still do, or you wouldn't have lied. Don't you see? If she no longer mattered, you wouldn't have cared. But you *do* care. You and she still have time together. Make it count, Philippe. I'll phone you in February. Goodbye."

Quietly Abby hung up the receiver. "I know I'm going to make the most of whatever time I have," she vowed to the empty room. "Whatever time Max is willing to give me. For however long he allows me to remain in his life.''

Tonight, in a pure revelation, the certain knowledge had come to Abby that this was what Kellie had wanted all along.

But it was knowledge meant for Abby alone, something to cherish and hug close to her heart.

"GOOD AFTERNOON, Philippe. How good of you to attend your wife's birthday party, even if you are late.''

Through the rain-spattered window of his car, Philippe had seen Georges in the cobblestoned courtyard long before he'd opened the door and climbed out.

He pulled up the collar of his overcoat and eyed his ex-secretary and friend. "It's good of you to stand in for me.''

"Don't worry. She is used to your habits and wouldn't be unduly concerned unless you decided not to show up at all. When I left her, she was in the salon, showing off her latest grandchild to the guests. So, how goes it with the American girl?''

Staring at the facade of the gracious château beyond Georges's shoulder, the family home he and his bride had lived in all these years, he said, "Actually, it's none of your business.

"But since you asked, I will tell you. She saw me as a father figure. Nothing more. She's in love with someone else. She plans to marry him. They are going to raise my child.''

For once Georges lost his sangfroid. After a minute he lowered his gaze. ''I will never whisper a word of this to Delphine.''

Philippe shut the car door and walked over to him. He put a hand on his rain-dampened shoulder. ''Whether you do or not makes no difference to me. I am going to tell Delphine everything.''

Georges looked completely taken aback.

''If she can forgive me, then I'm going to take the very sage advice of a beautiful young woman who prevented me from making the greatest mistake of my life. She reminded me that I love my wife.

''I do, you know,'' he murmured fervently. ''And God willing, I'll make the most of the years Delphine and I have left together.''

For the first time since Philippe had known him, Georges wept.

Intrigued, Philippe cocked his head. ''Georges, why the tears? After all, you're the person I have to thank for calling me to repent. I thought, of course, you'd gloat over the miserable state of my sin-filled soul.''

''Gloat?'' he shouted. ''You expect me to gloat?'' He shook his head. ''Don't you understand anything? What you've just told me has redeemed my faith in mankind.''

Philippe took a shuddering breath. ''I've only taken the first step. I have no idea where it will lead.''

"The point is, you *did* take it." Georges grabbed his arm and shook it. "Well done, my friend. Well done."

GETTING DOWN from Dr. Harvey's examining table had become a project that had to be thought out in advance. Without his nurse's help, Abby might have fallen headfirst. She flashed the other woman a grateful smile and started getting dressed.

"Come in, Abby," the doctor beckoned a few minutes later when he saw her exit the examining room. "Let's talk."

"This sounds serious." She took her place opposite his desk.

"In a way it is. Everything looks fine and your blood pressure's still within the normal range. But with Christmas practically upon us, you're less than eight weeks away from your due date.

"The closer it gets, the more often I need to see you. West Yellowstone is a long way from Rexburg, especially in the dead of winter. If you went into labor during a blizzard, I'd hate to think what might happen."

"Are you expecting the baby to come early?"

"No. But it doesn't hurt to plan for such a contingency."

"It never occurred to me."

Abby had been so despondent over Max's absence and the painful news that he wouldn't be home for Christmas, she hadn't thought about anything else. All the preparations they'd made, the decorating, the beautiful Christmas tree . . . And now he wouldn't be here to see any of it.

He'd become her whole world, yet he'd removed himself from his own world—his home, his life, his community. She knew why.

Last Christmas Kellie had been alive. He probably couldn't face the ranch at this time of year; there were too many painful associations.

Jesse and Ida were trying to make it a festive occasion. Several get-togethers were planned for neighbors and friends, among them Carole and Mike. With Abby's help, Ida had done a lot of baking. They'd all finished their shopping and had sent Giselle her gifts and received gifts in turn.

Abby had finally decided to make Max a stocking decorated with a felt deputy marshal wearing cowboy boots. She stuffed it with small personal things she knew he used and liked. But without him there, nothing would be the same. Nothing would be right.

Every so often, word would come via a phone call from Billings that all was well with him. The wait between calls was pure agony.

"Why don't you talk it over with your brother-in-law and see if you can't figure out something that'll make all of us a little less nervous. Maybe move into town for a few weeks."

Deep in her own painful thoughts, Abby hadn't realized the doctor was still talking to her. When his suggestion sank in, she wanted to leap across the table and give Dr. Harvey a hug. Finally she had a legitimate reason to get in touch with Max.

Since he'd left, she'd written him a dozen letters, only to throw them in the wastebasket the next morning. She didn't have the courage to send them, not when he hadn't sent *her* a personal message.

"I'll do that, Doctor." *Tonight.*

"Fine. See you next week."

She said goodbye and made her way to the reception area to make her appointment. When they saw her, Jesse and Ida put down the magazines they were reading and hurried toward her, full of eager questions.

The three of them trudged out to the Blazer, but at first, Abby couldn't even see the vehicle. Snow was falling heavily, and the parking lot had been buried under a fresh blanket of white. It made Dr. Harvey's concerns suddenly seem more real, more urgent; she had every intention of taking them seriously.

Once they were on the road, Abby told them what the doctor had said. "I'll need to contact Max right away," she finished.

"That's easy, honey," Jesse said. "Write him a letter tonight, and I'll take it to town in the morning. The sheriff's office can fax it to Billings, and they'll handle it from there. Max could be reading it by tomorrow night."

Abby was sitting in the back seat. But when she heard Jesse's plan, she unfastened her seatbelt and leaned forward, baby and all, to kiss the top of his head. "You're brilliant. And kind. And wonderful."

"Did you hear that, Ida?"

"I knew it long before Abby ever showed up at the ranch."

Abby sat back again and refastened her belt, remembering that first day as if it had happened in another lifetime. As if it had no bearing on the present.

"Tell me something, you two," she said. "When did you start to realize I wasn't Kellie?"

Ida turned in the seat and smiled. "I don't know about Jesse, but it was when I helped you to the bedroom and you said, 'You and Jesse are angels.' I thought, this isn't the Kellie I know. Not that your sister wasn't kind and thoughtful. She just didn't express herself that way."

Jesse nodded. "Ida's right. I knew something was different the minute I handed you the remote and you said you hated to put me out. The Kellie I knew would have said 'I owe you one, Jesse.'"

"We really are different—*were* different," she amended. Amazingly enough, the slip didn't make her feel like crying. Even Abby could tell she'd come a long way since her sister's funeral. "But most people we knew could never tell us apart."

"Probably because you were so close during your school years. Jesse and I had the advantage of getting to know you separately. If we have one regret, it was missing out on seeing the two of you together. Now *that* would have been some sight!"

Abby laughed delightedly. "We drove everyone crazy—always dressing the same, playing silly games to fool people. Kellie had worked out all these comedy acts and she made me do them with her. She got mad at me if I didn't want to join in."

Jesse flashed her a glance through the rearview mirror. "If you felt that way, why didn't you say no?"

Abby shrugged. "She was my older sister. You didn't say no to Kellie. Besides, we ended up having so much fun half the time I forgot why I was mad at her. There was no one more exciting to be with than Kellie.

"But according to Giselle, we intimidated boys because they felt they had to compete for our attention. Daddy agreed with her. They both worried that we'd never find a man we loved or whose company we enjoyed as much we did each other's."

"They didn't know about Max," Jesse muttered, his voice gruff with affection.

Abby took a shaky breath. "No."

The mention of his name seemed to put Jesse and Ida in a reflective mood, and they only made desultory conversation for the remainder of the drive home.

Abby was grateful for the quiet. She wanted time to compose her letter. She had so much to tell him....

CHAPTER THIRTEEN

THOUGH HE WAS OFF DUTY, Max tucked the .357 Magnum inside the waistband of his cutoffs. Then he grabbed a beer from the small refrigerator in his trailer home and walked outside, setting up the lawn chair to face the water.

This part of Florida was probably his least favorite place in the entire country. He put on his sunglasses, but the view didn't improve. The endless miles of flat sandy uninspiring beach made him yearn for the primitive terrain of home. He'd give a month's pay to breathe in the kind of dry winter air that froze your lungs and made you struggle for your next breath.

He chugged down half the can, picturing the ranch in his mind. It would be half-buried in snow by now. He could see the piles of wood stacked against the house, smoke curling from the chimney. Hell, he could smell it.

Wood smoke and Ida's coffee.

His mind wandered through the house, to each and every part of it, decorated for Christmas with pine boughs and wreaths and holly. He always ended up in the den, where the fire in the hearth crackled and flickered, sending dancing shadows against the walls.

He could see it playing over Abby's face, highlighting the gloss of her hair. He could picture her standing there, her pregnant shape rich and full.

But the real miracle was *touching* her—

He groaned at the memory and jumped out of the chair, finishing off his beer before he went in for a long cold shower.

He had no right to be fantasizing about her. The second Moreau had thrown the bait in the water, she'd swum for it. A marriage proposal was all she'd been waiting for.

There was no way he could spend Christmas with her, watching in silent agony while she counted the days until her baby was born so she could be free— free to leave him.

Max tried to shake off the thought. He walked slowly outside, glancing at the Christmas decorations on several nearby trailer homes. Maybe he should take Jesse's advice and find himself a woman. There were lots of them in Florida, attractive and available. He knew several in the trailer court who'd been giving him none-too-subtle signals since the first day he'd taken up residence there. All he had to do was smile.

He had nothing to smile about.

One day soon Abby and her baby would be gone. She'd be in France, married to the father of her baby.

How was he going to live with that? *How the hell was he going to live with that?*

"Paper, sir."

Max wheeled around as it dropped to his feet. His mind had been thousands of miles away. He hadn't seen Simmons coming until he'd already passed by on his bike.

The local marshal's office was using Greg Simmons as a go-between. He brought information, messages, orders. Any day now Max was expecting to be told that they were moving the whole operation to another state. He picked up the folded newspaper. Maybe the orders had been sent.

The witness he was guarding—a man who'd been shot up pretty badly in a drug bust—was about to be released from the hospital. Max's cover this time was a job in housekeeping. He'd volunteered to stay with the case for as long as they needed him. The way he felt about Abby, he couldn't go home. As it was, his jealousy had brought him close to violence; he'd come within a hairsbreadth of tearing Moreau apart.

Resting the chair against the trailer, he moved inside, locking the door behind him. He opened the newspaper and an envelope fell out.

Official business.

He tore it open, praying they were sending him as far from Florida as possible.

He frowned and took off his sunglasses.

These weren't orders.

He counted three pages of faxes, handwritten. But whose writing? Not Ida's or Jesse's. What the hell?

The "Dear Max," started his heart pounding. It was pounding out of control when he flipped to the last page and saw Abby's signature. He froze, half-terrified to find out she might be leaving before the baby was even born. As Jesse had pointed out, she had the right to do whatever she wanted with her life.

Tomorrow was Christmas. Maybe Moreau had come to the ranch to spend it with her.

Evening faded into night. Still, Max stood there as if in a trance. Finally, when he decided that not knowing was worse than learning the truth, he flicked the lamp switch and sank down in the chair by the table to read.

Dear Max,

I've tried to imagine where you'll be when you read this letter, what you might be eating, drinking, wearing (besides your holster, of course).

How lonely your work must get sometimes. Since I have no way of knowing what it's like, I can only pray you're well and content with your job.

As you know, I hate what you do for a living. (I know that's blunt and very rude, but I hope you'll forgive me.) All the reasons in the world, like "Someone has to do it," don't persuade me. The risks are just too great. The ranch would be enough for most men, but not you, apparently. There must be many people out there, grateful people, who owe you their lives. What makes you do it? One day I hope to hear—and under-stand—your reasons.

Max took a deep breath, reading everything over again, savoring her thoughts, her honesty.

Giselle finally phoned with wonderful news. Paul's attorney responded and there was a pre-trial. The court has ordered Paul to undergo psychiatric testing. He's now under a restraining order. You'll never know how relieved I am.

She can't leave Paris yet, but since Paul is no longer a threat, she may not want to. In any event, we can relax. I know you've been worried that he might be dangerous, but Giselle is confident the danger has passed.

Like a starving man, Max devoured every word, not realizing until now how much he craved this kind of news from home. From Abby. He didn't want the letter to end.

I saw Dr. Harvey today. He says everything looks good. I have a slightly different opinion and don't dare look in the mirror anymore, at least not a full-length one!

Max chuckled, remembering the feel of her even when she was bundled up in his parka, her skin and hair smelling like a high Montana meadow full of wildflowers.

Ida and Jesse drove me in. They've been kind enough not to mention my weight gain. It's a good thing they didn't see me trying to climb on and off the examining table. I know I looked like a beached whale, or maybe a turtle turned upside down.

At that, Max laughed out loud.

You know what they say about a turtle on its back. It's not going anywhere.

Which brings me to the point of this letter. You were probably wondering if I'd ever get to it.

Max's smile faded. He dropped the letter as if it had scorched him and shoved away from the table. She'd been building up to whatever blow she meant to deliver. Why the hell didn't she just get it over with?

He snatched the papers off the table and sat down again.

I'm due in less than eight weeks. Dr. Harvey is concerned that the ranch is too far away from town. Even though my blood pressure stabilized months ago, he's watching to see if it elevates again. Starting in mid-January he wants to see me twice a week. Then, when there's only two weeks left to go, he wants me to come in for a checkup every day until I give birth.

What do you think I should do, Max? Shall I

move to Rexburg? Thanks to your generosity, I still have enough money in my savings account to pay a month's rent on an apartment. Or do you think a motel room would be better?

Max leapt to his feet. He read and reread that part of the letter until he almost wore it out. *No mention of joining Moreau.*

He turned to the next page.

Another of Dr. Harvey's concerns is that I might go into early labor (not that he's expecting me to). I see his point, though. Today another blizzard made the highway look like a cow path in the Yukon. Without Jesse's skillful driving, I don't think we'd have returned at all. As it was, we were five hours on the road.

Five hours. If she developed complications, she might not have five *minutes*. That settled it. He was going home as soon as they could find a replacement.

I know I'm being long-winded. But I couldn't end this without thanking you for the two little sleepers. They look perfect with the sweater. Won't it be fun to see the baby in them?

I'm so glad you didn't buy the newborn ones. Dr. Harvey says it's a good-sized baby. That's why I started showing so early. The poor thing! There's no more room in there now! Like mother, like daughter (or son).

Smiling, Max shook his head.

The baby must be missing you, because I've never felt it kick as hard as it did the night the two of you got acquainted.

Oh, Abby...

I know I don't have the right to tell you to hurry home, so I won't. But in case you hadn't guessed, with Christmas here, everyone at the ranch needs you and misses you—especially little Kellie-Louise. Did you know my mother's name was Louise? Of course, I haven't said it out loud yet, in case my daughter hears me. (If it's a son, I'd like to call him Kelly. What do you think?)

Abby

P.S. A Rob Miller left a message on your voice mail. Something about having a bunny all lined up whenever you got there.

Damn.

I didn't know if it was important or not. Please don't be offended, but if you were thinking about getting a rabbit for the baby, I think he or she would probably prefer a puppy. My mother didn't like to be around animals, so we never had a pet.

I think pets are important. But I'm being selfish
again. I couldn't help noticing that all the ranch
hands have dogs—except you. Of course, it's
none of my business.

Oh, Abby, Abby.

P.P.S. Taylor Burton dropped by and said his
black Labrador is about ready to have her pups.
It's possible she's due around the same time I am.
I'd like to give you a pup for your Christmas
present. Of course, it'll have to be late for obvious reasons. I've tentatively arranged to pick out
one of the pups once they've been weaned. I've
even been thinking about a name for it. Valentine, perhaps. Or if you want a male, I thought it
might kind of fun to call him Deputy Dawg, like
the cartoon.

Max shook his head, both moved and amused. He
hardly knew what to do with all the feelings leaping
around inside him, screaming for release.

P.P.P.S. I have a confession to make. Please
don't get too mad. Your accountant called the
other day. He needed something looked up, and
since no one was around at the time, I got into
your files. They looked a little messy so I started
straightening them. I promise I didn't rearrange

anything. Well, maybe just a little bit. Nothing major.

Max blinked.

I had no idea running a ranch—even a small one—was such a huge business venture. I know you've got Jesse, but how do you manage to handle everything and be a marshal at the same time? Maybe there's something I can do to help earn my keep till the baby gets here. I used to be fairly fast on a computer keyboard. Think about it.

I'm not very good at taking and taking, you know, and never giving anything back. So please let me help—the way you've helped me. You've given the name of family a brand-new meaning.

Family. Max turned the word over in his mind. What did she mean by it? Was it her way of saying he could never be more than a brother-in-law to her? Was that what she meant?

He sighed. Maybe he was reading too much into this. After all, they *were* family.

Why didn't she say anything about her phone call to Moreau?

Maybe the two of them had agreed not to alter their situation until after the baby was born. Maybe Moreau had wanted to start paying her bills, and she'd refused to let him until they were married. But in the meantime, she didn't want to be beholden to Max.

Maybe that was why she was suddenly all fired up to pay her own way—until Moreau took over the job. It would explain why she mentioned using her own savings to find temporary housing in Rexburg. And why she was so keen to help with the ranch paperwork.

Hell, if she'd ever even hinted at it, I'd have given her some accounts to work on a long time ago.

With grim determination he tore up the pages and flushed them down the toilet. For once, the incriminating evidence needed to be destroyed so that *he* wouldn't have access to it, wouldn't be tempted to read it over and over again. A man could only take so much...

He needed to get home. He needed answers. And he needed to see her face when she gave them.

"ABBY? FEEL LIKE a little company?"

At the sound of Ida's voice, Abby, who'd been lying on the couch in the burgundy velvet robe Max had sent her for Christmas, sat up against the cushion. "Of course. I'm just taking a little rest, watching the weather channel before I peel the potatoes for dinner."

"What are you peeling potatoes for? I'll do that. Anyway, you didn't eat any lunch. I thought you might like some wassail."

Abby smiled at the housekeeper. "I've told you over and over again to stop spoiling me—but I won't say no."

She reached for the hot drink left over from Christmas dinner the night before and sipped it to please Ida, but in truth, ever since she'd given her letter to Jesse four days ago, she'd lost her appetite.

Five seconds after he'd left the house, she knew she'd made a mistake. She'd tried to call the sheriff's office to stop him from faxing it to Max. But high winds and heavy drifting had interrupted phone service to the ranch, and she'd assumed the fax couldn't be sent, either. Her spirits improved slightly.

But two hours later, a pleased-looking Jesse walked in the back door, stomping the snow from his boots. In a loud voice he announced, "Mission accomplished."

Her heart plunged to her feet.

She'd all but told Max she was in love with him.

She'd been too bold, too forthright.

Once she'd started expressing her feelings, she couldn't seem to stop. Now she had to live in agony wondering if she'd revolted him by stepping over the lines drawn by his marriage to Kellie in a different lifetime.

"You're brooding," Ida observed. "I know the bad weather's made you nervous, so I'll tell you what. As soon as the roads are cleared, we'll drive to Rexburg and check into a motel. We'll stay there until you go into labor. It'll be fun, like a vacation. We'll rent videos and buy lots of magazines and books."

"Ida, stop worrying about my state of mind. I'm fine. Everything I've read on expectant mothers says you go through a restless period before the end. Something about the nesting instinct.''

Ida made a tsking sound. "You must feel very cooped up."

"No. I love the snow, the snug feeling of being safe and warm in this house." Her gaze strayed to the tree where Max's gifts sat waiting to be opened. "There's a coziness, a feeling of love that draws you in. Just like an old-fashioned Christmas card. You know the kind—with the hearth and the frost on the windows."

She gave Ida a loving smile. "That first day, when you helped me into the house, I—I felt like I'd come home." Her voice caught, and she took a steadying breath. "Christmas with you two has made me feel as if I belong. It's hard to explain. But believe me, I could *never* feel stifled here."

"I'm happy to hear it."

Abby gasped. She knew that voice. She turned her head toward the door.

"Well, what do you know!" Ida hurried toward Max and gave him a hug. "Are you ever a sight for sore eyes. Just what the doctor ordered. I'm going to go get you a cup of wassail."

Max looked so good to Abby she had to avert her eyes. She didn't even notice Ida's departure from the room.

"That was some letter." He shrugged off his sheepskin coat and walked toward her, his hands on his hips. He must have just flown in, for he was still wearing a pair of well-worn dark gray sweats.

"Wh-what did I say that would bring you home this fast?" She couldn't control the quiver in her voice. His eyes were traveling all over her, assessing the changes since he'd last seen her. She felt unaccountably shy.

"Your letter coincided with a new development in the case, which gave me an opportunity to come home. When you mentioned the accounts, it reminded me of some ranch business I've been putting off. I decided now would be the best time to take care of everything."

His half-veiled eyes slid over her. "I'm glad to see you're wearing my present."

She ran a palm down the material. "I love it, even if I do look like a plump partridge. Your gifts are over there, under the tree."

He either didn't hear her or chose to ignore her comment. In the next instant he'd moved to the couch and knelt beside her, searching her eyes with a solemnity that made her tremble.

"How's Kellie-Louise?"

Abby never knew if it was her own shocked reaction to his deep husky voice, or if the baby really did recognize it, but suddenly there was a burst of activity in her womb, visible beneath the soft material.

This time Max didn't wait for an invitation.

At the first contact, a soft gasp escaped her throat. She saw a quickening in his eyes before he said, "You're so full and hard, I can follow every little movement the baby makes. What does it feel like, Abby?"

She attempted to sit up a little more, striving in vain not to think about his touch and the effect it was having on her. "I don't know how to explain it," she whispered.

"I want to know."

Her breath came in pants. "Try to imagine it's the inside of your stomach picking up the sensations you can feel against your fingers. Think of a baby curled up in a ball, squirming this way and that, its feet and hands bumping against your ribs."

Before she knew it, his hand left her stomach and he was caressing her forehead, smoothing the hair away. Then he paused. "Are you scared, too?"

He was completely serious. This man, who protected other people's lives and never counted the cost to his own, was actually scared.

Dear God, how she loved him! Her mouth curved in an ecstatic smile.

"No. Excited. Nervous maybe. But never scared."

He took a shuddering breath and got to his feet, staring down at her. "How can you be so calm?"

"How do *you* go running off to face professional killers without hesitation?" There was real distress in her voice. He regularly subjected himself to dangers most people couldn't conceive of.

"That's not the same thing."

"Then explain it to me."

He took so long to answer she was afraid she'd angered him. Finally he spoke, his voice low and controlled.

"My father had an only brother who retired from the forest service, but still helped out by keeping a fire watch over in the Gallatin area. He'd cover for some of the other guys who wanted time off for summer vacations.

"My uncle Owen loved the outdoors. Some of my greatest childhood memories are the hiking trips and rafting we did together.

"I was seventeen the summer he died. Dad hadn't heard from him in a while, so we took a drive over to see how he was doing."

As he spoke, the color drained from his face.

"Max..." She shook her head, dreading to hear what she guessed was coming. "Don't—"

"You wanted to know why I do what I do. When we arrived at the ranger station, we found him inside." After a tension-filled silence he said, "His killer had worked him over pretty good. And his dog. It may not make sense, but it's why I haven't got a dog myself. The poor thing suffered. And my uncle..." Max passed a hand over his eyes. "The shock killed my father, who died of a fatal heart attack the following morning."

"Oh, Max—"

"Pneumonia took Mother a year later. At the time, Jesse was one of our ranch hands. I told him I was going to find my uncle's killer. He put his arm around me and said, "You do it! You get him for me, too!""

Abby was in shock. Tears burned her eyes. "And did you find him?" she asked.

"No. But someone else did, thank God."

And you've gone on saving lives ever since.

Without conscious thought Abby got off the couch, wanting to comfort him, not knowing how. "Forgive me for passing judgment. Forgive me for mentioning anything about a dog. Kellie never told me."

"Kellie didn't know. Before I got around to telling her, our marriage fell apart. There was no more communication, no opportunity to tell her what had happened."

His eyes looked haunted. "I don't know why I told you. It all happened such a long time ago."

"I needed to hear it, to understand." The pain he'd endured—it had refined him, had made him so strong she stood in awe of him.

"Hey, you two!" Ida popped her head inside the door, jerking them both back to the present. "Come into the kitchen and help Jesse and me eat the scones I've been baking. We want to hear what you've decided to do about moving closer to the hospital."

CHAPTER FOURTEEN

As THEY DROVE AWAY from Dr. Harvey's office, Abby felt too warm. She worked her arms out of Max's parka.

He shot her a glance. "If you're hot, I'll turn the heater off."

"Then you'll freeze. Don't mind me. Lately I get warm for no reason."

"Did you ask the doctor about it?"

"Heavens, no." She smiled secretly, loving his concern. "It's normal."

"How do you know?"

"Because I read it in that new book you bought me last week."

Max had been a busy man since his return. Every day since New Year's, her bedroom had grown a little smaller. First came the crib, then the sheets and blankets. After that, clothes, diapers, nightgowns, everything the well-dressed baby was wearing this year.

"While you were being examined, I checked out the furnished apartments and found one that should suit you. The husband's being transferred to the East Coast and they have to leave before their lease is up. I paid them the difference. We can move you in next weekend when you come for your appointment.''

Abby tried to quell the frantic beating of her heart. She'd have the last four weeks of her pregnancy to herself. Knowing Max, he'd drop in to see her. They'd be alone. That was what she needed, what she craved.

"Can I see it?"

"We'll drive by. The couple who live there are in a mess right now, and the wife is sick in bed with the flu. I don't think they'd appreciate my disturbing them again today."

"Then let's not. I can wait."

They'd only gone three blocks when he pulled up in front of a substantial-looking brick house. "The apartment is around back. Everything looks secure. There's a locked gate and burglar alarm. The retired couple in the front own the house, and they're always on hand."

Abby continually marveled at his generosity and thoughtfulness, the way he watched over her. "It's a lovely home. I'm sure it will be perfect."

"So you think you could stand to stay here for a month?"

"Of course."

"Ida's willing to keep you company."

"Ida needs to keep Jesse company. I'll be just fine reading and knitting and watching soap operas."

"I bet if you asked her, Carole would come and stay weekends."

"Max—I lived in New York by myself for a year."

"You weren't pregnant—and you weren't living through one of the worst winters of the century."

Then why don't you offer to move in with me?

She bit her lip and looked out the window, wishing she had the courage to say it.

MAX SLIPPED out of the house at dawn, pulling his collar up around his mouth and nose. During the night the temperature had dropped to twenty below. His feet made crunching sounds on the frozen snow.

"You'll be lucky if the truck starts," Jesse muttered through his wool scarf. "How long are you going to be gone?"

"Barring complications, I should be back the day after tomorrow. If something holds me up, I'll be here the morning after. Make sure Abby's packed with everything she needs for the next four weeks."

"We'll get her ready."

"I've notified Giselle that her ticket's been prepaid. When it's Abby's time, all we have to do is phone and she'll be on the next flight to the States."

"Does Abby know?"

Max opened the door of the truck and climbed in. "I told her last night."

"Ida heard her wandering around about three in the morning."

"She had a backache and couldn't sleep." He twisted the key in the ignition till the engine kicked over. "I sat up with her until it went away." *We talked about everything except Philippe Moreau.* "She finally drifted off on the couch."

"That's where she ends up sleeping most nights lately."

"She can't breathe lying down anymore."

"Don't reckon I could, either, if I was carrying that load."

As he revved the engine, Max flashed him a wry smile. "In her letter, she referred to herself as a beached whale."

Jesse chuckled. "I suppose it feels that way to her. But it won't be long now."

That was what worried Max. For the next four weeks or so, he had her where he could keep an eye on her. But once the baby came and no more restrictions kept her from doing what she wanted, everything would change. He knew it in his gut, and there wasn't a damn thing he could do about it.

"Another big storm's supposed to hit tonight."

"I couldn't have planned things better, Jesse. By the time I'm back, it'll be all over and we're home free."

"How come *you* have to be the one transporting that prisoner? You barely got home from your last case."

"I owe A.J. a favor for all the times he covered for me while we were waiting for word on Kellie."

Jesse's eyes narrowed. "Max, you're as restless as Abby. I hope it ain't catching."

"I've never been a father before."

"You're not the father, Max."

His heart slammed to a stop. "Tell me something I don't know," he lashed out, and gunned the engine loud enough to wake the dead.

"Then when are you going to tell her you *want* to be?"

"Mind your own fool business, Jesse."

"*You* happen to be my own fool business," Jesse shot back. "I knew you were in love with her months ago."

"Don't say that," Max whispered.

"Kellie's gone, son. It seems to me she gave you permission when she talked Abby into trading places with her."

"Lord, Jesse." His voice shook with emotion. "Can you hear it? Off with old, his wife hardly even in the ground..." He almost strangled getting the words out.

"Since when did you ever care about gossip? Your marriage ended more than a year ago, and except for their looks, Abby's as different from Kellie as the sun from the moon."

Max ground his teeth. He had to get out of there. Fast. "I don't why we're even having this discussion. Moreau's waiting in the wings, just biding his time."

"I don't think so."

"I've got to go."

"You're too upset. Call someone else to take this case."

"Get out of the way, Jesse. Don't force me to knock an old man down."

"ABBY? IT'S FOUR. We've decided we'd better leave for town now or we might not beat the storm. Are you sure you don't want me to pick anything up for you?"

Abby walked out of the bedroom, aware of a twinge of pain in her lower back. She hoped the pain wouldn't come back full force. Dr. Harvey had warned her that this close to her due date she'd experience various aches and pains. All it meant was that her body was getting ready for the big event. She hadn't dared tell Max how severe some of the pains had been or he'd have panicked and driven her to the hospital.

"No. I'm fine. I hope there's a letter from Giselle."

"I do, too." Ida patted her cheek. "You look a little flushed."

"I'm always warm these days."

Ida's gaze didn't miss much. "Jesse says the roads are clear. We should be back in an hour and a half."

Abby walked with Ida to the back door and watched as they drove off in the Blazer. Then she shut the door and locked it.

This would be a good time to work on a couple of the less complicated accounts Max had left for her. Grateful to have something to occupy her mind, she padded into the den in her slippers. Now that her feet were swollen all the time, the slippers were the only things that fit.

She hadn't been working a half hour when the back pain increased dramatically, forcing her out of the chair. Surprised at its intensity, she walked around for a while, expecting it to ease. But if anything, it felt worse.

While she contemplated calling the doctor, the phone rang. It could be anyone of course, but there was always the chance it was Max.

Every time she thought of him, her heart raced, leaving her breathless.

Not wanting to miss the call in case it *was* Max, she hurried to get it. But she couldn't move quickly, and it had rung four times and was picked up by the answering machine before she could grab the receiver. She hoped whoever was calling would leave a message.

She punched in the code to listen to the message. The first thing she heard was static. Then, "This is the dispatcher in Great Falls reporting to anyone there that Deputy Sutherland was injured on duty. He's been transported to the hospital in Rexburg. We have no information on his status, but will keep you posted. Stand by."

"No! Max!" she cried to the empty room. "I can't lose you. I need you. I love you—I can't live without you! You can't die. I won't let you!"

Reaching for a pen, she wrote a note, but her hands were shaking so badly her writing was hard to decipher:

"Ida and Jesse," she scrawled, "Max is hurt. They've taken him to the hospital in Rexburg. I'm leaving in the other car. Come quickly!"

She rummaged for the keys Max had left in the desk drawer, grabbed his parka and a pair of boots, and headed out the door, heedless of everything but her need to get to him.

The freezing air hit her lungs and caused her to gasp, but she made it to the garage where Max's car was parked. At first, the car wouldn't start, and she was frantic.

But she knew that if she panicked, she'd flood the engine. For minutes, she sat in agony, waiting, then tried again. It finally turned over.

With a shiver of relief, she pressed on the gas and backed down the snowy drive. She used the remote Max kept on the visor to open the gate.

The sky had grown darker, which meant the storm wouldn't be long in coming. But the roads weren't too bad and there was virtually no traffic. She could go fifty miles an hour down the middle of the highway— no more, or she'd lose control of the car.

Once the heater started pouring out warm air, Abby became aware that the pain in her lower back had moved around to the front. It felt like a ring of pressure that was growing by degrees.

Every time she had to slow down to round a curve, she found it harder and harder to shift her foot from the accelerator to the brake.

At one point the pain was so severe she had to stop. Her stomach was rock-hard and she literally couldn't move.

She was having her first contraction.

It had to be false labor. It wasn't time for her baby to be born yet.

When the pain eased, she was soaked with sweat. She began driving again, more slowly now because the road inclined into the forest and snow had started to fall.

A car passed her—the only car she'd seen—flashing its brights. She hurriedly turned hers on, not having realized how dark it had grown. Within minutes all she could see now was snow, coming down harder and harder, all around her.

Another contraction hit, paralyzing her. She didn't have time to pull off to the side. She felt a sharp twinge, and suddenly her water broke.

Warm liquid gushed all over the seat, up her back, down her legs. This was the real thing. She'd never felt so helpless in her life. The baby was coming and Max could be dying.

Please, God. Don't let him die. Help me. Help the baby. Please.

She had to think. The small town of Island Park was only about ten miles from here. She could make it. She had to make it. She had to get help.

Struggling for control, she put the car in gear and started out once more, praying the contractions would hold off.

Gusts of wind splattered the windshield with fresh snow. If anything happened to the wipers, she wouldn't be able to drive on. *Please don't let anything happen to the wipers.*

Another contraction. She braked the car and groaned out loud, overwhelmed by its length and intensity. When it subsided, she was again soaked with sweat.

The contractions were coming closer together.

She drove faster, knowing she had to make up for the time lost. *Oh, Max, why did I let you leave without telling you how much I love you?*

With her eyes riveted on the road, she didn't see the bull moose until it moved into the path of her car. She lifted her foot off the gas to brake, but it was too late. There was a thud and the car veered off the road and into the embankment.

All went quiet.

Another contraction began. Shē sat there, powerless to move, groaning from the incredible power of muscles working to expel the baby from her body.

She couldn't move, couldn't get out of the car to see if the poor moose was lying in the road or not.

New terror clutched at her heart. If someone should come along and hit it, there'd be another accident. She turned on the hazard lights, praying that if the moose was still on the road, he was dead. She couldn't bear to think of its suffering.

She couldn't bear to think of losing Max.

"Kellie-Louise," she groaned, "what made you pick *this* moment? Please, God. Help me."

Another contraction hardened her belly and she lost all sense of time and place. When it ended, she was limp from exhaustion.

Her entire body trembling, she turned on the engine and tried to drive the car back onto the road, but the tires spun. She was well and truly stuck.

A turtle on its back, she thought hysterically. *I have to get out of the car and flag down a motorist for help.*

But she'd only seen one car. Who in their right mind would be out in this blizzard? What if no one else came?

She had to help herself. She and her baby would have to do it all by themselves. She needed to climb into the back seat where there was room.

The contractions were coming faster. If she waited any longer, she might not be able to get out from behind the steering wheel.

She had to move *now!*

Please God, give me the strength to do it. Keep Max alive for us.

BY THE TIME Max passed Island Park, the novocaine had worn off. His left eyebrow throbbed where they'd put in a couple of stitches. He'd refused any pain killers because he needed to stay alert for the drive home.

Carefully he felt around the edges, satisfied that the swelling didn't seem any worse. A split second before the knife came, he'd seen it and been able to deflect it before any real damage could be done.

When he thought of the two thugs who'd tried without success to free his prisoner, a dangerous smile broke out on his face. They hadn't fared nearly as well.

It felt good to have put three more away for the duration. Damn good.

But when that knife had missed his eye by the merest fraction, it came to him like a revelation that one day, a bullet with his name on it would finally find its mark. He wasn't ready for that. Something much more important awaited him at home. Someone vitally important to his existence. He was tired of fighting for everyone else's safety. It was time to start fighting for what *he* wanted.

Picking up the car phone of the department's Bronco, he called the ranch for what was probably the twentieth time, but continued to get the answering machine. Ida had probably turned the phone's ringer off because Abby was sleeping.

He hadn't been able to get anyone on the Blazer phone, either. With this weather, Jesse would stay put. He figured he'd try it one more time on the off chance Jesse was working on something in the garage and happened to hear it.

After the first ring, he connected and heard, "Max? Is that you?" Jesse's frightened tone stunned him.

"It's me. Wha—"

"Thank the Lord!"

"Are you all right?" Ida cried into the phone.

"Would somebody tell me what's going on?"

"Stop being a hero and tell us how bad it is." Jesse took over again. "We know you're in the hospital."

Max's hand tightened on the steering wheel. "I was there to get a cut stitched. I'm on my way home.

Passed Island Park five minutes ago. How did you know about it, anyway?"

"Listen, we went into town a couple of hours ago, and when we got back, Abby was gone."

Gone?

Max felt like someone had just kicked him in the gut. *No. This just couldn't be happening.*

"She left a note saying you'd been hurt and were at the hospital in Rexburg. She took off in your car. Told us to hurry."

Abby's coming to me because I'm hurt? Max shook his head, trying to take it in. "Lord, that means she's on the road now!"

The blizzard required all his concentration. When he thought of her pregnant and alone in that car, his heart almost failed him.

"Thank God you called, Max. We're somewhere behind her. You're heading toward her from the other side. Whoever catches up with her first, let the other know."

"I've only passed one car." He struggled to remember. No, it hadn't been his. "What damn fool called the ranch and told her that? Must be a rookie on tonight who's too stupid to know better. This is exactly the kind of thing I've tried to avoid. When I get my hands on whoever it was—"

"Take it easy, son."

"If anything happens to—" He stopped midsentence. He could see lights up ahead on the left, but they weren't coming closer. A few more yards and he saw a car stuck in the embankment at an angle. It was his car!

"I found her, Jesse!"

"Thank the dear Lord," he heard Ida's voice. Her prayer echoed his own.

"She's off the road. She's hit something. Car's dented. I'm seven miles north of Island Park and pulling to a stop on the other side of the highway. As soon as I talk to her and make sure she's okay, I'll call you back."

"Right."

He set his brake and leapt out of the Bronco. Snow had been piling on the car, covering the windows. She'd been here awhile.

"Abby?" He tapped on the glass, then opened the door, expecting to see her in the front seat. *"Abby?"*

He heard a hoarse voice crying, "Help my baby. Someone, please help my baby. She's not breathing."

Max didn't remember turning on the overhead light or opening the rear door. But for the rest of his life, he would never forget seeing his courageous Abby lying naked from the waist down, the afterbirth expelled, her newly born infant still covered with amniotic fluid and blood as she tried desperately to breathe life into her.

"I'm here, darling. Let me." He crept inside, placing one foot on the floor. With his other leg, he wedged his knee between hers where he could get a good hold on the baby.

"Max," Abby moaned his name weakly. "You came— But how could you— I was afraid I'd lost you— You were in the hospital— My baby—"

"Don't talk, Abby. Save your strength."

He lifted the baby carefully, aware the umbilical cord still needed to be severed. Inserting his finger in the tiny mouth, he felt around, clearing the throat passage, which was full of fluid.

Once that was accomplished, he cradled the baby in his hand with its feet against his chest and breathed into her mouth and nose. The lungs filled, but she still wasn't breathing on her own. He took two fingers and traced her rib cage to the sternum, then pressed. "One, two, three, four, five."

He repeated the process three times, then took her by the ankles and tipped her upside down. "Come on, Kellie-Louise." He gave her a slap. "Cry for me, sweetheart. Come on. You can do it for me."

He slapped her one more time. There was a gurgling noise. Then she let go with a lusty cry. It was the most beautiful sound he'd ever heard. Before his eyes he watched her perfect little body come to life.

The baby seemed outraged by the torture he was inflicting on her and wailed vehemently in protest.

Max let out a yelp of pure happiness. Abby's cries of joy mingled with his, and she began to sob.

"Let me see her. Let me see my baby girl."

"Here she is," Max whispered, his tears dripping onto her cheeks, "just as eager to meet her mommy." He cradled the baby's head and neck in one hand while he lowered her ankles with the other, then placed her in Abby's arms. Almost immediately the baby responded and grew quiet.

"You're beautiful," she murmured in awe. "So perfect." As she talked, the baby made little noises that tugged at his heart. "I can't believe she's here, that she's alive." Abby's eyes suddenly lifted to his. They radiated a glow he'd never seen before. "I thank God for you."

Max could find no words. Without conscious thought he leaned over and brushed her mouth with his own. "This is the supreme moment of my life," he whispered against her lips.

Reluctantly he raised his head. "Now I've got to cut the cord and get you two warm."

While she crooned to the baby, who was making tiny whimpering sounds, he dealt with the cord. Then he peeled off his sheepskin coat, unbuttoned his flannel shirt and took it off. "Let me wrap the baby so she'll stay nice and cozy. That's it. Now let's take care of you."

He could see his parka on the floor. He reached for it and covered both of them, then wrapped his jacket around her legs and feet.

"I'm going to start the car and we'll have heat. Then I'm going to phone for an ambulance."

"We already did that when you didn't call us back," Jesse said from behind him. "The ambulance should be here in a few minutes. We talked to Dr. Harvey, too. He'll meet us at the hospital. So will the pediatrician. You take care of Abby and the babe. I'll see to everything else.''

''Is the moose dead?'' Abby asked anxiously.

''So that's what made the dent,'' Max muttered. ''I didn't see any sign of it.''

''I hope it isn't suffering somewhere.''

Max didn't know he could love a woman so much. After what she'd been through, she was worrying about a moose...

''I'm sure it isn't,'' he said emotionally. ''The dent's not big enough.''

It was a night of miracles.

Within seconds, Jesse and Ida had climbed in front. Jesse started the engine and turned the heater on high. Ida got up on her knees to see over the seat. ''Ah, will you look at that?''

''She's wonderful, isn't she, Ida?''

Max was thinking the same thing about Abby, whose tired pale beautiful face radiated joy. He couldn't take his eyes off her.

''Indeed she is, honey. And so are you.''

''Amen,'' Jesse croaked.

CHAPTER FIFTEEN

WHEN THE PEDIATRICIAN walked into the hospital waiting area, Max stood up, along with Jesse and Ida. His anxiety was at its peak. Any minute now he expected Dr. Harvey to come out and tell them how Abby's surgery had gone. She'd been torn during the birth and needed to be repaired.

"Mr. Sutherland?" Max nodded. "I'm Dr. Rich." He extended his hand. "I understand you're the one who arrived in the nick of time and got that baby breathing on her own. A nifty piece of work under circumstances that would have daunted anyone, even a deputy marshal. My congratulations."

Max appreciated the compliment, but he needed to hear that the baby was going to be okay. "What's the verdict?"

"All the right parts are there." He smiled. "As far as I can tell, she's responding like a healthy full-term baby. Her lungs are doing fine, her color's good, she's a good size, and she's hungry. If she keeps this up, I don't see why she can't go home with her mother in a few days."

"Max!" Ida cried for joy and hugged him. Max held on while relief spread through him like sunshine after a freezing rain.

In a cracked voice Jesse asked, "How much does she weigh?"

"Seven pounds two ounces. She's twenty inches long."

Jesse punched Max's arm, his face beaming. "How soon can we see her?"

"You can walk down there right now and watch through the nursery window. Good night now. Call me if you have any questions."

Max murmured his thanks, while Ida and Jesse gave him a hearty handshake.

"Come on, Max. Let's take a peek at our new baby."

"You two go on ahead. I'll be there in a minute. I'm going to wait here for Dr. Harvey."

Ida put a gentle hand on his arm. "I know you're anxious about Abby. But even if they've finished, she'll be in the recovery room for a while. It could be a long wait."

Jesse pulled his wife away. "Come on, honey. I've seen that look on Max's face before. He's not budging."

Max flashed Jesse a private signal of gratitude and sat back down, clasping his hands between his knees. There was an air of unreality about the whole night, like a strangely vivid dream. He kept remembering how Abby had looked—so terrified when the baby wasn't breathing. Then afterward, so brave and beautiful, pale with exhaustion, yet shining with joy. He needed to see her. He needed to touch her, hold her.

"Max?"

At the sound of Dr. Harvey's voice he sprang to his feet. "How is she?"

"She's going to be fine. They'll be taking her to her room in a little while. It's you I'm worried about. Didn't I hear you were in the emergency unit earlier?"

"Just a cut."

"Do me a favor, Deputy?"

"What's that?"

"Follow me to the doctor's lounge and lie down for a while. I promise to send the clerk for you the moment Abby's back in her room and awake. She went through an extraordinary ordeal tonight. She needs rest. So you do. How about it?"

If he hadn't felt as if he was going to black out at any minute, Max would have resisted.

ABBY COULD TELL it was daylight, even though the blinds at the window of her private room were closed. Part of her knew there'd been nurses throughout the night, checking her temperature and her blood pressure, changing the pad beneath her. Dr. Harvey had made his rounds, too. But her exhaustion had been total, and the pain killer they'd given her had done its job.

Her eyes opened a little wider as a nurse she didn't recognize came into the room.

"Hi, Abby. My name is Georgia and I'm taking care of you today. Are you still having pains?"

"No. They've subsided, thank heaven."

"Great. But I bet those stitches are starting to hurt again. I'll give you something for that in a minute."

"I'm not sure what's hurting more. And I need to use the bathroom."

"That doesn't surprise me. I'll show you how to get out of bed. A shower's going to make you feel better, too."

Abby didn't think she was ready for any of this, but she didn't want Max to see her looking like a hag.

She averted her eyes. "Has my brother-in-law come yet?"

"No. But I know he's here. I was told he's been asleep on a cot in the doctor's lounge. When you say the word, I'll get him for you. You can have lunch together if you like. Then they'll be bringing your baby over from the nursery."

"I can't wait!"

"Dr. Harvey says you're planning to breast-feed. After you've had your visit, I'll help you get started."

The ordeal of the next half hour was something Abby had no desire to repeat. But when she got back into bed, with her hair freshly washed, wearing a little makeup and a clean hospital gown, she had to admit she felt much better. The effort had worn her out, though, and she lay back against the pillow, exhausted.

"Looking at you right now, nobody would dream where you were and what you were doing last night," the nurse remarked.

"I can hardly believe it myself," Abby murmured with a smile, too tired to open her eyes.

"Here's some juice. Take this tablet with it." Abby complied. "Now I'll go see about your lunch and then try to rouse your brother-in-law. He's a big hero around here."

He would always be Abby's hero.

But before she saw him, she needed to phone Philippe. He had the right to know his daughter had just been born, and this was the perfect time, with no one else around.

She reached for the phone and made a credit-card call. It didn't take long for the overseas operator to get Philippe's office number in Nice and ring through.

Abby had worried Philippe might be out for a late lunch or a meeting. She sighed in relief to discover he was in.

"Abby? I didn't expect a call until next month. Is something wrong?"

"No. The baby came early. She's beautiful." Abby broke into rapid French and registered his gasp as she told him as much as she could to satisfy his curiosity. "I promised you I would call when she was born. I need to know what you've decided to do. I'd like to tell you what *I'm* prepared to do."

MAX WALKED toward her room with so much excitement he thought he might jump out of his skin. Thanks to Jesse and Ida, who'd left the hospital last night to make a few purchases and get a motel room, he'd been able to slip over there this morning for a shower, a shave and a new T-shirt. The sound night's sleep had rejuvenated him.

Her door had been left ajar. He lifted his hand to knock so he wouldn't startle her, but he didn't complete the motion.

It was like déjà vu. She was in bed, speaking French in her soft husky voice. Her face was turned so she couldn't see him, but he could see her.

What was more, he could hear her. He couldn't understand the words; he certainly understood the way she was saying them. Her conversation was low and confidential. Without conscious thought he crushed the tissue around the long-stemmed red roses he carried, drawing blood.

She had every right to speak to anyone she wanted. Every right in the world. He just hadn't expected her to call Philippe this fast.

Last night had been the stuff miracles were made of. But today represented a whole other reality. It now seemed the miracle had happened *only* to him.

He had to get out of here.

"Max! Wait!"

She'd seen him.

Just keep walking and don't look back.

Suddenly he heard a bloodcurdling scream.

Abby?

Wheeling around, he raced back down the hall toward her room, unaware that the roses had dropped from his hand. In the background he could hear someone running.

Abby smiled when he entered the room. So much the better that he'd gone pale from fright. It told her everything she wanted to know.

"Abby?" His chest heaved from fear and exertion. "What's wrong?"

"Everything," she answered calmly from her half-prone position on the hospital bed. "Since you wouldn't come when I called, I had to do something. Shut the door and don't let anyone in."

His shocked expression would have been comical if the situation wasn't so poignant. "I don't need help. I need you," she said, "Tell them to go away."

Forced to think fast, Max stood in the doorway to face two anxious-looking nurses. "It's all right. She thought she saw a spider."

"A spider? In here?" one of them said, then both nurses burst out laughing and hurried off to their duties.

Max shut the door, then turned to Abby, his expression grim. "Do you want to tell me what this is all about?"

"Do you want to tell me why you ignored me when I called out to you?" she fired back, noticing the tiny plaster on his brow. She'd ask him about it later.

His eyes narrowed on her mouth. "You were busy."

She studied his taut features for a moment. "I was on the phone with Philippe."

"I gathered as much," he said woodenly.

"How did you know it wasn't Giselle?"

"Because I called her just before I came to your room. I told her you'd phone her later, when you were awake."

"Thank you for getting in touch with her. I wanted to, but the phone call to Philippe took priority. I promised I'd let him know when she was born. He *is* the natural father of my baby."

He glanced away. He'd had no idea she could be so cruel. "You think I need to be reminded of that?"

"Yes." Her voice trembled, then grew stronger. "You see, he's agreed to give up all rights to her because... because I've told him *you* want to be Kellie-Louise's father."

The blood pounded in his ears so loudly he wasn't sure he'd heard her right.

"You do, don't you?" Her eyes, her voice, her whole body begged for his answer. "I told him you'd earned the right from the moment I set foot on your ranch. The only problem is, Kellie-Louise is a package deal. If you want her, you have to take me, too."

"Do you have any idea what you're saying?" he demanded.

Her beautiful green eyes drew him closer. "Surely you know how I feel. I'm in love with you. I have been, for a long time. But you loved Kellie desperately. I know that, and I—I've been so afraid your love for her would blind you to what we could have together.'' Tears spilled down her cheeks, but she didn't bother to brush them away.

"You want to hear how long I've been aching for you?" In a swift movement he approached the bed and took her flushed face in his hands. "Do you want to know how long I've been agonizing over what I've done—fallen in love with my own sister-in-law? The *twin* sister of my wife?"

She felt him shudder. "Do you want to hear how close I came to doing real damage to Philippe? Do you want to—"

She shook her head, then lifted her arms and wrapped them around his neck, pulling him down, down. "Kiss me, Max...darling. Really kiss me. I can't wait any longer."

Max felt her mouth move to meet his, and he was lost. Her breathtaking response answered every question. He found himself drowning in her luscious warmth. Suddenly her mouth wasn't enough. He needed to taste her skin, her eyes, the sweet curve of her neck where the damp red-gold tendrils clung.

"Marry me as soon as we get back to the ranch," he whispered against her ear. "I can't possibly take you home unless I know you'll be in my bed every night."

Abby kissed him again, long and passionately, never wanting this ecstasy to stop. "Maybe we could get married in the hospital chapel," she finally whispered back. "But I think it's fair to warn you that I'm not supposed to...go to bed with you for the next six weeks.''

Max groaned and lifted his head, staring into her glazed eyes, his own a smoldering gray.

"Did you make that up to torture me?"

Her mouth curved into a smile. "No. Dr. Harvey mentioned it this morning. He figured things out— about us—a long time ago.''

"Six weeks. I'm going to have a talk with that man."

Abby sighed and her heavy eyelids closed. "You do that, darling." She settled back against the pillow, her strength spent. "I love the way you handle everything. I love the way you love me and our baby. I love you. Don't ever leave me. I love you, I love you, I love...'' her voice trailed off.

CHAPTER SIXTEEN

THERE WAS A GENTLE TAP on the door of the guest bedroom, rousing the new puppy Taylor Burton had given them. Valentine—they'd chosen that name although she was born February first—was sleeping on a small rug beside the cradle.

"Abby?" Ida whispered, opening the door. "Hush, Val!" She scooped up the puppy. "You have a visitor. It's Carole."

"Oh, good! I've been hoping she'd come over."

Abby had been home from the hospital four weeks without a word from her friend. "Send her in. I've just finished nursing the baby. Carole can put her down for the night."

The next little while went by in a kind of blur as Carole hugged Abby, then went crazy over Kellie-Louise. The woman was baby-hungry. Abby wondered if she'd ever considered adopting. It would be wonderful to raise their children together. One day soon she'd discuss it with her.

"I'm sorry the baby's asleep. You can't tell what a terrific personality she has until her eyes are open."

Carole chuckled. "Spoken like a mother. Oh, Abby, she's so precious. I would have come by sooner, but

Mike and I have been vacationing with his parents in Boise. We got back yesterday. That's when I heard the news. Is it true Max saved the baby's life?"

"Yes." Abby blinked back tears. "My knight in shining armor. I'm the luckiest woman in the world."

Her friend studied her for a moment. "You're... radiant. Like a woman with a wonderful secret."

Abby started to feel nervous. "That's because I've got one. I've been keeping it until I could try it out on you."

"You're not teasing, are you."

"No."

"Tell me."

"You might hate me."

"Abby, you're not making sense."

"What would you say if I told you Max and I were married before I left the hospital?"

Carole stared at her with a shocked expression. "You're kidding me," she whispered.

"No," Abby murmured, wounded by her reaction.

"Oh, my gosh. I've got to go, but I'll be back."

"Carole? What's the matter? Where are you going?" Her friend was already halfway out the door.

"I won't be long. I promise. Where's Max?"

"He's out doing some chores."

"Tell him to come in. Promise me you'll both be up when I return. Give me a half hour, all right?"

"I promise," Abby said, shaking her head in bewilderment. For the next little while she stood by the crib watching her daughter sleep, all the time trying to understand Carole's bizarre behavior.

Finally she gave up and kissed the baby's forehead, then turned off the light and tiptoed out of the room.

"Where do you think you're going?" She heard her husband's deep beloved voice in the darkness.

Abby's heart leapt every time she felt his presence. His hands came around her from behind, caressing her hips and stomach, sending a private message of wanting. She let out a quiet gasp.

Last night, after Max had told her he'd resigned from his deputy marshal's job to become a full-time rancher, they'd made love for the first time, then promised each other that they wouldn't let it happen again until she'd been to see the doctor.

But they both knew it was a lie. They couldn't wait to break their promise, again and again.

"We can't, darling." She was out of breath. "Carole's coming over in a few minutes."

"I have to."

"Heaven help me, so do I."

He turned her in his arms, loving her low moan of surrender as his mouth descended.

ABBY HEARD a tap on the door of the master bedroom. "Carole's in the living room. Jesse made a fire."

She tore her lips from Max's. "Thanks, Ida. We'll be there in a minute.. Hurry, darling," she whispered, struggling to fasten the zipper of her jeans. Oh, boy.

Max flashed her a heart-stopping smile and pulled on a hooded sweatshirt over jeans. "What's up with Carole?"

"I don't know, but let's not keep her waiting." Abby started for the door, but he pulled her back for a moment to give her a hard kiss on the mouth. Then he followed her through the house to the living room.

Carole gazed at both of them as though she was seeing them for the first time. "I understand congratulations are in order, Max. I couldn't be happier for you."

He gave her a hug, then his expression sobered. "Even if you disapprove?" he said quietly.

"Max, you hurt me when you ask a question like that. I *hoped* you two would get together. I've just been waiting."

One dark brow dipped. "You and Kellie were close, Carole. You would have every right to feel we betrayed her memory. Abby and I realize that once our marriage is made public, there will be negative gossip. We can handle that from everyone except our closest friends."

As Carole stood there staring at them, a strange almost palpable tension emanated from her. "I have something to tell you. I think maybe you'd both better sit down."

Worried by the change in her friend, Abby automatically clung to her husband, who pulled her onto the couch beside him. Carole remained standing.

"We wouldn't be having this conversation if Abby hadn't told me you were married. It relieves me of a great burden."

"Burden?" Max repeated. "What are you talking about? Whatever you have to say, just say it." Abby felt his hand grasp hers tightly.

"Kellie lied to you when she said she spent the night with me that time."

It was like a bomb going off.

Abby wasn't sure she wanted to hear this and started to get up, but Max held her in place and told Carole to go on.

"She never went to West Yellowstone. Instead, she drove to University Hospital in Salt Lake to consult a doctor about her blurred vision, which, of course, she'd never told anyone about. They ran tests and discovered an inoperable brain tumor that they said would kill her within the next six months to a year."

"She went to Salt Lake..." Abby whispered in pain. "Why didn't we think of that?"

"More to the point, why didn't you tell me, Carole?" Max's eyes were accusing.

"Please, let me finish. Then you can ask all the questions you want."

Abby cringed at the tremor that shook Max's body.

"I knew nothing about any of it until she phoned me from Salt Lake and told me the ghastly news. She didn't want you to know anything until she'd had time to think. She swore me to secrecy and asked if I would manufacture an alibi for her.

"A few days later, she came into the store and said that I was to continue keeping everything a secret. She told me that if I truly loved her, this was the one thing I could do for her before she died."

Abby nodded sadly. "I know how persuasive Kellie was. She got me to change places with her and fly to the ranch."

"It was a horrible time for me, watching her push all of you away, withdrawing from life," Carole admitted. Her tear-filled eyes focused on Max. "I can only imagine what it must have been like for you. I hoped, I prayed, that one day she'd relent and go to you for comfort.

"We argued about it. I threatened to break my promise to her, but at the last second, I couldn't do it. She left after that. I never saw her again. Then one day, *this* came for me in the mail." She reached into her purse and pulled out a brown envelope, which had been opened.

Max released Abby's hand and got to his feet.

"As you can see, there's a Paris postmark. It's dated three days before her death. Inside are two sealed envelopes and a brief letter to me. Read it."

Abby stood up, too, and her gaze met her husband's. *The pain was starting all over again.*

Alarmed at his pallor, Abby slid her arm around his waist. His hand shaking, he reached for the stationery. Seeing familiar handwriting brought back her sister with a sharp jab of pain. Together they read:

Dearest friend of mine,

I know you're still my dearest friend because Max knows nothing, and that's the way I want things to stay.

I have one more favor to ask. The last one, I promise.

If Max and my sister should ever marry, please give them the sealed letters inside this envelope. If that never comes to pass, then show them to no one.

Do this for me, and one day in the great hereafter, I'll come looking for you and throw my arms around you, my dearest friend.

All my love,
Kellie.

When Abby finally looked up, Carole handed her an envelope. On the front, in Kellie's flamboyant script was the word Romulus. Her vision blurred as she read Beloved Husband on the other.

"I'm going home," Carole said. "If either of you ever feels like talking to me again, you know where I live." Quietly she left the room.

"Abby—" Max's voice was almost unrecognizable. "I—"

"At last my sister has chosen to talk to you. Take your letter into the bedroom, darling. Whatever she's written, those words are for you alone."

"I can't bear to hurt you . . ." he whispered.

Compassion filled her heart to see him struggle with the overpowering—and conflicting—emotions of love, loyalty and guilt.

"If it were anyone but Remus, I wouldn't be as charitable. But she's my other self."

Abby turned her back on him, freeing him to leave. She waited long minutes before she heard his footsteps. When they faded, she opened the sealed letter. It was just like Kellie to be so dramatic, playing out a part, even to the bitter end. Tears rolled down her cheeks.

Romulus—
If you're reading this letter, it means my plan worked, in spades!

I knew it, Abby whispered to herself.

It's what I prayed for, what I'll go on praying for after I'm on the other side. The two people I love most in this world will always be together now. My elaborate strategy wasn't in vain, after all.

"Kellie!" Abby cried, and sank down on the couch to finish reading.

It was awful to find out I was going to die. I won't kid you about that. AWFUL. At first I wondered if you had the same thing. But I was always careful to ask about your health and you never had my symptoms. Not one. So my doctor told me to stop worrying.

After I got over the initial shock, I realized what the news would do to you. Let's face it, Romulus, no one ever knew how it was with us. Only the Bobbsey Twins, right?

Abby laughed in spite of her tears. They'd both hated the Bobbsey Twin stories and had planned to write the Clarke Twin stories in their old age. They'd always joked about dying together in their rocking chairs, side by side, holding hands.

"So I schemed and came up with what I can now announce was the infallible plan. I knew that if I'd told Max the truth, his heart would have been broken ten months earlier than it needed to be.

But Max's heart *was* broken, Abby thought sadly. It was broken when Kellie first turned away from him, when she shut him out.

She returned to the letter.

Then I put myself in your place. I knew that if I'd told you, you would have flown out to the ranch to live with me to the end, and you'd probably have died a week later from sympathetic pain. Don't laugh. It could have happened.

Abby wasn't laughing. Every word she spoke was the truth.

I had to keep you two away from each other for a couple of reasons. First, I needed time to turn my husband against me so that when I died, he wouldn't grieve so long.

Second, I knew that if the three of us had spent the last ten months together, you two would never have been able to throw off the guilt you'd suffer for falling in love with each other after I'd gone. I knew you'd both go your separate ways out of loyalty to me, always suffering in silence.

Let's be honest, Abby. If you'd seen him first...

I told you I was scared of you. It was the truth. I didn't want you anywhere around him for the first few months. Not until I was completely certain of our love, our marriage. That's why I didn't let you come to the ranch. I couldn't afford anything to go wrong. So I had to keep you apart as long as I dared. Sorry about the phone rules, Romulus, but there was no other way.

Remind me to thank Philippe one day when he joins me on the other side. I was kind of rough on him when I saw him in Paris. I liked him and felt kind of sorry for him in spite of his cowardice. Instinct tells me he's probably a decent human being if you forget his fatal flaw.

What? When did Kellie ever see Philippe?

Getting you pregnant was the best piece of work he ever did. You supplied me with an even better strategy than my original one to get you out to the ranch. Max has always wanted children. It was perfect! By the way, you'd better name that baby after me, or I'll want to know the reason why when I see you again.

Abby was sobbing so hard she could no longer read the words.

Giselle knew nothing. I couldn't trust her not to break down. And Jesse and Ida are such sweethearts they wouldn't have been able to stand it. So the awful task was given to Carole, who's a saint and deserves a houseful of children. When it seems the right time, urge her to go for adoption.

Oh, Kellie, Kellie.

Romulus—you and I have always shared everything. As your older sister, I give you permission to love Max Sutherland, the most wonderful man alive.

We didn't have long enough together for him to come to know me as well as you do. Help him, Abby. You're the only one who can. Help him understand why I did what I did. He's probably gone off somewhere private with my letter to lick his wounds. Probably to Jesse and Ida's cabin.

I spilled my guts to him in the letter I wrote, but I know he'll never really understand, not without you there. You were always the brave one, the strong one.

Love him, Abby, my darling dearest other self. Love him with all the generosity of your soul and you will have joy!

I ought to know, because when I met Max, I discovered the meaning of the word.

Love,
Remus

P.S. I *knew* my plan would work. I had no doubts. What's mine is yours. That's the way it was with us, the way it always will be. You have to give Giselle credit. She tried valiantly, didn't she? But she didn't know what she was up against when she met the Clarke twins. Who has more fun than we do, Romulus?

P.P.S. Don't ever let anything happen to you. But when it finally does, remember—I'll be waiting, little sister. And I'm going to want a full report!

Clutching Kellie's letter in her hand, Abby got up from the couch and started running, her feet barely touching the floor. She only made it as far as the end of the living room when she saw her husband hurrying down the hall toward her, joy written on his face.

Thank you, Remus. Bless you for the gift of peace. The greatest gift of all.

HARLEQUIN SUPERROMANCE®

WOMEN WHO DARE
They take chances, make changes
and follow their hearts!

FORBIDDEN
by Ellen James

Having proposed marriage and been turned down flat,
Dana Morgan says to hell with security, her ex-lover and
her old life. Out for adventure, she's prepared for difficulties
and discomfort—and she's eagerly looking forward to the
unpredictable.

What she isn't prepared for is Nick Petrie. Talk about *unpredictable*... And Nick knows it; in fact, he enjoys his reputation.
While Dana tells him to his face that he's a "royal pain," privately she has to admit he's the handsomest, sexiest, most
exciting man she's ever met. Unfortunately, Nick swears
there's no room in his life for love.

Dana's taking the chance that he's wrong.

Watch for *Forbidden* by Ellen James.
Available in April 1995,
wherever Harlequin books are sold.

MILLION DOLLAR SWEEPSTAKES (III)

No purchase necessary. To enter, follow the directions published. Method of entry may vary. For eligibility, entries must be received no later than March 31, 1996. No liability is assumed for printing errors, lost, late or misdirected entries. Odds of winning are determined by the number of eligible entries distributed and received. Prizewinners will be determined no later than June 30, 1996.

Sweepstakes open to residents of the U.S. (except Puerto Rico), Canada, Europe and Taiwan who are 18 years of age or older. All applicable laws and regulations apply. Sweepstakes offer void wherever prohibited by law. Values of all prizes are in U.S. currency. This sweepstakes is presented by Torstar Corp., its subsidiaries and affiliates, in conjunction with book, merchandise and/or product offerings. For a copy of the Official Rules send a self-addressed, stamped envelope (WA residents need not affix return postage) to: MILLION DOLLAR SWEEPSTAKES (III) Rules, P.O. Box 4573, Blair, NE 68009, USA.

EXTRA BONUS PRIZE DRAWING

No purchase necessary. The Extra Bonus Prize will be awarded in a random drawing to be conducted no later than 5/30/96 from among all entries received. To qualify, entries must be received by 3/31/96 and comply with published directions. Drawing open to residents of the U.S. (except Puerto Rico), Canada, Europe and Taiwan who are 18 years of age or older. All applicable laws and regulations apply; offer void wherever prohibited by law. Odds of winning are dependent upon number of eligible entries received. Prize is valued in U.S. currency. The offer is presented by Torstar Corp., its subsidiaries and affiliates in conjunction with book, merchandise and/or product offering. For a copy of the Official Rules governing this sweepstakes, send a self-addressed, stamped envelope (WA residents need not affix return postage) to: Extra Bonus Prize Drawing Rules, P.O. Box 4590, Blair, NE 68009, USA.

SWP-H395

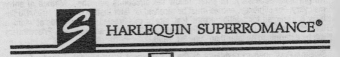

HARLEQUIN SUPERROMANCE®

A Superromance *Showcase* book.

THE SECRET YEARS
by
Margot Dalton

Kate Daniels is beginning to regret her impulsive move to the
small town of Fox Creek, Alberta. The locals are less than
friendly and seem determined to thwart Kate's efforts to revive
the old Fox Creek Inn. Only the mysterious—and gorgeous—
Nathan Cameron is prepared to help. Then Kate finds a
treasure hidden in the walls of her hotel—a diary kept by
another young woman who had come alone to Fox Creek ninety
years ago. From the diary, Kate learns answers to questions
that have plagued her since her arrival. Answers that cause
her to view Nathan Cameron in an entirely new light...

Watch for THE SECRET YEARS
by Margot Dalton.
Available April 1995, wherever
Harlequin Superromance books are sold.

HARLEQUIN SUPERROMANCE®

Introduces

Laura Abbot

This talented author's first Superromance, *Mating for Life*, appears in April 1995. You'll meet Josie Calhoun and Mackenzie Scott—and their story will involve you, move you and warm your heart!

Watch for it next month, wherever Harlequin books are sold.